D0513725

Untimely Graves

Also by Marjorie Eccles:

Cast a Cold Eye
Death of a Good Woman
Requiem for a Dove
More Deaths Than One
Late of This Parish
The Company She Kept
An Accidental Shroud
A Death of Distinction
A Species of Revenge
Killing me Softly
The Superintendent's Daughter
A Sunset Touch
Echoes of Silence

UNTIMELY GRAVES

Marjorie Eccles

Constable · London

First published in Great Britain 2001
by Constable, an imprint of Constable & Robinson Ltd,
3 The Lanchesters, 162 Fulham Palace Road,
London, W6 9ER
www.constablerobinson.com

Copyright © 2001 Marjorie Eccles

The right of Marjorie Eccles to be identified as the author
of this work has been asserted by her in accordance with
the Copyright, Designs and Patents Act 1988

ISBN 1-84119-370-4

Printed and bound in Great Britain

A CIP catalogue record for this book is available from the
British Library

1

The water swirled beneath the bridge, thick as pea soup after the recent floods.

She stood leaning against the parapet, hands and feet frozen, gazing downwards at the little waterway that dared to call itself a river, and moreover, had a name, the Kyne. The level was at last beginning to go down: you could see the footpath alongside now, muddy and strewn with debris after being under water for so long. Dog walkers were wisely avoiding it, and keeping to the tarmac paths instead of cutting across the playing fields where the grass was still deeply squelchy underfoot. The March morning was bitter, with a raw wind, and the sparrow-bitten crocuses under the bare trees had a defeated, drowned look, as if it had hardly been worth their trouble to emerge at all.

Cleo watched a little boy and girl playing Pooh sticks alongside the bridge. The undercurrent beneath the swollen surface of the water was still strong, and they were beginning to get fed up with trying to run fast enough to see the sticks they threw in at one side emerging from under the bridge at the other. Their mother, waiting impatiently for them with a toddler in a pushchair, shouted again for them to come *on*, and Cleo gave them the nearly full packet of Maltesers in her pocket to make up for their disappointment. The little family disappeared towards the swings, and she went back to staring at the water, gazing at what looked like part of a cot mattress being borne along before being caught in the eddy as the surge of water hit the bridge, closely followed by several lumps of indestructible polystyrene packaging pushed along by the limb of a tree, with the remains of a chicken coop perched rakishly among its branches.

Spring had been terrible this year – rain, more rain and floods, pictures on television showing the havoc wrought all over the Midlands. It was nearly impossible to imagine that this rush of water, yellow with churned-up mud, could be the same gentle stream that normally flowed harmlessly through this municipal recreation ground. She leaned further forward and stared down, mesmerised by its relentless sweep. Would they ever be the same again, those farms and villages, those new housing developments scattered in the low-lying fields upriver, all of which had suffered the brunt of the floods? No more than she could ever again go back to being her old self, she thought gloomily. But not quite as gloomily as yesterday, and the day before. Perhaps things were getting a little better, after all. Yet still she shivered, despite her fleece jacket, a big scarf and the woolly hat pulled down over her ears.

'Don't do it, it's not worth it. Life's still sweet.' A hand descended on her shoulder.

She didn't need to turn around to know who the voice belonged to and she forced what she hoped was a cheerful smile. 'Hi, Dad. What are you doing here?'

Daft question. George always walked through the rec on the way to his office in the morning. 'Want a coffee?' he asked.

'Why not?' He invariably called at Stan's caff for a coffee before opening up the agency. Did that indicate a certain reluctance to do this last, or was she being paranoic? A year ago, he'd reached compulsory retirement age in the police force. No longer Detective Inspector George Atkins, he'd set himself up as a private enquiry agent, and she still wasn't sure whether it had been a good idea or not. Nor, she suspected, was he.

When they got to Stan's, she found a table while he went to the counter. He came back with the coffee and three currant buns, one of which he slid across to her. 'I don't suppose you had any breakfast.' He didn't ask why she'd got out of bed at six on a freezing morning and let herself quietly out of the house, nor where she'd been since then. He'd know she'd been walking, something she did a lot, lately. A compulsion had come over her to keep on the move; she'd thought it might help her to sort herself out, but it didn't seem to be having that effect.

The bun was good, with a sugary crust, stuffed with currants, and the coffee was strong in its thick pint mug. Stan's place wasn't the Ritz but he knew his customers – mostly lorry drivers, building site workers and the like – and how to feed them. Her father was an expert at sussing out these sort of things. Like where to get a hot drink and a hearty snack most hours of the day or night, and where all the public loos were. You learnt self-preservation, he said, when you'd worked in the CID for as long as he had.

He offered her half of the third bun but she declined, so he took it himself. 'Don't tell your mother.' Daphne periodically inflicted upon him one of her diets, though never with much success, it had to be said. He stayed solidly comfortable, his girth not appreciably less than it had ever been.

She felt a bit more cheerful now that she was full of comfort food, and she sat back, sipping her coffee. They both spoke together.

'Cleo.'

'Dad.'

'You first,' she said, and braced herself for what was coming.

'What's wrong, m'duck?' he asked. The way he deliberately clung to his local accent embarrassed Daphne. She thought by now he should have risen above it, but Cleo found it familiar and comforting.

'I'm all right.'

He shook his head. 'You haven't been all right since you left college.'

And that had been in the summer. After which, she'd bummed around a bit, knocked sideways by what had happened, and then, not knowing what else to do with herself, come home. Home, the place you go back to when all else fails.

She knew that her parents were really worried about her. But she wasn't ready to talk about it, not yet, if she ever would be ready. They thought it was her abysmal exam results that were causing her misery, and that did have more than a bit to do with it, but not everything. That she'd done so badly had shaken her to her roots, but the bald truth was that she just hadn't worked hard enough during her last year at university, though there had been reasons for that, too. Love. Oh yes, love, among other things, beyond which nothing else had seemed to matter, the feeling of being lost in a dream that could go on for ever. She couldn't blame anyone but herself.

'Come on, love, you can tell me,' George coaxed.

'Sorry, Dad, I can't. Really.'

He sighed, and she avoided his eye and stared at the suicide breakfast menu chalked up on a slate hanging over the counter: bacon, sausage, fried egg, tomatoes, black pudding and a fried

7

slice, £2.95, it said. Tea and toast included, chips and baked beans 50p extra. Several hunky-looking types were availing themselves of the full works.

They'd know sooner or later what was wrong, anyway, she'd told herself, though she was becoming less and less inclined to believe it, because it involved Jenna. Her twin. Born two minutes before her, and scooping all the advantages ever since.

People always assumed that if you were a twin, you were two halves of the same apple, she thought, sipping coffee from the huge mug, both hands wrapped around it. Maybe that was so if you were identical twins, but they were not. They didn't think or act alike, or have the same ambitions. They didn't even look alike, except in the way that sisters often do. They were both roughly the same build, small and slim, and once they'd both had long, silky dark hair and blue-green eyes, but there it stopped. Cleo had chopped her own hair off, as nearly short as it could get without being a crew cut, which had made her mother freak out the first time she saw it. It was growing out though, having reached the shaggy dog stage. Looking even worse – awful – but that was the price you paid for attempting to look different. And whereas, if they were being truthful, Cleo knew herself to be skinny rather than slim, Jenna's figure was just drop-dead gorgeous. She worked at it, of course, with her daily exercises and her Wonder Bras and those figure-flattering clothes that Cleo really, really despised, but she had the basic advantages to start with.

All of which made Jenna sound like some sort of bimbo, which couldn't be more misleading. As if it wasn't bad enough, Cleo coming such a cropper in her exams, Jenna had to go and get a First in Law at Cambridge, and she was now all set for a brilliant career. They'd actually been queuing up to offer her jobs as soon as she graduated, and she was still considering which City of London law firm she would grace with her presence.

And what was Toby feeling about that? Oh yes, Toby, right. In the end, he'd done worse in his exams than she herself had. Which ought to be giving her some sort of satisfaction, but made her feel rather worse about her own contribution to that.

'Come on, Glory, we've always been able to talk, you and me, eh?' George said.

She managed a wobbly smile. She'd thought there'd been

some mistake, it couldn't really be true, when she'd found out, aged about ten, that Cleo was in actual fact a diminutive for *Cleopatra*. Oh horrors! Truly? 'I'm not *really* called Cleopatra, Dad, am I?'

'No, it's Cleo on your birth certificate – after Cleo Laine. I was mad about her at that time. Like your mum got Jenna from *Dallas*. Anyway, what if it was? Cleopatra means "glory of her father",' George had said, smiling. 'A useless piece of information I once came across.' They'd made it their private joke. No one else had ever twigged why he sometimes called her Glory, not even Jenna.

'OK,' George said now, with the helpless sort of shrug he used sometimes to convey he'd never understand women, especially the three who made up his family. Cleo wasn't taken in by that, she knew it was a ploy. George understood a lot more than he ever let on. 'OK, I've had my go, now it's your turn. You were going to say something as well.'

Cleo had changed her mind by now, but she couldn't say 'Oh, nothing' again, so she said, 'I just wondered if you'd managed to get anybody in to help, yet, that's all.'

And that too was the wrong thing to say, she knew it as soon as she heard it come out of her mouth. 'You've been reconsidering?' he asked, his face brightening.

No, she told herself, she absolutely *didn't* want to go and work in his office. Not even until Muriel came back – if she ever did. Once there, there'd be no telling when she'd be able to leave. I shall be like the woman Jenna and I used to call Miss Frowze at the library, stamping books till I die, she thought in a panic. Only she wouldn't be stamping books, of course. Answering the telephone, typing up George's reports for his customers, addressing envelopes. Riveting stuff like that.

But to her consternation, she heard herself saying, 'Well, I know you're in a hole – so maybe, just until Muriel comes back.'

He smiled. Cleo thought, with a rush of affection, he's not so bad, even at fifty-six. Going bald on top, and the rest of it needing a trim. A big man, tall and a bit overweight, but still nice-looking, and kind. Untidy. If her mother had been there, she'd have straightened his tie, or more likely told him to chuck it away. Already the shirt collar she'd ironed so beautifully was turning up at the points. He looked no different from when he'd been working all those unsocial hours and taking irregular meals. But at least he'd astonished everyone who knew him by giving up smoking – or very nearly. His old pipe, though it still dangled from his mouth most of the time, rarely had tobacco in it now. Maybe he didn't need it, now that he was free of the stress of police work. It was probably more to do with the fact that her mother had suddenly decided she'd had enough of it now that he was at home more, and made him go outside every time he wanted to light up.

'You're a good girl, Cleo. Come on, let's go.'

She trailed after him. Me and my big mouth, she thought. It was frightening, sometimes, the way she had no control over what she said.

He was in a cheerful mood and she had to quicken up and trot beside him, trying to keep up with his long strides. Despite his weight he was no slouch. Though the sun had forced its way through the clouds it had no strength to it, and the wind won out, blowing grit and takeaway cartons, chocolate wrappers, old crisp bags along the pavements, rattling empty Coke cans in the gutters as they neared the sleazy end of Victoria Road where his private investigation agency was situated. Neighbouring with a branch of the Bank of Ireland, a halal butcher's, a Joe Coral betting shop, a pungent Indian tandoori restaurant and several charity shops on short leases, it stood out with its shiny new paintwork and nameplate. The traffic ground past unceasingly, and the general public still mostly passed it by, too.

The agency's premises were small, having once been a wool shop. But it was tastefully decorated inside, too, because Cleo's mother had had a hand in it and Daphne was good with that sort of thing. Greens and blues predominated, lots of pot plants stood about and there were comfortable chairs for clients to sit on while they put their problems to George. But small, all the same. Mainly because what had been the original shop had been divided into two, one part now being the reception area where Muriel's desk was, the other George's office. Behind was as it had always been, a cloakroom with a sink and a tiny storeroom with an electric point for making coffee. Its size hadn't posed any problems in accommodating customers yet. Like most places

10

around this quarter, it was doing less business than the Millennium Dome.

The wool shop had actually belonged to Muriel until she'd decided to sell, on account of not many people having time or inclination to knit nowadays, she said, plus her own increasing rheumatism and Hermione's advancing years. She came in part time and had her desk at right angles to one of the windows, which had been artistically painted over half-way in dark blue, lettered in gold, so that the interior was private and passers-by couldn't see Muriel knitting when her day's work was done. Which was still quite a lot of every day.

Muriel Seton was a round, comfortable woman with sharp eyes and hair like a Brillo pad. Since George had come to her financial rescue by buying her shop, she'd have done anything for him. Anything, that is, except come into the office until she was sure Hermione had fully recovered from her hysterectomy. This seemed likely to be a lot longer, remarked Daphne with some asperity, than the time Daphne herself had taken to recover from the same op, Muriel maintaining that dogs didn't get over that sort of thing like humans did. Hermione was her long-haired miniature dachshund, around whom Muriel's entire life revolved.

When they arrived, Cleo picked up the post and put it on her father's desk. She didn't think he'd want her to open it, especially since she couldn't help noticing that most of it seemed to be bills.

Well, anyone knew that starting up a business from scratch took time, especially a private enquiry agency in a smallish town not all that far from Birmingham. Most of the work so far consisted of surveillance: following erring wives with signs of wanderlust, sussing out people who were skiving off work and drawing sick pay or compensation while digging the garden or putting up a do-it-yourself conservatory. Insurance scams, process-serving, employees creaming goods off the boss's stock to sell at car boot sales. You name it.

It was nothing more than he'd expected, George said, but it was all a far cry from the real thing for ex-Detective Inspector Atkins, stalwart of the Lavenstock CID for more years than Daphne, for one, cared to remember. Hardly knowing he had a home to go to, she added tartly. Cleo suspected his heart wasn't truly in his new venture, that he missed his police work more than he'd ever admit. But it was better, he said, than spending his life trying to knock a little hard ball into a small round hole with a long stick. Or worse, partnering Daphne to the Bowls Club. Things would eventually look up, Cleo hoped. Perhaps a nice juicy murder would come his way, and he could solve it before the police did, like Hercule Poirot.

The first call she took was from Maid to Order, the contract cleaning firm who came in once a week to give the offices a spit and polish. 'Muriel?' queried Val Storey, the owner, an efficient woman who was an old school friend of Daphne's.

'No, it's Cleo.' She explained she was standing in for Muriel.

'Cleo! It's ages since I saw you, how are you?' Without waiting for a reply she went on, 'Look, I'm sorry about this, love, but you'll have noticed we haven't been able to get in this morning.' Cleo rolled her eyes. It was obvious Val hadn't been talking to her mother about her. 'We're another girl short, it's this chickenpox epidemic. All the mums are having to stay at home to look after their kids, so you see my problem.'

During the school holidays or in winter, when coughs and colds spread like wildfire through the classrooms, Val had a hard time finding enough staff to keep her increasingly successful business going, since a lot of her 'girls' were young mothers, working for her on a temporary basis.

'That's all right,' Cleo told her, looking round the reception area and through the open door into George's office, thus taking in the whole of the premises at a glance. As long as she flicked a duster round the most obvious places, no one would ever notice a missed week.

'I'm really sorry,' Val said. 'I'm at my wits' end. If you hear of anyone who wants a job . . .'

Cleo assured her she would, knowing how unlikely *that* was.

Val's call was the first thing that happened that morning. The other, just before lunch, was that George had a new client. In between, Cleo watched the tops of lorries and the upper decks of corporation buses cruise past. She read last night's paper.

There were a lot of pictures of the floods, showing plenty of reason to be thankful to be living down here, near the town, where it sloped to the Stockwell valley. There were pictures of farms further up looking like paddy fields, people crossing the streets of small housing developments and villages in boats. No one was shown actually sitting on the roof, but many families had fled upstairs until church halls could be opened as emergency quarters. Livestock had drowned. Several adventurous children had fallen out of boats. One human life had been lost.

There was quite a bit about this poor woman, whose body had been found floating one morning like a Pre-Raphaelite *Ophelia* down the very same stream into which Cleo had been gazing earlier. The Mystery Woman, they were calling her, since no one had yet come forward to identify her.

Cleo folded the paper hurriedly and picked up a stack of forms and a pen as she heard signs of George's client leaving. She was a middle-aged woman who'd obviously been crying, but as she left she smiled a rather watery thank-you at Cleo as she sprang up to open the outer door for her. It looked as though she'd been too worried before she came out to do anything but put on the first things that had come to hand – a shocking pink scarf tied anyhow over her greying hair, a coral lipstick that hadn't been designed for someone with her colouring and had smeared on her lips. Her emerald green jacket, though smart, went with neither. All the same, Cleo noticed her noticing her own admittedly scruffy jeans and baggy sweater. Oh Lor'! If her appearance was enough to make someone in that state give her a reproving glance, she was going to have to raid Jenna's wardrobe for something more suitable to come to the office in.

She made some tea and took a mug into her father. He told her the woman was called Ruby and she wanted him to try and find her daughter.

'Ruby what?'

'It's Mrs Ruby. Evelyn Ruby. Her daughter Sara left home about three months ago without leaving a note or taking any of her clothes. Her mum's aggrieved that the police don't want to know. But that's how it is, Sara's over twenty-one and if she's left home of her own accord, there isn't really a lot anybody can do.'

'You can't afford not to take the case, though, can you? It's business.'

She sounded just like her mother, but he smiled. 'So it is. I've told Mrs Ruby I'll do what I can but not to be surprised if I can't find Sara. If anyone of her age doesn't want to be found, she won't be. I'll either find her straight away or not at all. If I do succeed, it's odds on she won't want to go home. Ten to one she's gone off with some man her family wouldn't approve of.'

Cleo felt sorry for Mrs Ruby – and for her father, come to that, lumbered with such a thankless task. But Sara Ruby had her sympathy too, wanting to hide away. There'd been times, lately, when she'd felt like doing exactly the same thing.

2

He'd just finished breakfast and was shrugging himself into his jacket when the phone in the kitchen rang. 'Mayo.'

'Thought I might catch you before you left, Gil. Sorry I didn't ring last night.'

'Alex!' His mouth lifted in an involuntary smile, just at the sound of her voice. Especially since she was ringing him before eight, mornings never being her best time. Even more especially considering her previous assertions that she and her fellow course-members were kept up until all hours every night, up to the eyebrows in work. But touched, and, knowing Alex, not having far to look for the reason: though she'd never admit it openly, she was worried about him, unable to forget what hell the last few weeks had been for him. He felt warmed by this unnecessary concern, but it had to be admitted that, though he'd toughed it out, as usual, it had been no picnic. And not only for himself as detective superintendent, but for every other senior officer in the Division also.

They talked for a while, catching up on what had happened the day before. When they'd just about exhausted that, she asked, 'What did you have for dinner last night?'

'Dinner?' he repeated, momentarily thrown.

'Food. You know, the stuff that fuels the body and keeps it going.'

'Oh, that!' He laughed. 'I had one of those M & S microwave things you left in the freezer.' He cast a guilty glance over his shoulder towards his supper – and breakfast – dishes still stacked unrinsed and forgotten in the sink. Still waiting to be put in the dishwasher, an unthinkable sin to Alex. He thanked the Lord his life hadn't yet encompassed the horrors of video telephones.

'Which one?'

'Which one what?'

'Which meal did you have?'

He found he had to search his memory. 'The beef. *Boeuf*

bourgnignon. It was delicious.' He was able to say this with perfect truth and felt it absolved him from adding that half an hour after midnight, he'd found it necessary to get up out of bed and make a large cheese and pickle sandwich to fill up the yawning spaces. His friend Henry Ison, the police doctor, had once told him that a low blood-sugar level was not conducive to proper sleep. Alex's understanding of how much food was good for him and his waistline didn't necessarily coincide with his own. In his opinion, one-portion, microwaved meals were meant only for women and weeds. Someone of his size needed more than that to keep body and soul together.

She went on, uncannily percipient, 'Sleep well?'

'Like a log,' he lied.

'Hmm.' Never mind video, he couldn't deceive her, though it was partly true.

It wasn't an empty stomach alone that had kept him awake. But the sandwich, and a cup of tea, had helped him put a brake on the merry-go-round of unprofitable thoughts which had prevented him dropping off. After it, his stomach comfortably full, his thoughts in proportion again, he'd slept at least better than he had in a month.

The cold-blooded murder of a local football star, shot through the passenger window of his car when he drew up at a red light at 3 a.m. one morning, had sent earthquake tremors throughout the Division, not without justification. Danny Fermanagh had been a lad of Irish immigrant parentage and native charm who was going places, a clean-cut boy hero, whose murder had touched a collective local nerve. His adoring public hadn't wanted to believe the truth that emerged, that Danny, when he wasn't playing for Lavenstock United, had been involved in small-time drugs dealing. When the killer wasn't immediately apprehended, the police became the scapegoat: they'd had a tip-off about Fermanagh's drug-dealing connections some time ago, it was alleged in the press – without revealing how this knowledge had been come by – and had apparently ignored it. The truth was something different, but it wasn't expedient to say so. The footballer had been watched for months, with one particular undercover detective detailed to get matey with him in an attempt to net the bigger fish who were supplying him: Danny-boy was notoriously loose-lipped when he'd had a noggin or

16

two. Unfortunately, those behind him had taken matters into their own hands and shut him up permanently before he could say anything too revealing.

There'd been mistakes, yes, a reluctance to act quickly, failures of communication. Allegations of CID bullying in their attempts to pull in witnesses. However unfounded, and most of the accusations were, as Mayo knew full well, it was no surprise that Joe Public, goaded by some sections of the media, saw the whole affair as a typical police cock-up which the Division as a whole was having to live down. There was to be the inevitable enquiry, though it was felt within the Division that Mayo had been dealt a tough hand. He had a very good private idea of the killer – or, more correctly, those who were behind the murder – but that didn't mean, even if more resources had been available – which they were not – that he'd ever get the person who'd pulled the trigger. This, he felt ominously, was going to be one of the few stickers of his career, one of those cases which were never solved. Not one that he'd ever forget, though.

But inevitably other crimes were waiting, other problems had come along and Danny had now been consigned to that limbo labelled 'Pending'.

He looked at his watch, not wanting to be the one who terminated the conversation, but Alex seemed reluctant to let him go. 'You're looking after Moses all right? Don't forget his vitamin supplements, will you?'

This was just filling in time! She knew better than he that there was no chance whatever of him not looking after the cat – Moses himself would see to that, self-preservation being his middle name. As for vitamin supplements . . . 'That cat's going to live to 120, vitamins or not,' he said. 'I'm the one who needs the supplements.'

Alex laughed, and at last said she must go. 'Back to the salt mines. I'll be home tomorrow. Two whole days' rest from this madhouse!' She didn't sound overwhelmed by it. 'Love you, Gil.'

'Love you, and miss you, too,' he answered, inadequate as this was to express what he wanted to say. Unable, as always, to say more. 'Enjoy yourself.'

'I'll do my best,' she said drily, 'I'll really try.'

In line with the recommendations of her new job, she'd been

sent on this two-week training course, with a weekend break in the middle. He hoped she was enjoying it: the idea of dramatis personae from the Crown Prosecution Service gathered together for two weeks of each other's company filled him with a horrified amusement, but Alex had said she was actually looking forward to it – and it sounded as though she was in fact relishing it. Unfairly, this made him feel badly done by. She knew that he, along with most other police officers, trod warily with the CPS, who, like as not, saw fit to throw out as unsafe for prosecution, due to what they considered insufficient evidence or whatever, cases the police had toiled over for months. He appreciated that her new career was giving her a buzz and he was glad for her, but he didn't have to like what she was doing. It smelled too much of collusion. Sleeping with the enemy.

Because he felt guilty, thinking like that, he dutifully stacked the dishes in the machine before he went out. He also went to feed the parrot, who was tuning up for his morning recital, his shrieks sounding even more demonic than usual. Sometimes Mayo thought he'd be better off living in Oxford Circus than in this menagerie, where the occupants did not live in harmony. It would certainly be quieter.

Moses was sitting in front of Bert's cage, his eyes lit with an unblinking, malevolent yellow glint. No wonder the parrot was losing it. One day I'll get you, the cat's gaze said. Try it, said Bert's mad glare. Mayo resisted temptation, and shut the cat in the kitchen.

It was just on eight when he walked into Milford Road Divisional Headquarters, having decided to make time to walk down the hill to work, loosen up, clear his head and maybe tune into some of that feel good factor he heard so much about. He was met with the usual controlled hubbub associated with changing shifts that issued from the office behind the front desk – doors banging, telephones ringing, exchange of banter. He asked, as he normally did, to see the night duty officer's occurrence book, and glanced through the usual depressing spate of crimes – drunk and disorderlies, acts of vandalism, car thefts. Routine stuff. And housebreaking. It looked very much as though Lavenstock's finest were signally failing to come to grips with this last.

'There's a lot of it about,' pointed out the desk sergeant, Light by name, miserable old sod by nature, when he saw Mayo's eyes resting thoughtfully on the entries. 'Four again last night. All that grief, just for drug money! I'd show 'em.'

'Hmm. Inspector Moon in, yet?'

'No, sir, not yet,' Light answered with relish, looking point-edly at the clock. Tough as old boots, he hated all policewomen on principle, and Abigail Moon in particular, since she didn't put up with his old buck and gave as good as she got.

'Right. Tell her I'd like to see her when she gets in, will you?'

Light said it would be a pleasure.

The door next to Mayo was flung open and a hefty young policewoman bounced through, nearly knocking him over. He dimly remembered seeing her around. A big girl. Beefy red arms under a short-sleeved white shirt, moon face, mouse-brown hair streaked blonde and pulled tight back in a scrunch. 'Nobody ever tell you standing behind doors is an unsocial act?' she demanded, before she saw who it was. 'Whoops, sorry, sir – I thought it was someone else!' Her face turned as red as her arms.

'My fault, shouldn't have been standing there. No harm done.' He regained his balance, nodded to show there was no ill feeling and turned to make his way up the stairs.

'Tracey,' he heard Sergeant Light ponderously behind him, 'a word in your shell-like.'

Who was she?

No one had yet come forward to identify the woman found in the flooded uplands.

She had been discovered by two small brothers, indulging in forbidden activity. It was Saturday morning and they'd been intent on making the most of being off school on a day miracu-lously free from rain, and set off to fish in what at that point was normally a dismal trickle of water yielding nothing more inter-esting than sticklebacks and tadpoles. Now, it had suddenly, magically, become a river. Had they but known it, the Kyne had

19

always been officially classed as a river, though it was never much more than a brook anywhere along its course, sliding lazily along in its upper reaches, becoming somewhat swifter and wider before joining the more robust Stockwell in its own deep valley . . . where Lavenstock, back in the mists of time, had started as a medieval river-bank settlement, expanded when it was drawn into the Black Country industrial developmental sprawl, and now spread its residential suburbs inexorably upwards towards the hills on either side.

The two boys, from one of the estates past which the Kyne meandered, had got more than their act of disobedience warranted. Inexpertly casting their lines, they'd convinced themselves that the thing on which one of their hooks had fastened must at least be a huge salmon, if not a shark, swimming around in there. Reeling in his line, shrill with excitement, the ten-year-old at last drew forward what was attached to it: a horrid, bloated thing which had drifted into the far bank, become wedged under a group of low-branched alders and balsam, and was now freed.

The boys, who'd been warned they'd be given what for, and not half, if their parents caught them messing around near the floods, had abruptly abandoned their tackle and fled in terror, as quickly as their wellies sinking into the squelchy mud would allow. Shane wasn't for telling what they'd seen, but Darren, who was only eight, was blubbing for his mum (something he'd hotly deny later) and in the end Shane was glad they *had* told when the police cars and ambulance arrived and he had the kudos of telling his story to the police. It was as well he didn't know then that he'd remember it in his dreams for years to come.

Five days later, nothing had yet come of appeals in the media for anyone who might have information on a missing woman, but that was perhaps understandable, in view of what the post-mortem had revealed – what had now, inevitably, become public knowledge. It could no longer be assumed that her death was an accident, or that she'd been one of those poor unfortunates who had finally surrendered to the water a life that had proved too much to endure.

Mayo opened the pathologist's report and flipped through it again. The unknown woman hadn't drowned, either by accident or intent, as had at first seemed, but had been murdered before being tipped into the water, two days before she was found, it was estimated. Which meant she had died a week ago today.

She was about forty years of age, previously healthy and well-nourished. A tall woman, five foot eight inches, having fair, shoulder-length hair, blue eyes and an unusually perfect set of teeth, without any extractions, fillings, crowns or cappings, so that the possibility of ever tracing her through dental records was remote. Nothing on her clothing helped to identify her: Marks and Spencer underwear and tights, a grey skirt from the same source, a sweater and shirt without distinguishing labels. When she had been found, she'd been shoeless, and so far the shoes had not been found, probably never would be. There was no ring on her wedding finger, but the condition of her swollen flesh made it impossible to say whether there ever had been one which had been removed. Although it had still been possible to obtain prints from her fingers, these hadn't been found to match any in the National Computer index of criminal fingerprints. Truly The Mystery Woman the newspapers had dubbed her.

He pushed his chair back and walked over to the large-scale map of the area hanging on the wall. The murder, when it had been revealed as such, had at least served to deflect the relentless attentions of the press from the Fermanagh affair. Which couldn't fail to be welcome, notwithstanding the choked feelings of rage and pity the untimely death of a fellow human being never failed to provoke in Mayo, however many he encountered, and by now they were numberless. But, as usual, he summoned up a pragmatic detachment, the only way he knew how to cope with it, knowing the next few days would demand total dedication from him, and from all his team: the slog of endless and mostly unproductive questioning, snatched, irregular meals, a willingness to forgo sleep, when and if necessary.

But this time it hadn't happened that way. Frustration was all that had happened, like butting your head into a feather pillow. Despite a well-mounted enquiry, the woman might as well have appeared from below the water as magically as Excalibur. The days went by and nothing turned up. Not a soul admitted to having seen or heard anything suspicious in the vicinity of where the body had been found, no gunshot had been heard, no untoward disturbances had occurred anywhere nearby. No one resembling her had been seen around the place either, as far as this could be ascertained from the police artist's impression of what she might have looked like when she was alive. But this didn't really convey anything, except that she'd looked like a million other women. Nondescript, eyes blue, hair fair. No distinguishing features. Misper – the Missing Persons Register – had been consulted, with negative results. One thing was certain, however – she hadn't put herself into the water, and common sense said she must have gone in not too far away from where she'd been found.

Someone, somewhere, must have known her. She couldn't simply have slipped out of life and left no ripples. Or could she? People did. In London, floaters were regularly brought in from the Thames and never identified, known only, and eventually buried, by numbers: DB 548. Dead Body 548. A sad, small, insignificant detail, but unthinkable, shocking, even to those not easily shocked. But that was the Met, big city policing, and this was Lavenstock, Mayo's bailiwick, under his jurisdiction, where it was his job to oversee the keeping of the peace, and where a drowned person was, thank God, still a rarity.

Only she hadn't drowned, had she? She had been shot through the heart.

The day, unsurprisingly, brought forth no more information. But, though routine matters filled the hours, the mystery woman was with Mayo, occupying the back of his mind like the shadow behind him, and he was once again studying the map on the wall when Abigail came in, in answer to his summons, about half-past five.

'Tea?' He waved a hand towards the teapot on his desk which his secretary, Delia, always brought in last thing before going home. Having experienced this beverage before, Abigail hesitated, but eventually poured herself a cup and refilled his empty one and took both over to where he stood. She sipped cautiously at the strong Indian brew which was what a Yorkshireman like Mayo considered to be a good cup of tea. It was also stewed, but she managed not to pucker her lips.

'Have a look at this, Abigail.'

It was a detailed, coloured map showing the whole of the

Division. Limited by the yellow snake of the M6 on one side, on the other the industrial sprawl of Holden Hill and the old scars of steelworks, abandoned coal and clay mines as the roads reached out to the Birmingham suburbs. The map-markings, circled by the bypass, showed dense in the town centre, then thinned out towards the residential areas. In and amongst were the green islands of parks and recreation grounds: the Stockwell and its tributaries showed blue; the canal wound lazily through the whole area. The one-dimensional map gave no indication of the undulations of the area, how the streets of its old quarter sloped gently down to the river; how the blue hills rose on one side, from the top of which it was possible to see right into Wales on a clear day. How the land lay flat for the most part on the other, before its descent into the valley.

The map was large-scale, and also showed the course of the Kyne, its total length not more than seven or eight miles, down which the body had floated, though not far enough. Abigail tried to envisage the land as it was in reality: the source of the stream was several miles out of the town, the only indication of its whereabouts a wet patch surrounded by reeds in the middle of a field, unless those same fields became waterlogged with excessive rain; then water spread outwards and channelled itself into a stream, flowing down the slope past Covert Farm and alongside Wych Cottage, until it spread out again on the flat land of the Kyneford estate.

Twenty years ago, Kyneford had been little more than a hamlet surrounded by an undistinguished tract of scrubland. Now, since the land had been released for development, it had become a great spread of houses, set out in crescents, avenues and closes. Of particular interest in view of their easy access to the stream was Pinfold Lane, a row of bungalows, where several of the small gardens reached right down to its edge. Built on land that had always been prone to flooding (a fact which the developer had failed to point out to intending buyers), most of the gardens had been under water during the recent floods, if not most of the houses themselves. But enquiries had drawn a blank there, like everywhere else.

After leaving the estate, the stream flowed alongside an abandoned brickworks and then down into Lavenstock's outer suburbs. Crossing a recreation ground, through a culvert under the main railway line, it emerged in the industrial park, passed the brewery and finally flowed into the Stockwell. All the while gathering momentum, especially when swollen, as it had been recently, with flood water.

'But why?' Abigail murmured thoughtfully.

'Why was she put in *there*? Or why was she put in the river at all? You tell me. What puzzles me,' he said, stabbing his forefinger at the map, allowing her to take away his empty cup and giving her the opportunity to tip her own into a rubber plant, 'is why anybody should have dumped her at that particular point. Between where she was found and the source of the Kyne, there's only Covert Farm, Wych Cottage and the beginning of the housing estate, there, on Pinfold Lane. Whoever chose the spot must have realised she might be found quite soon, and that would pretty well define the limits of our search.'

'Yes, they'd have done better to have put her in lower down, where the current gathers force. Unless they hoped she'd be swept down with the other debris and carried right down into the Stockwell? Which, but for getting snagged on that tree, she probably would have been.'

Mayo rubbed a hand across his face. 'It's a bugger, this, and right, isn't it? We're on a hiding to nothing until we find out who she was. And don't tell me what I already know – that we're running out of steam.' The hollow feeling in his guts told him that this, another shooting, could well join the Fermanagh file. A thought insinuated itself. Could the murder of Miss X have been another drug-related crime? It was a depressing thought which he didn't care to examine at that particular moment.

'Have another look at this, will you?' He slid the discouragingly thin buff folder which held all the dead woman's case notes across to Abigail. 'On the offchance that anything strikes you.'

While she scanned it for the umpteenth time, he sat at his desk, picking things up and putting them down again, staring absent-mindedly through the window at his old familiar foes, the scruffy pigeons, settling on the Town Hall for the night. He watched one land on a narrow window ledge, close to three others already perched there. Like fastidious old ladies moving away from an unwelcome tramp who'd decided to occupy the same park bench, the three began a shuffling, sideways progress,

24

closely followed by the intruder, which resulted in them being forced off the far edge one by one, leaving the victor alone to preen himself. Obviously a natural for heading the pecking order. Like some humans he knew.

As she read, Abigail absently munched through two of the peanut butter cookies which had come with the tea. 'Nothing new,' she said, closing the file.

Neither said anything more for a moment and then, as if continuing that previous thought of his own, she said casually, 'The promotion board's been fixed for next month.'

He breathed a silent, selfish and entirely unworthy wish that she might not be successful, then cancelled it. It wasn't possible she wouldn't be, anyway. He, and everyone else, would just have to get used to not seeing her energetic, sparky presence about the place. He'd miss her quick intuition and her capacity for unquestioning hard slog when it was necessary – even her sometimes too blunt outspokenness. On a more frivolous note, attractive faces and shining bronze hair were thin on the ground in CID – and there was no one else who could deal with Farrar at his most obnoxious, though Farrar was, if anyone dared hope, becoming less of a pain. At least treading more circumspectly since his long-awaited appointment to acting sergeant.

God, what was he thinking of? He'd always known Abigail wouldn't be with him for ever – she was university-educated, a high-flyer on her way up. He'd been lucky that she'd stayed here so long, he supposed – without flattering himself that it was due to the attractions of the Lavenstock Division. Or even his charisma as a boss. Part of the reason why she'd stayed was because promotion would almost certainly mean a move away from the area, and that would mean a move away from that journalist, the editor of the local newspaper. Which wouldn't necessarily be a bad thing, in Mayo's admittedly jaundiced opinion.

However, though her own ambitions were paramount, he, Ben Appleyard, probably *was* a factor in Abigail's decision to apply for promotion. Mayo suspected a certain conflict of interest had arisen between them over the reportage of the Fermanagh murder. Actually, he knew it had. Alex, who was close friends with Abigail, had told him there was a coolness between Ben and Abigail lately, and she was certain that was the reason. Left to himself, Mayo might never even have thought of it, but when it was pointed out to him, he couldn't help noticing certain signs that confirmed it.

Then, coming very opportunely, a vacancy had arisen for a detective chief inspector in the next Division, in Hurstfield, which wasn't more than a spit and a jump away. And since Detective Superintendent Glenda ('Flossie') Nightingale had retired, there'd been nothing to stop Abigail applying for the job. Mayo couldn't visualise any way she would ever have worked voluntarily again under Nightingale, after having been compelled to do so when the woman had been seconded here a couple of years ago. As it was, now, she wouldn't need to. There was nothing to stop her getting the promotion, and therefore the job, he was convinced. And so, evidently, was she. Like the old toothpaste ad, she had that ring of confidence about her. She was going to need all her not inconsiderable powers of push, but when had that ever stopped Abigail from doing anything?

'Good luck,' he said and yes, he really did mean it.

'Thanks.' She looked radiant. 'Maybe it was tempting fate, but I stopped and looked in Tixall's Estate Agents in Sheep Street on the way here this morning. My God, you should see what houses round here are fetching!'

'So now's the time to sell.'

'Looks like that, but I don't know if I could bear to – I've put my soul into that house.' She smiled ironically, though it was near the truth. She'd bought her cottage for a song, against all advice, when it was a near ruin, and she'd never regretted putting all her spare money into having it gradually repaired and restored. She'd had to make do with scouring markets and car boot sales for furnishings, but she'd had great fun learning how to do them up. It was a long way from perfect yet, but it was comfortable and appealing, and now that she'd opened up its possibilities, she hoped that prospective buyers wouldn't be slow to see its further potential. It would be a wrench, leaving it, but there were other houses.

Oh, but the garden, that she'd so lovingly created, that she loved almost more than the house!

And then there was Ben. Well, yes, Ben.

The truth was, let's face it, she thought, leaving both house and garden would be more traumatic than leaving Ben. Mainly because she wouldn't really be leaving him at all, only moving a bit further away – Hurstfield wasn't far. It might be better for both of them to be further apart, in the circumstances. They'd never quite got it together, the idea of sharing a home. It suited them, living separately, as they did. Especially now, when they were not exactly seeing eye to eye, or to put it more bluntly, in the middle of a major row. Words had been bandied, unforgivable things said, words like 'lack of integrity' and 'bloody ambitious females' hurled between them. It was time for distancing, at least until tempers cooled.

And in any case, Ben had never had any scruples about abandoning her in the past, when some more exciting job prospect had presented itself . . . Now it was her turn, Abigail told herself, feeling childish but unrepentant.

On the whole, however, more adult feelings prevailed, that it was time to put to the test a theory she'd had for some time: she'd railed against their enforced separations in the past but perhaps that was what kept their relationship alive. It wasn't the first time she'd thought this, but it was the first time she'd thought it seriously.

She closed the file and shifted on her seat. She looked at Mayo. Should she, or shouldn't she?

Then, with an impetuosity worthy of her fellow inspector, Martin Kite, she blurted out: 'That leak, to the press. I'd just like to say that – it didn't come from me.'

He put down the pen he'd been clicking and regarded her steadily. 'I never for a moment thought it had, Abigail.'

Whether he was speaking the strict truth or not, it sounded genuine – at least indicated he wasn't saving anything up for some future occasion. She felt a rush of relief, unnecessary, for since when had Mayo ever been one to hold a grudge? You might get a right bollocking at the time, if you did the wrong thing, but he never bore malice. Bluntly north country, he said what he thought, and then forgot it. 'Nothing more we can do here tonight. Go home, and have an early night, while you've got the chance.'

She heard herself saying, 'No rush, Ben's away at the moment.'

She hadn't been fishing, honest she hadn't, but now was the chance for him to suggest that since Alex was too, they could grab a meal together, but he merely said, with a smile, 'An even earlier night, then.'

She could have suggested the meal herself, of course she could, but she was, as always, wary that it might have been construed wrongly. The thought that she could easily, if she let herself, find him very attractive, was intermittent, but never all that far away. Nor was the thought that he was her best chum's man. Rubbish! A quick meal with a colleague, what was wrong with that? Nothing, if the colleague wasn't Mayo.

He said kindly, 'You're looking tired, lass. Do as I suggested, and get off home. And that's an order.'

They just didn't have any idea, did they, men?

3

'I know the house is going to rack and ruin, my lovey, I know it is, but what can I do?'

Eileen Totterbridge poured Sam a mug of her thick, bracing tea, added milk, sweetened it the way she knew he'd always liked it and passed it across the kitchen table. Sam leaned his broad shoulders against the high-backed kitchen chair, raised his mug to her and sipped. Nectar! He never felt he was really home again until he'd been rejuvenated by Mrs Totty's tea and entertained by her conversation. She was just the same, too, his lovely Mrs Totty, whom he'd known all his life. Burbling on, comforting, kind, her round face concerned as she tried to excuse the deteriorating condition of 16 Kelsey Road, even though it wasn't remotely her responsibility.

'You can't do any more than you do,' he reassured her. 'Which is more than any of us have a right to expect in the circumstances.'

'Oh, rubbish! If I can't manage two mornings a week, after all these years, I don't know what. I'd come in more, willingly, you know I would, but there's my other cleaning job, and Joe, and there's the grandchildren. Seven of 'em, now, and their mums have to go out to work, Sam, you know how it is. Nobody can live on one wage nowadays, or nobody wants to, and that's the truth.'

Sam reached out for a chocolate Hobnob and thought it wiser not to mention her increasing age, which must also be a contributing factor. She really ought to be retired altogether. Her fingers were knobbly with arthritis, and he'd noticed how much more stiffly she was moving, but he knew she hated the idea of not being as active as she had been all her life: she was into her seventies but she'd always said it would be the beginning of the end if she'd nothing better to do than discuss her ailments. Apart from that, she wasn't looking a scrap different – her hair had been resolutely dyed and was as richly brown as ever, done up in a neat perm. The nylon overall over the checked, pleated skirt and a pink, round-necked jumper, the little gilt studs in her ears and the scent of violet talc were reassuringly as they'd always been.

'I'm sure Dorrie's only too glad you can come in at all,' he said.

'Yes, well.' She looked as though she was about to say more, but hesitated, then changed the subject, smiling at him. 'I must say, it's grand to see you looking so well, Sam, dear. How've you got so brown, then, when they don't have any sun down there? Come on, have another biscuit, you need feeding, a big chap like you, though you don't look as though they've been starving you, I'll say that! Isn't it wonderful what they can do nowadays? Even down at the South Pole.'

Sam smiled his slow, attractive smile and stretched his long legs. He hadn't exactly been living on the fat of the land recently, while working as a geophysicist, part of an inter-disciplinary research unit on the Polar Ice Cap, but life had been reasonably civilised, the food had been quite amazing, considering. 'There's a lot more sun down there than up here, sometimes, and no, we haven't been living on whale meat and pemmican, exactly.'

'I can see that – oh, it's grand to have you back, my lovey, we've all missed you, especially Dorrie. She's been like a dog with two tails ever since she heard you were coming home, and no wonder. It'll do her the world of good to have you here. Three years, it's a long time when you're knocking on, like we are.'

He smiled, wondering what his Aunt Dorrie would think of that comparison. Mrs Totty could give Dorrie ten years, though despite that, and her hard life, she'd come out better on the whole. Dorrie had changed, not physically, but in some other, indefinable way . . . she was still the same odd, eccentric little person he'd always known, soft floppy hair pulled back from her face into a knot, a thick fringe falling over her eyes and seriously interfering with the big, round, owlish glasses. Still with the same soft, slow, solemn way of talking, and the sudden smile that, had he known it, echoed his own. A sweet contentment had always seemed part of her, though sometimes he thought he'd detected faint echoes of sadness. A regret, perhaps, for something that had never been, but it was hard to say what, so faintly and so occasionally was it glimpsed. Missed opportunities perhaps. Dorrie had never had a career, never married, never, so far as he was aware, even had a love affair.

Sam Leadbetter had been orphaned at an early age, and though he'd spent most of his time at boarding school, the house in Kelsey Road was home to him, the place he'd always come back to in the holidays, back to Dorrie. His beloved aunt, his mother's sister, was his only living relative, the person he'd loved most in the world, despite realising, as he grew older, that she wasn't quite like other people. The amused glances that followed them whenever they went out had first told him that, Dorrie looking like a bag lady in a haphazard collection of garments, with her hair escaping from its knot into straggling wisps round her face. Sometimes wellingtons on her feet with an old cotton dress, if she'd forgotten to change them after gardening, or dressed up in ancient finery, as if for a garden party, to go and buy vegetables. Her mother's tatty old musquash fur coat and her strange hats. The indulgent way the shopkeepers treated her, the way the vicar humoured her because she was more than generous with her donations to church funds – but also, Sam had come to believe, because he was fond of her as well. Anyone who really knew Dorrie couldn't help loving her. Old Dorrie Lockett, mad as a hatter.

But no, even as a child he'd known that wasn't right, and fiercely defended her against anyone who even hinted at it – just living on another plane, but even so quite often able to cut through the conventional ways of looking at things that hampered other people, and to give one a sharp glance and a surprisingly wise judgement. Not mad. Just someone happy not to live her life by other people's prescribed rules.

Was she still happy, though? Coming home again after a long absence, Sam had immediately sensed a jitteriness that was foreign to her, a worry at the back of her eyes, an uncertainty that surely hadn't been there before he went away. She'd never mentioned in her letters that anything was troubling her, though, and he'd read nothing between the lines of her almost impossible to decipher backward script.

'Though of course,' said Mrs Totty, as if a party to his thoughts, 'there isn't as much for me to do as there used to be. Sensible, if you think about it, though, shutting most of the place up. Who needs all that space, living on their own, when all's said

31

and done? Better live in two tidy rooms than in twelve like a pigsty I say, though I'd never let her come to that, not me, never, you can bank on that, Sam.'

It didn't need saying. The kitchen here, though so old-fashioned it might qualify for a Heritage award, was spotlessly clean, as was the bathroom, and the two bedrooms still in use. The bright and sunny former morning room Dorrie had chosen to live in was untidy, as anything around Dorrie was bound to be, but hoovered and polished within an inch of its life by Mrs Totty. But he had been shocked all the same, to see how bad a state of repair the rest of the house was in when he'd gone poking around, searching for his own left-behind belongings on the morning after his arrival. So familiar he hadn't noticed anything untoward before he went away, but impossible to miss now, with the furniture sheeted up, the pictures removed. Broken cornices, peeling wallpaper, wet and dry rot, mice scuttling behind the wainscotting. It didn't need Mrs Totty to tell him it had slid into neglect, and he was ashamed he'd never really looked at it seriously before; it couldn't have reached that stage so quickly. But those few years had signalled for him the passing of the borderline into more responsible attitudes: before then, he'd never noticed such things, and in any case, leaving England so precipitously, so preoccupied with his own troubled mind, he'd been in no state to be thinking about the house, so far were his concerns fixed on other things, or at any rate, on one other person . . .

'She'll have to sell, you know, sooner or later, she'll have to give in. The school keeps pestering her, they've offered her a good price, and she could get herself a nice little bungalow, one of those retirement homes up by the rec . . .' But even Mrs Totty's optimism faltered at the idea of Dorrie away from Kelsey Road, living in a bungalow. 'Well, maybe not,' she admitted with a sigh. 'It'd be too much to expect of her, wouldn't it?'

'So why *are* the school so anxious to buy?'

The house backed on to the playing fields of Lavenstock College, the minor public school whose Victorian buildings could be seen in the distance, surrounding the chapel and its clock tower. A familiar, well-loved view. Across the sweep of green turf, the irregular yet orderly grouping of buildings looked serene, peaceful and traditional, especially when a cricket match was in progress, though in truth more pleasing from afar than they did on closer inspection. Once, at a time when the Butterfield-style, polychrome, brick-and-stone-banded school had just been built in the High Victorian Gothic tradition, when the great horse chestnuts surrounding the playing fields were new, Lavenstock College had stood with its back to open fields, the town and its industry falling away below it to the river; now the town had crept upwards and outwards and spread itself around the school, a new housing estate having filled in the last empty space to complete its encirclement.

He'd asked Dorrie the same question last night – why did the school want to buy? – but she'd shrugged and evaded a proper answer. Mrs Totty, on the other hand, could hardly wait to inform him. 'Well, you know, they've already bought three of the houses either side of here – oh yes, they have, starting when him at number 12 retired and put his house on the market! When the folks next door to him saw what price he'd got from the school, they weren't slow to follow suit, I can tell you! The school bought that as well, and made an offer for this and for number 18, which 18 jumped at – but not Dorrie! A real thorn in their flesh, she is!' she finished, not without satisfaction.

Sam, too, felt indignant on Dorrie's behalf. She'd been born in the house sixty-odd years ago, and had lived there with every expectation of staying there until she died. Why should pressure be put on her to move if she didn't want to?

'What it is, you see, lovey, once they've got all four, they mean to have them down, to make a new entrance for the school. That new estate that's been built either side the Tilbourne Road, see, near the present school entrance, well, it's lowered the tone! Don't want the posh parents in their Rolls Royces and their Bentleys having to drive through *that*, do they? They want to make a new entrance along here, and then put up some school-rooms or whachoumaycallems where the present entrance is, to screen the estate.'

Sam could see now what the school was after. Kelsey Road was generally regarded as one of the best roads in Lavenstock, quiet, tree-lined, unassuming, houses of different styles and ages mingling easily together, some of them substantial properties with big gardens, some less so. A school entrance leading off Kelsey Road would form a very pleasant and dignified approach

33

to the school. On the other hand, buying four houses to pull down simply for that purpose was going a bit over the top. Wasn't it?

'. . . but you know, Sam,' Mrs Totty was going on, 'those Tilbourne Road houses *aren't* an eyesore, they're lovely, really. Wouldn't mind one myself, anyway.' She sighed. 'Chance'd be a fine thing, eh?'

So it would, Sam thought, with Joe Totterbridge, her useless husband, around. Bone idle before he became entitled to his state retirement pension, he did virtually nothing now except sit on his backside and watch television.

'It'd break Dorrie's heart to leave this house, Mrs Totty.'

She paused in the act of picking up the teapot, and stared at him. 'Sam, I'm as fond of you as I am of my own, but I've always said it and I'll say it again. There's nobody so daft as a man when he doesn't want to see what's right in front of his eyes!'

With this Delphic utterance, she raised her own eyes to heaven, leaving Sam, for the moment, at a loss, until she went on, 'Break her heart? Lord love us, she hates this house, always has done, and it's nothing but a burden to her now! The only thing it'd break her heart to leave is her garden, and I'd like to see the one who could make her do that!'

Sam blinked and turned a disbelieving regard on the jungle outside the window. At one time, Joe Totterbridge had kept it in reasonable order, until superannuation from his job as a store-keeper down at the glassworks had signalled his abdication from almost any form of physical activity except walking down to the pub. It came as a shock to see what even such a relatively short spell of neglect could do – if a prime example of exponential growth was needed, look no further. It hadn't been tidied up before the winter and looked forlorn, pathetic and abandoned. Dead herbaceous stems stuck up like witches' brooms and with-ered grasses waved in an unending prairie. A rotting pergola had collapsed under the weight of a great, unchecked rambler. Willow herb that was rosily beautiful in summer was ominous in its spread and the threat of its feathery seed heads. Brambles had taken over entirely in one corner. The paths were invisible.

But even as he surveyed this scene of desolation, determined to set about and tackle it the very next day, he realised Mrs Totty wasn't speaking of Dorrie's garden. She meant Dorrie's *garden*, a different proposition altogether: the other garden, where once a wide drive and a double coach house had existed, a sunken plot constructed on the site of a shallow bomb crater, the result of a bomb dropped on Lavenstock during the war. Jettisoned at random by a crippled, home-going German bomber after the raid on nearby Coventry, less than twenty miles away, on the infamous night when a beautiful, medieval city centre and its cathedral had been reduced to rubble, this particular bomb had landed, injuring no one, while Coventry, already mourning its dead and injured, was in flames.

A few years later Dorrie, with who knew what compulsion, had set about making a wild garden of the ugly, empty space which had once been the Victorian coach house and stables. She'd employed workmen to cart the rubble away and to create a randomly shaped pond over the shallow crater, had tons of topsoil dumped around its edges, then dismissed everyone and set to work planting the wild plants she loved: now teasel, red clover, wild sorrel and yellow rattle grew among the pluming grasses. Self-woven into a wattle fence were dog roses, black-thorn and elder, within it in season there grew bluebells, wild scabious, white wood anemones and celandines. A substantial part of her days in the summer was spent on her knees, happily grubbing in the earth, talking to her plants and coaxing small seedlings to grow, aiding nature by art. Blackbirds, tits and pond life colonised what had become a small miracle. The side of the house had become a secluded, sheltered, scented haven, screened from both the road and the next house by sweet-smelling hedges, a living and beautiful thing risen from ashes and destruction.

No, Sam wouldn't like to be the one who tried to prise her away from it. Once Dorrie set her mind on anything, she could be as stubborn as a mule, and this time Sam found himself in sympathy with her. More than that, he couldn't help feeling that Dorrie without her garden was likely to lose even more hold on reality.

4

When Cleo announced, after having worked for her father for just two days, that she was going to work for Maid to Order, Daphne lifted her eyes to heaven. And well she might, she told herself. As a teenager, Cleo *had* occasionally been known to tidy her room, under duress, and now it had to be admitted that she kept it in order – more or less – saying off-handedly that life was made easier if you knew just where to put your hands on a clean pair of knickers when you needed them. Daphne saw to it that she helped with the housework when she was around, though truly she found her daughter more of a hindrance than a help to her own efficiency. And nowadays, Cleo occasionally cleared the table after meals and put the dishes in the dishwasher without needing to be reminded. But dedicated to domesticity she was not.

'Val must be desperate,' was all Daphne allowed herself to say, in a jokey sort of way, as she whisked around, getting ready to go out. She'd learned to hold her tongue, and sometimes her tight-lipped disapproval. She did try, she really did. As she did now, by changing the subject. 'Do you like my new bowling skirt?'

It was important to Daphne that she always looked exactly right, even just playing bowls with her friends, a game they were all currently mad about. She'd have liked George to go with her and had been at pains to explain that it wasn't just a game for the wrinklies, and what great skill it required, but George only rolled his eyes.

'Mmm, yes,' said Cleo. 'Very stylish.' Like all Daphne's clothes, the skirt was well chosen and perfectly fitting. She'd kept her figure and the natural strands of silver in her well-styled fair hair only served to give it a fashionably streaky look. People often took her and her daughters for sisters. 'Nice for me,' Daphne would say with a light laugh, 'but poor you. Unfair.'

'It isn't Val that's desperate,' Cleo said now, 'it's me. Now that

36

Muriel's come back, Dad doesn't need me. I have to find another job.' In fact, she rather suspected that Muriel's sudden return wasn't unconnected with her own unexpected arrival on the scene.

'Oh, now, look –'

'Don't, Mum.'

Cleo began to rummage through the stacks of CDs on the rack. There was nothing to be ashamed of in living on the Social if there weren't any jobs around. Or living at home with your parents. But she'd been independent during the last three years and she'd no intention of going back on that. She'd thought that maybe the best solution would be to buzz off and find some-where to live in London, like Jenna, who was flat-sharing there, and where a lot of her friends were, but she couldn't even begin to think of affording that without a job, even if she was sharing, which for one important reason she didn't want to do.

'That Muriel!' Daphne was saying, as if what Cleo had said had just registered. 'And that Hermione! Anybody would think nobody had ever had a hysterectomy before.' She sniffed. Even she thought of Hermione as a person. Then she looked at Cleo more closely, her eyes worried. 'Cleo, you could get yourself a good position anywhere, if only you'd . . .'

Be content with what there is, she'd been going to say, but she bit it back just in time, seeing the expression on Cleo's face, which said that was just what she *wasn't* going to do. If she couldn't get the sort of job that demanded a good degree, then perversely, she'd said more than once, she didn't care what she did. One day she might, Daphne fervently hoped, she just might be persuaded to go back to university and begin again where she'd left off, because, contrary to what recent events had shown, Cleo was every bit as bright as Jenna. Jenna was just more clever at passing exams. On the other hand, Daphne sighed, it was more likely Cleo might not. She seemed to have changed and, in some way, grown older, even more secretive than usual. Cer-tainly more independent, and stubborn. Well, university apart, there were plenty of other opportunities open to clever girls. But going out cleaning wasn't one of them.

'Oh, Cleo!' she said helplessly. 'Maid to Order – I ask you!'

'Mum, I haven't signed my life away! It's only *temporary*! Just until Val gets herself sorted.'

Having disarranged all her mother's carefully ordered CDs and not found anything worthy of playing, Cleo knew exactly what Daphne was thinking. But she was never ever going to settle for being somebody's secretary. That seemed to her more like an admission of failure than taking a job with Maid to Order. And once there, she'd be trapped. She couldn't say this to her mother, however, who was very proud of her own job as part-time secretary (almost full-time, the hours she put in) to the Bursar at Lavenstock College. The Maid to Order job wasn't going to do anything to reinforce the impression that she was serious about getting herself together, yet how could she explain that this was something more than just a silly whim? That doing something undemanding would give her a breathing space while trying to do the one thing she really wanted to do?

'There's a letter from Jenna on the mantelpiece, she's going to take the job with that big law firm,' Daphne said at last with a sigh, realising she'd lost the battle yet again. She patted her already immaculate hair in the mirror before going out, looking neat and trim in her white skirt and navy blazer. 'She might be coming home next weekend.' She fluffed up a few cushions and blew some imaginary specks of dust off her Lladru collection on the display shelves. Cleo half expected the same treatment, but Daphne only looked at her, then left, with instructions about what time to switch on the oven for the evening meal, and how to peel the potatoes.

Cleo didn't read the letter for an hour and a half – an hour and thirty-four minutes, to be precise. She let it sit there, while she gazed out at the semi-detached houses opposite, a mirror image of their own, then back at the neat, familiar script on the envelope, telling herself she wouldn't read it. In the end, of course, she did. If she'd known what it would contain she could have saved herself one hour and thirty-four minutes biting her nails.

What had she expected? That Jenna was going to pour it all out, how she'd gone across to visit Cleo at Norwich, met her lover and stolen him? No, she wouldn't. Not Jenna. Well, not many people would, Cleo had to admit. No one would willingly admit to such perfidy. Perhaps she'd thought Jenna was simply writing to say she'd met this perfectly wonderful man, Toby Armitage, and was going to marry him and could she bring him home and please would Cleo keep out of the way? Preferably for the rest of their lives?

Cleo would keep out of the way, all right. She'd seen Jenna only once since that spectacular fight. Toby she hadn't seen at all. He'd dissolved like Scotch mist when all the trouble arose, leaving Jenna to face the music.

Oh Lord, thought Cleo. Never mind they weren't alike, she and Jenna did understand one another, there was a special sort of sibling bond between them whatever they said; until this last thing had happened, they'd always been best friends. Until that night when Jenna had admitted that on those weekends Toby had told Cleo he was going home to see his parents, he'd been seeing her in Cambridge, that they'd developed this grand passion.

Cleo's work had already suffered during the last year when she and Toby had no time for anything else except each other, and after he was gone and her exams loomed she was too miserable to apply herself to catching up at that late stage. She'd sort of been running backwards for a long time, anyway. Fighting against the admission that perhaps she wasn't really university material, which was something just too hard to swallow. You don't need a degree to be a writer, she'd told herself fiercely, think of all those famous names who've never been near a university. Think of Shakespeare. Think of Charlotte Brontë. Think of almost anyone. All the same, it was mortifying for someone who'd intended to be a writer for as long as she could remember to fail in Eng.Lit.

She was glad that nobody – except Jenna – knew about her ambitions. Still unconfident, unpublished, she wasn't sure even George would have understood. She knew despondently that her biggest battle was against her own lack of confidence. Why should anybody be interested in what she had to write? With so little experience of the world, did she even have the right to think she could be a novelist?

She knew that her parents knew perfectly well that, exam results apart, there was something else wrong, too. She was almost certain Daphne suspected some sort of broken love affair, and thought that was why she was moping around like a lovesick cow, though Cleo had never told them about Toby, wanting to keep him to herself for as long as she could. But her mother was wrong. Splitting up with Toby had hurt like an abscessed tooth, of course it had, but several months later, she knew the condition wasn't terminal. It was just that losing him had left her feeling so *empty*, hollow with unsatisfied longings for . . . she didn't know what. Well, she could always write.

She wasn't due to start with Maid to Order until Monday, so she went out and spent the morning once more looking for somewhere to live – a flat, or a bed-sit, anything. By now she wasn't all that fussy as long as it afforded her some privacy. Not that she was anti-social, but if she was going to be serious about writing, she needed her own space.

Near Birmingham, or Coventry, there was plenty of student-type accommodation available near the universities, but that absolutely wasn't what Cleo was looking for. She felt very definitely that she'd left that scene behind, to get involved in it again, however peripherally, would be a markedly backward step. But she found nothing else she could remotely afford, and after a depressing sandwich in a pizza bar (she should have stuck to the pizza) she wandered down to the agency, to give in her notice to her father, so to speak. He hadn't heard about her alternative proposals for employment yet.

He wasn't as rude about her qualifications for the job as Daphne had been, but he wasn't thrilled with the idea, even when she pointed out that there was nothing for her to do at the agency, now that Muriel was back.

'I know,' he said, 'and I wish she'd made up her bloomin' mind to stay away. It was good of her to think I'd be needing her, but I'm not mad about having Hermione around the place.'

Who would be? The little dog had been spoiled to death before her major op, and was worse now, enjoying the rewards of being an invalid without any of the disadvantages. Cleo had noticed her trotting around the back yard on her short legs without a care in the world, not to mention chasing the butcher's cat from next door, but she was canny enough not to push her luck by letting Muriel see her doing this. She even stayed curled in the little basket at Muriel's feet when anyone came in, gazing at them with soulful eyes rather than snapping as was her wont, when there was nothing she enjoyed more than seeing people shrink back in fear of her sharp little teeth. She'd been tyrannising her mistress for years. Muriel had always sworn that her previous bad temper was due to the poor little thing having had hot flushes for years, and how could anyone prove she hadn't? True or not, the dog obviously knew she was on to a good thing now. Minced fillet steak and Choccie Chews. Warm milk to drink. Hottie bottles in her basket. Hermione had obviously become power drunk, with every intention of spinning this out indefinitely.

'I wish I could give you some real work here,' George said, 'but you know how it is.' There was barely enough work for Muriel, never mind Cleo into the bargain. 'You've done well,' he added, and she felt a certain amount of pride, despite herself.

Muriel, it had to be said, though well-intentioned, and capable in her own way, was a muddler, and the office was in better order than when Cleo started. Maybe she could have made a good secretary after all. Perish the thought.

It didn't take her long to turn over everything back to Muriel, and before she left, she assured her father she'd done this – including the Sara Ruby case. She'd wondered at first if the woman who'd drowned could have been Sara Ruby, but the dead woman had been several inches too tall and many years too old. How terrible such a death was, thought Cleo, haunted by a sadness she couldn't explain whenever she thought about her, the fact that no one yet had claimed to have known her. How lonely.

'Don't you worry about me, Dad,' she told George when she was ready to leave. 'It's just that I have to earn some money, I can't go on living with you and Mum indefinitely.'

'Why not? It's your home, and always will be,' he said, but he was just being kind. Strained politeness had ruled at 26 Ellwood Street for the last few weeks, but they all knew that it was only a matter of time before Cleo and Daphne began to have some very real differences of opinion. Her mother, thought Cleo, expected too much. They got on fine, when they were apart. It was living together they couldn't stand.

'All right,' George said suddenly, with the air of a man coming to a decision. 'I might as well tell you now. I wasn't going to mention it until your mum and I had given it a bit more thought. But we've already decided, really. Phoebe's house has just come vacant.'

'The Honeybuns are leaving?' Cleo could never remember

their real name, a lovey-dovey married couple, Americans who'd come to live in her great-aunt's house after she died. The one time she'd met Mrs H she'd thought her a silly, wilting sort of creature who looked as if she wouldn't say boo to a goose. What was her name? Oh yes, Angela. Mr Honeybun had called her Angel.

'They've already gone. Back to America. The people at the place he worked for over there suddenly decided they wanted him back, urgently, and the college agreed to let him go. I don't know the details.'

Cleo remembered that Brad – Hunnicliffe, that was it – had been over here on some sort of exchange. Teaching science or something at Lavenstock College. When Daphne, working in the Bursar's office, had heard that he and his wife were seeking accommodation, it had seemed to her that Phoebe's house, which was standing empty after her death, though still furnished, could be of some use to someone, rather than standing idle . . . not to mention bringing in some cash.

'You might just as well stay in the house until we get another tenant – or for as long as you like as far as I'm concerned, Cleo,' George said now.

Cleo could hardly speak, unable to believe that her luck could change so dramatically. Phoebe's lovely little house! Not lovely in the sense that most people would regard as such, but lovely to her because it had been dear and familiar all her life, just as Phoebe had been.

Phoebe had been George's aunt. She had married just before the war. Hardly had the wedding bells ceased to ring, however, than war had been declared and Jack, her young husband, had been called up into the Navy, where he'd gone down with his ship almost as soon as he'd finished training. Poor Phoebe. She and her Jack had had so little time together, but at least he'd never known that she'd lost the baby she was expecting. After that, she'd just gone back to work, never remarried, and lived alone, until she was eighty-four, in the house she'd come to as a bride. In many ways she'd had a sad life, but a busy, and in the end, Cleo thought, a contented one. When she died, she left the house and contents to George. He'd had some idea of tarting it up, like some of the neighbouring houses, before selling it, but Phoebe, quiet, determined, austere little Phoebe, had been very special to him, and to all the family, and he hadn't yet been able to bring himself to get rid of all her furniture and belongings. However, as Daphne pointed out, it wasn't very sensible to leave the place unlived in, and so he'd agreed to rent it to the Hunnicliffes as temporary furnished accommodation.

It was the end one of a row of pint-sized artisan-type dwellings, as the house agents referred to them, meaning two up and one down, with a kitchen tacked on and bathroom made from the tiny second bedroom. Now wedged in between blocks of council flats on the one hand and fairly swanky properties on the other . . . but nothing was perfect, Cleo told herself. It was here, in Lavenstock, not far from either the library or a bus route. You could walk into the town centre easily if you were so minded. Everything she needed, really. But . . .

'You'll have to pay me rent,' George said sternly, and Cleo nodded happily, seeing this face-saving gesture for what it was, knowing he wouldn't overcharge. 'So I hope this cleaning job pays well. Otherwise you'll have to get a proper one, won't you?'

'That's blackmail!'

'I know.' He grinned.

He was a good egg, really. Her mum, too. They must have been cooking this thing up for some time.

Filled with a new energy, she couldn't wait, and walked on air up to her new abode, stopping only to get in a few essential supplies at Sainsbury's. Brandishing the keys like a trophy, she unlocked the front door.

She felt a little choked as she stepped in, and stood blinking for a moment. She'd never been inside the place since Phoebe had died, and the sight of all her familiar things brought her vividly back to mind: the embroidered cushions, her footstool, the crocheted duchess set on the sideboard. There also Cleo saw evidence of the quiet continuance of her modest life in the collection of knick-knacks, valueless to anyone else, but which had meant so much to Phoebe, as well as the clock presented to her father on his retirement and, in pride of place, her wedding photograph.

Going into her aunt's house had always seemed like entering

43

a time warp, and seemed even more so, now that she was no longer here, part of it. Phoebe had lived in this little house for well over sixty years, and practically everything in it was exactly as it was when she and Jack had set up home when they were first married. She'd never seen the need for much modernisation.

The front room was all geometric shapes, fashionable at the time, the fireplace a perfect semicircle of fawn and eau-de-nil Art Deco tiling, without a mantelpiece, set against what Phoebe had called 'a nice biscuit-coloured wallpaper'. The square dining suite was in limed oak. A matching step-sided china cabinet stood in one alcove, in the other a square-columned standard lamp, complete with its original parchment shade painted with flying ducks. Three more flew diagonally across one wall.

But people went in for this sort of thing nowadays, paid a lot of money for it, and the Honeybuns had probably been charmed, seen the whole thing as a genuine period piece, which is just what it was. Cleo looked at the only picture in the room, placed high on the wall, a curious depiction of Spaniards apparently about to do the tango, made from coloured silver paper mounted on black velvet, occupying the wall over the sideboard. The mirror over the fireplace had peach-coloured glass insets either side. Good Lord, she might well be living in an Aladdin's cave! Every time she sat down on the fawn uncut moquette three-piece suite with its curved-to-the-floor padded arms, she'd be terrified of spilling her coffee on it.

Talking of which . . . she went to make herself a coffee, as a sort of rite of ownership, to carry around while she inspected the entire place and thought how she might adjust it, without disrespect to Phoebe, to her own more chaotic living requirements.

The kettle boiled, and as she reached for a mug, she noticed with shocked disapproval that Angel Honeybun had been using Phoebe's good, Greek key-patterned tea service for every day. Her aunt must be turning in her grave. Not that it was Crown Derby, but Phoebe had treasured it. Cleo was furious when she saw a small chip on one of the cups – though she told herself you had to be prepared for worse than that when you rented a furnished house to anyone. There and then, she returned the cups and saucers prissily to the china cabinet in the front room where they'd always lived, and as she did so, she noticed something else. The Clarice Cliff candlestick was missing.

She stared at the place where it had stood for as long as she could remember. Perhaps Angel had broken it, perhaps George had taken it home for safe keeping. But Daphne wouldn't have given it house room, she'd been united in loathing it with Phoebe, who'd said often enough she'd have thrown it out years ago, had it not been given to her as a wedding present in 1939. Cleo could understand anybody who went in for Greek key-patterned china hating it; she was hardly enamoured herself. The chunky, two-branched pottery candlestick was OK if you admired angular, geometric affairs, decorated splashily in orangey-red, dark blue and bilious shades of green, outlined in black. But Cleo knew that anything with the Clarice Cliff name attached to it fetched high prices these days. Why was a mystery to her, but Daphne said they did. She'd seen something almost identical to this candlestick on the *Antiques Road Show*.

She poked around a bit more, went upstairs, where drawers and wardrobe were empty. The large cupboard built into the fireplace alcove was locked and her keys downstairs, but it could wait, she certainly wouldn't need more space. She went back to the kitchen to finish making her coffee, stood on a stool to take a better look in the top cupboards and there, behind a tall jug, was the candlestick. Slightly offended to find even such an object so relegated, she picked it up to return it to its rightful place, wondering if Phoebe's spirit wasn't hanging around there somewhere, already insinuating itself into her in an effort to make her great-niece as fussy as she herself had always been about that sort of thing, like people get, living alone. But as Cleo reached to put the candlestick back into the cabinet, she hesitated. Something was telling her – just what it was she didn't know, she was no expert on those things – that all was not quite right about it. The shape? The design? It looked just the same. Had it, perhaps, like the china cup, acquired a chip? She turned it over.

The 'Rudyard' pattern, a number, and the designer's name and mark. She'd have to show it to her mother to know whether there was anything wrong there, but what if there were? If it turned out to be a copy? Wasn't there some subtle difference between the legality of copying something, and making a deliberate fake? Why should anyone worry, anyway, if you couldn't tell either from the real thing? Apart, of course, from the differences in price. She looked at the candlestick before putting it back. That was it, she thought, the colours looked just too *new*.

Well, well, who would've thought it? Not such an angel, after all, little Mrs Honeybun. Had she broken the original, and been scared to own up?

Or what?

Cleo wondered briefly if anything else had been substituted, but Phoebe had never been one for amassing possessions, valuable or otherwise. She'd left the house and contents, family photographs and Jack's gold watch to George, and all the money she had in the bank – a surprising amount, but she'd worked all her life and always been thrifty – to a children's charity. She'd willed her engagement ring and a cameo that had belonged to her mother to Daphne, a turquoise ring and all the books she had to Cleo, and a string of cultured pearls to Jenna. And that was it, as far as Cleo knew.

5

Dorrie normally did her own cooking, but tonight Mrs Totty, as a gesture of goodwill or in deference to Sam's needs, had left a substantial and savoury casserole for supper. When they'd finished – though Dorrie had eaten no more than a spoonful, leaving Sam to demolish the rest – he decided to broach the subject of the school's offer for the house once more. He'd brought in a bottle of wine, she'd had two glasses and he thought she might be prepared to talk about it. But she wasn't.

'I don't even want to think about it, Sam, I don't need the money, I've more than enough to live on and I'm quite happy here, so why should I let them bully me into selling my home? Just because the school's suddenly decided they need to build a big new science block?' Seated in the depths of the big armchair, she managed to look small and defenceless, but stubborn, and more owlish than ever, taking refuge behind the huge specs which hid her eyes.

'So it's a new science block, is it? That's why they need to resite the entrance? Not simply to spare the school from the horrid sight of the estate?'

'You've been listening to Eileen, and she's prejudiced!' Dorrie's lips twitched, though, and she added slyly, 'Though naturally, new buildings would effectively do that, wouldn't they?'

Nobody could seriously believe that was the prime reason, snobbery didn't extend so far, even for institutions with a far more exalted reputation than Lavenstock College, Sam told himself. Or could they? For years, Lavenstock had teetered a little nervously between being a minor public school with a good reputation and being a rather better one; then the installation of the present Headmaster had brought academic successes and achievements which sent it soaring up the scholastic league tables. Improved science facilities were likely to be even more of an inducement to well-off people to send their sons to the school, though the extent of both the wealth and the snobbery of such parents was almost certainly exaggerated.

The evening was chilly and Sam had made up a fire in the morning room. Resin hissed and boiled from the big log set on its glowing embers and Dorrie poked at it, sending sparks flying up the chimney. Several flew the other way, on to the hearthrug, and one began to smoulder. Casually, she stamped it out, but not before it had made yet another scorch mark to join the dozens of others already there, leaving behind a smell of singed wool. 'It's not convenient, they say, to have the new buildings over on this side, so far away from the others, right across the other side of the playing fields from the main school. It would also mean laying new services and everything – by which I suppose they mean drains and electricity. It's easier to put in a new drive, this side. Well, they've already got the other three houses around me. Why don't they pull them down and leave mine alone?'

'Could it be because this one is bang in the middle? Which effectively stymies any chance of a new entrance?'

'Maybe it could,' said Dorrie, with another guileless smile. She reached out and twisted the knob on the old-fashioned radio by her chair until she found a concert on Radio 3. 'All right?' she asked, as the first notes of the Dvorak cello concerto flooded into the room, offering him the choice of a Murraymint to suck, or a piece of Cadbury's Fruit and Nut. Sam said yes to the music and declined the sweets, seeing both actions as signalling Dorrie's wish not to continue the conversation, but as he stretched his legs to the fire and let the tide of music sweep over him, and Dorrie snuggled into the warmth of her comfortable, sagging old chair like a sleepy tabby, he thought yet again about what Mrs Totty had said. Could it really be that Dorrie had always hated this house? She'd lived here all her life, alone in it for at least twenty years since her father, his grandfather, had died. Loyalty, or perhaps subservience, to that terrible old man had kept her living here while he was still alive, but she'd had no reason to stay afterwards. It couldn't simply be that garden which was keeping her, he told himself. But he was afraid that it might be. She had always formed odd, unaccountable attachments to places, as well as people.

But if the school had offered a good price, which seemed likely, she could surely find a suitable, small house, where she could make another garden? Would leaving this be so terrible? How long could she stand out? The school's plans, he felt, were unlikely to be given up quite so easily.

He said gently, when the concerto had finished and she'd switched off, 'Ignoring this business won't just make it go away, you know.'

She looked away and began fussing with the evening paper. 'I've told you what I think.'

'Come on, Dorrie,' he said more firmly, 'wouldn't it be better to have it resolved, one way or the other? Let me have a look at the correspondence for a start, and see if I can't suggest something.'

Her face assumed a hunted, secretive look. He felt as though he was hurting a child. Then she said suddenly, uncaring, 'Oh, go on, have a look if you want, it won't make any difference.'

'What have you done with the letters?'

'I don't know, they're somewhere around.' She gestured vaguely towards the ancient, battered desk in the corner. 'In one of those drawers, I think.' She leaned back and closed her eyes for sleep. 'Three or four, I think there are. Unless I've thrown one or two away. I might have.'

'Dorrie!'

'Well, they made me so *angry.*'

It took him twenty minutes, rummaging through seed catalogues, some of his own old letters, recipes torn from newspapers, sweet wrappers, communications from the bank, before he came up with three or four letters with the Lavenstock College heading. He sorted them into date order, then read the first one through, until he came to the large, almost illegible signature at the bottom. He stared at it, mesmerised, then propped his elbow on the desk, his hand supporting his head. It felt incredibly heavy. Eventually, he looked up to see Dorrie gazing at him, blinking through her round glasses.

'Wetherby,' he said when he could speak, 'Charles Wetherby's still Bursar here? I was told he'd moved on.'

'You must have been mistaken.'

But Sam knew he wasn't. Charles Wetherby was the reason he'd joined the Antarctic expedition, the reason he'd sworn never to return to Lavenstock as long as the man was there. Two months later, he'd heard that he was leaving. Nothing would have induced Sam to come back had he known he was still here.

He sat still, while a sense of hopelessness invaded him. That man, still here, when, if justice had been done and decency had its way, he should have been wiped from the face of the earth. His time in the frozen miles of Antarctica had purged Sam, healed the scars – or so he had thought. He was a young man in any case slow to anger, an easy-going fellow who believed in live and let live. But when he did lose his temper, it was monumentally. Now, it overtook his hopelessness, seethed up inside him like boiling sugar, until an even more terrible thought forced a certain calmness on him.

He shuffled the letters together. 'Dorrie,' he began, 'Dorrie, do you know –' But then he stopped. Dorrie wouldn't, of course, know. She'd never had anything to do with the school, or the people there, or wanted to. Look how she'd chucked those letters into a drawer, almost without reading them.

'What's wrong, Sam?'

He roused himself, took a grip on his mind, and made himself say, 'Oh, nothing, Dorrie, dear. Just a rather nasty goose walked over my grave.'

Hannah Wetherby sat in the darkened school hall, with only the stage lights switched on, wondering at the inanity that had caused Roger Barmforth, deputy head of English, director *manqué*, to choose *The Beggar's Opera* for the end-of-term production – or to be more accurate, wondering why she'd ever allowed herself to be roped in to help with the costumes. Making her own clothes was one thing, this was something else.

Roger Barmforth was an amiable idiot and nothing he did should have surprised her, but the choice of this bawdy entertainment for a school production, with its endless possibilities for innuendo and sniggers, was asking for trouble, when even the author's name, John Gay, caused the adolescent cast to fall about. Nor had it been the world's best idea to invite the sixth-form girls from the Princess Mary High School to participate. Though it had to be said that Rosie Deventer made a splendid Polly Peachum, hardly needing to act at all – and it was better than encouraging some of the boys to dress up, certainly better than Douthwaite with his blond baby face in the part. There was no need for false boobs where Rosie was concerned.

Right choice or wrong, things had advanced too far to go back now. Hannah leaned back and closed her eyes. Subconsciously, she fingered the gauzy scarf around her throat, very aware of the letter in her pocket and the warm rush of feeling whenever she thought of it, though it had hardly been what she would have expected, or hoped for.

'Our Polly is a sad slut! nor heeds what we have taught her. I wonder any man alive will ever rear a daughter!' sang Polly Peachum's father, to accompanying cat-calls from the wings and a compliant flounce, a rolling of eyes and various other body parts from Polly on the stage.

Hannah had never expected to see Sam Leadbetter again, had fully expected they'd be gone from Lavenstock before his stint in the Antarctic was finished. She felt quite dizzy at the thought of seeing him again, and overwhelmed by what it would inevitably mean. Had all the anguish of these last years been for nothing?

What would Sam think of her, now? Once she'd glowed with health, love had lent her warmth and vitality, but now she felt herself a spent thing, who'd lost too much weight and was too pale. She often had a bruised look under her eyes, which she'd once thought echoed those other bruises . . . in her heart . . . Immediately the thought was formed, she'd scorned herself for such sentimental twaddle, but it was too late: she'd already thought it. And it was in any case exactly what she felt.

But it was an uncomfortable analogy which she skittered away from. She looked sometimes at the album containing her wedding photograph, like probing a sore tooth, and couldn't believe what she'd once been: slight, even then, with big brown eyes and soft brown hair falling to her shoulders, but glowing and vibrant in a cream silk frock and her grandmother's lace veil, standing on the steps of Our Lady's Roman Catholic church – glowing with what she'd then thought was love. Adoring love for Charles, the tall, good-looking man beside her. Looking at the photo with hindsight, she could see that even then he was complacent, though she had never noticed it through the haze of her infatuation.

They had met when he was standing as the prospective candidate for the Surrey constituency where she lived, and where she'd drifted in as a helper. She was eighteen, messing around after leaving school with nothing to fill in her time, not knowing what she wanted to do – a condition, had she but known it then, that was fatally endemic to her character. Here she was, still messing around at forty, still being roped in to lend a hand whenever there was no one else to do it, not knowing what she wanted to do with her life – except that, quite passionately, she wanted to live it without Charles, wrong though her religion said that was.

Her mother had never wanted her to marry him, and within two years would have been able to say, 'I told you so,' had she not been dead by then of a secondary cancer.

After Charles left school, his father had found him a job in a City bank, but though he had undoubted abilities, he had never felt he received the acclaim from it he thought he undoubtedly deserved, and eventually decided a life at Westminster would suit him better. He had convinced the selection committee of his solid worth (or perhaps dazzled some of the women as much as he'd dazzled Hannah) and achieved considerable publicity during the subsequent campaign, when his suave manner and photogenic good looks had made him apparently very popular. The seat he was contesting was thought to be a safe one, but the people of the constituency he was meant to represent had thought otherwise, and presumably seen through him. He had lost by a large margin.

Some people could cope with disappointment, but Charles was not one who fell into this category, never having been allowed to know what disappointment meant by either of his parents, who had spoiled him outrageously all his life. After failing in his bid for Westminster, he had stayed with the bank for some years then found an administrative job in industry, which was a mistake of the first order. He had lasted barely eighteen months among people who were quick to spot a supercilious phoney.

God knows what would have happened had the post of school Bursar not conveniently become vacant at that particular moment. The then Headmaster of Lavenstock had shortly been due to retire, and was happy enough to push the appointment of a man who seemed to have the required financial and administrative acumen, without going too deeply into his background, other than to note with satisfaction that he was an Old Boy of his own school.

The post of Bursar, and the authority it conferred, had persuaded Charles that he had finally found a niche that suited him, and he filled the post with admirable efficiency. But he had never seen the advantage of showing circumspection, and was less and less able to curb his arrogance, even in public. He made few friends, of the sort he thought worthy of his upbringing, certainly none among his colleagues at the school. None of this went unnoticed; he was tolerated because of his undoubted abilities, but he could not be unaware that he was not popular.

Hannah was dimly aware of all this but dared not say anything lest she precipitated one of his rages with himself. The effect on their marriage was disastrous. The more his complacency became dented, his personal inadequacies revealed, the angrier he became. Hannah had not been able to bear it, but she bore it better than what came after . . . She could scarcely believe that they had once been happy, or how wretched their lives had since then become.

When Sam had come into her life, it had been like letting in the sun. He was too young for her, ten years in age and twenty in experience. What did age matter, said Sam, and she'd believed him. Until he'd gone berserk and nearly killed Charles when Charles found out what was happening. What would he do now, when he discovered nothing had changed? That she was still too spineless to have made the move to leave Charles, even though Paul was now old enough to lead his own life? That, trapped in an unhappy marriage, she had allowed herself to get lost in a labyrinth of introspection, which had led to much worse?

So much worse that she wouldn't even allow herself to think about it.

6

Cleo had often before passed, but never had reason to enter, the premises of Maid to Order, which were situated on a busy road, lined with shops and houses of Edwardian vintage: the business was run from Val Storey's own house, the yard being the back garden which had been concreted over. That first morning, there were four snazzy white vans drawn up in the yard, with Maid to Order written across the sides in black and scarlet.

It was a large, double-fronted, villa-type house and Cleo found Val distractedly supervising operations in what had once been a sitting-room and was now her office. It was thronged with women talking fifty to the dozen, receiving their instructions through a haze of cigarette smoke, being issued with invoice pads and replenishing cleaning kits from the bulk supply cartons lying around the room and spilling out to line the passage to the back door. Not knowing what to do, Cleo stood hesitantly to one side until Val, looking up and running a hand through her hair, saw her, smiled and told her to make herself comfortable and she'd be with her in a minute.

She found a chair and tried to squeeze herself out of the way, ordering herself to remember that this was going to be *fun*, resolutely squashing her doubts that she'd be in any way suitable for the job. Too late for that, she was committed, but if she couldn't actually enjoy the work, at least she would be earning some money, not only to pay her parents the modest rent they were asking for Phoebe's house, but also to live on.

Gradually the room emptied and she was able to inspect her surroundings properly. There wasn't much to look at, other than Val's desk, occupied by a small PC surrounded by a sea of papers, and a stack of filing cabinets to one side. After a while, her eyes were drawn to the wall above the fireplace, still papered in a psychedelic 1970s wallpaper, where an A4 sheet of the firm's headed notepaper was pinned. Underneath the heading, 'MAID TO ORDER', was an accomplished sketch in black felt tip of a saucy French maid wearing a very short skirt and a suggestive wink.

Ring Fifi, maid to order, it said, and gave a telephone number. Underneath, somebody had scrawled, 'We should be so lucky!'

'Don't take any notice of that,' Val said, seeing her smiling at it when the rest of the women had gone. 'It's only *someone* thinking they're being funny,' she added, nodding towards the corner, not seeming in the least put out by it.

'I've been trying to get her to accept it as the firm's logo but she won't listen,' said the languid person to whom she'd obviously been referring, a youth of about seventeen or eighteen, who was smoking and lounging in a chair tipped on its back legs, his feet propped up against the wall.

He was seriously weird. Ear-rings and an eyebrow stud and cropped-off dyed carroty hair were par for the course, but that was only the start. It wasn't only that he was as thin as a broomstick, either, with the pale eyes and complexion that go with ginger hair, not to mention ears that stuck out like bat-wings. A deep scar ran across his forehead and lifted one side of his face, so that his features looked somehow uncoordinated, as though one half was saying one thing and one another.

'This is Tone, Tony Gilchrist,' Val said, 'Cleo Atkins.'

'Hi, Cleo.' It sounded as though the simple effort of getting the words out had exhausted him.

'You'll be working together, with Sue – that's Sue Thomas – when she gets here. She's your team leader,' Val added, glancing at her watch, looking worried, while Cleo was trying to believe that, appearances to the contrary, Tone might well be a whizz with a squeezy mop, for all she knew. 'I hope she isn't going to let me down. She's usually so reliable. Well, let's get you sorted, Cleo, before she comes.'

She tossed Cleo a black sweatshirt with MO monogrammed on it in red, and a pair of black jogging pants, the uniform she must wear every time she went to a job. 'That way, people know who you are,' Val said, seeming confident that it was enough for the people who employed them to accept without question this evidence of any lack of evil intent. She was shown to a little washroom where she could change.

As she emerged, Val was throwing open a window, though it was another clear, piercingly sharp, blowy March morning and the wind immediately began to blow the papers on her desk about. 'Oh, close the bloomin' thing again, Tone, will you?' she said resignedly, chasing papers, wrinkling her nose. 'I don't allow smoking on the job, so they all get as much in as they can before they start, never mind that I might die of passive smoking.'

She shot an accusing look at Tone, who was about to light up again. He mumbled sorry, put the packet away and shut the window. At that moment, the door burst open and Sue surged in, full of apologies for being late.

Like many fat people, she moved lightly on her feet, bouncing as energetically as a sorbo rubber ball. She was very pretty, with a round, pink-cheeked face, dark eyes and curly brown hair, and within a few minutes she had Cleo and Tone outside in the yard, the cleaning gear stacked in the back of her van and herself in the driving seat.

'I'll go in the back,' Tone offered, insinuating himself in amongst the bottles of Flash and the plastic mop-buckets and the industrial vac, sitting on the floor, thus relieving Cleo of one anxiety at least. She hadn't fancied being wedged in the front seat of the van between him and Sue. Even though there wasn't all that much of Tone, there was more than enough of Sue.

He was very quiet on the way there, but Sue became chatty, once out on the road, explaining how the system worked for MO. 'We mostly have regular calls, but we do have one-offs as well, like cleaning before somebody moves in and that. Domestic jobs are best,' she added, 'doctors' and dentists' surgeries mean getting up early, and office cleaning generally means working late.' She threw Cleo a speculative glance. 'We often get students helping out, between terms, they're always hard up. That's why you're doing it?'

'That's right, money,' Cleo said, and Sue nodded with understanding, seeing this as an entirely satisfactory explanation which needed no elaboration. She had three children, she added, you wouldn't believe what they cost.

'Hope you don't mind mucky jobs,' she remarked, after a few minutes. 'This one we're going to, it'll be pretty rotten. It's not a regular, though Val thinks we'll likely have to come at least twice.' It was only then that Cleo learned they'd been earmarked for work at one of the houses which had been flooded.

It had a desolate feeling, she thought when they arrived, this

56

place where the Kyne began. So near Lavenstock, yet it might have been fifty miles away. Even the quality of the light was different, suggesting that the sharp, brilliant sunshine of the morning was only transient. Although the water levels were everywhere going down rapidly, here it was less apparent. Light reflected on flat sheets of still, dirty yellow water that stretched across the reedy terrain, riffled by the wind. Sparse groups of alders still stood with their feet submerged. But the sky was eggshell-blue and clumps of wild daffodils blew on the few patches of higher ground, and in the distance could be heard the calls of spring lambs and ewes.

A tall, narrow farmhouse, gaunt and unadorned, stood like a grim fortress a few hundred yards away at the end of the lane into which they turned. There was no doubt what sort of farm it was. Tone sniffed the rich aroma as he uncurled himself from the back of the van, announcing 'Pigs!' Unnecessarily, since a nearby signboard advertised itself as 'Covert Farm, Organic Pig Rearing'.

Val had drawn the van up, not at the farm but in front of a cottage, crouching low to the ground and suddenly appearing in an unexpected dip in the lane. It had probably been two, or even three tiny cottages at one time, where farm-workers had brought up broods of children in rural squalor. The pump still stood picturesquely outside what had once been a barn attached to the end of the row. Now knocked into one house, modernised, centrally heated and with indoor plumbing installed, even in its present surrounding sea of mud, the cottage, with rosy bricks between black beams and wavy, pantiled roofs that sloped nearly to the ground at the back, unexpected windows and crooked chimneys, was the sort that fetched mega prices. It had a twee ceramic plaque on its gatepost, decorated with flowers of unknown origin, proclaiming it to be Wych Cottage.

No one who has ever experienced their home being flooded can have any idea what it's like, Cleo thought as they surveyed the task they were to undertake. Daphne's washing machine had once flooded the kitchen at home, and what seemed like tons of water had reached right across into the dining-area, where it had lifted the parquet flooring. The carpet tiles in the kitchen, despite their claim to be washable, had taken weeks to dry. But at least it was clean, soapy water and there was only a measurable amount of it.

The ground floor of old Mrs Osborne's home had been under eighteen inches of dirty river water for over a week, and now that it had receded it had left a thick, stinking layer of alluvial mud over everything. Somebody had already got rid of at least the top layers of it, but a lot – and the stink – remained. She told them tearfully that the upholstery on her sofa and three chairs had been utterly ruined, though her precious Persian rugs, now at the cleaners, might be salvaged. What still had to be assessed was the damage done to her other furniture. Luckily, the boys from the farm had come over and carried the more portable pieces upstairs before the worst of the water came seeping in. Lucky was the word, Cleo thought when she saw those tables and chairs. Most of them had to be antique, and expensive antique at that.

Mrs Osborne, a deceptively frail-looking old woman in her seventies, insisted on making them mugs of coffee, which they drank while they worked, since it would otherwise cut into their cleaning time.

'She's getting under the feet, I know, but never mind. Drink it or the old duck'll be offended,' Sue whispered to Cleo as they attempted to make inroads into the devastation, while Mrs Osborne sat on the window seat and chatted, drawing her legs to one side every time anyone came near her. Perhaps she wanted to keep her undoubtedly sharp eyes on them: if they looked like missing a corner, she wasn't slow to point it out.

She told them she'd once lived up at the farm proper, up the lane, but it had been sold when her husband died and she'd moved down here into this cottage. She seemed an unlikely farmer's wife, and not averse to the change; the cottage was obviously the pride of her life. She sighed as she said, 'I was never much of a farmer's wife. To tell the truth, I never was one, very much. I've occupied my life with much more interesting things.' What they were, she didn't say, as she smoothed her coral pink skirt and matching jacket and adjusted the string of pearls around her neck.

Cleo could imagine the interior of the cottage as it had been before the flood: the chintz and china, the pretty ornaments on the walnut tables and chests, the Persian rugs on the polished stone floors. These thick stone slabs made getting the mud off much easier than if they'd been wooden floorboards, and with all the windows and doors open to let the brisk, blowy wind through they were drying quickly, after several sluicings followed by a thorough scrub. It surprised Cleo what six hours brisk work could accomplish. Once they'd managed to make the floors presentable, they had washed down the walls right up to the low, beamed ceilings so as not to leave further tidemarks. 'No way can you wash half a wall,' said Sue, speaking from experience.

'We can get some of your furniture down for you now, seeing the floor's nicely dry,' she told Mrs Osborne at last. 'Then we can give a quick once-over upstairs, and next time we come, do a proper spit and polish on everything. A good rub-up and these flags'll come up a treat.'

'Oh, could you? But no, it isn't really necessary for you to move the furniture back. The boys will do it!'

'We've time to shift some of the smaller bits, anyway, so it'll start looking more like home,' Sue said, conscientious about not wasting time they were being paid for.

'You've done marvels already. Wait until my daughter sees it! She'll be coming down to pick me up presently. I've been staying with her since that dreadful night. She's a teacher and she has a lovely new house over at Lattimer. Even so, I shall be glad to get back into my own home. Just do as I want, you know, without bothering anyone else,' Mrs Osborne added wistfully.

'You shouldn't live out here all on your own,' said Tone suddenly. 'Aren't you scared?'

'No, why should I be? I've got some good door locks and a telephone, and I'd never answer the door after dark.'

'All the same, nasty things can happen to old ladies living on their own.' He mooched off upstairs and in a moment, the sounds of furniture being moved penetrated through the ceiling.

'Don't mind him,' Sue said, 'His mother never taught him to mind his manners. He's not as bad as he looks.'

'Oh, I've already cottoned on to that! His heart seems to be in the right place. And he's a good worker.'

Cleo didn't know about his heart being in the right place – it might have been anywhere, looking at Tone – but to her surprise, her cynical private observations about his capacity for hard work had proved quite unjustified. When he took his jacket off, she could see he had strong muscles and he used them to good effect. And being so tall, he could reach as far as the low ceilings, which had been a help. He didn't say much, but got on with the job, chugging away like a steam engine. Sue worked just as briskly. They seemed tireless. Cleo's back was breaking, her arms ached with the unaccustomed exercise. But she thought she might get used to it, given time. Providing she didn't drop dead first.

In the end, Mrs Osborne surrendered to Sue's persuasions about moving some of the smaller furniture down, and followed Tone nimbly upstairs to indicate what was what. He had already manoeuvred a walnut chest of drawers to the top of the stairs, and he and Sue began to assess the logistics of getting it downstairs. Cleo could see the old lady looking at the chest nervously and couldn't blame her. Neither Sue nor Tone were weaklings but the stairs were narrow and twisting, and the chest looked valuable.

'If you took the drawers out it wouldn't be as heavy,' she ventured, pulling out one of the top ones as she spoke and carrying it over to rest it on the bed.

Mrs Osborne gave a little scream. 'Oh goodness, they're in such a mess, let me tidy them a bit first!' She darted over to the one Cleo had pulled out. She hadn't seemed to be the sort to be prudish about anyone seeing her winceyette nightdresses and thermal bloomers, and it turned out that wasn't the reason she'd grabbed a woolly bedjacket and thrown it over the contents of the drawer – which weren't undergarments, anyway, but table linen. Quick as a little sparrow, she still hadn't been quite quick enough to conceal what Cleo had seen lying there.

A car drew up outside.

'Oh, there's Eleanor,' Mrs Osborne said, with evident relief. 'Just you leave everything, now. Eleanor and the boys will see to it.'

'You're sure?' Sue asked.

'Quite sure,' Mrs Osborne said firmly.

They followed her downstairs, collected their belongings and Mrs Osborne was just writing out the cheque for their services and arranging for the next visit when Eleanor Robson walked in.

Her critical glance swept around the room. 'Well,' she announced grudgingly, after a moment or two, 'you've made a start, I'll say that.' She glanced at her watch and saw that there was still five minutes to go, which Cleo supposed meant fifteen in real terms, and said pointedly, 'Didn't you have time to get the furniture downstairs, then?'

Sue began to explain, though Cleo was sure it wasn't part of their job requirements to go lugging furniture around. Any offers to do so had been made out of the goodness of Sue's heart, but Mrs Osborne cut her explanations short. 'Eleanor,' she began warningly, 'it's been a perfectly filthy job, they've worked wonders and I'm delighted with what they've done. The furniture will stay where it is, for now.'

Little Mrs Osborne, Cleo saw, could insert an edge of steel into her voice with the best of them when necessary. Her large, forbidding daughter, obviously having had experience of this before, shut up.

Cleo was rather glad to see her put down. She didn't take to Mrs Robson at all.

She was tall, with a big bosom and her dark hair drawn back from her face into a low bun on her neck, her mouth set in an uncompromising line. You could imagine her swishing a cane in her hand. She looked like the sort who'd enjoy terrorising unwilling children. I'll bet it's maths she teaches, Cleo thought.

'Let's get off, then,' Mrs Osborne said.

'We can't go, yet, Mother. The police are here, wanting a word with you.'

All eyes in the room followed her glance out of the window, where a couple of large, uniformed men were standing beside the police car that was parked on the muddy frontage of the cottage, next to the MO van, and Eleanor's own car. 'The *police*?' Mrs Osborne's voice rose to a squeak. 'What do they want with me?'

'It's all right, don't look so worried, Mother, they're questioning everyone in the neighbourhood. It's that woman who was drowned. They seem to think her body went into the water somewhere just below here.'

61

One of these days, thought Charles Wetherby, he was going to inform Mrs Atkins, in no uncertain terms, that he loathed the smell of the air freshener she insisted on spraying around the office, and forbid her to use it. But unpalatable though it was for him to admit this, she was one of the few people who intimidated him – he'd never even been able to bring himself to call her by her Christian name, Daphne, though everyone else around the office seemed to manage it. He would have found some reason to dismiss her before now, except that she was so damned efficient and besides, she'd been appointed by Conyngham, the school Secretary, who not only thought the sun shone out of her, but called her Daph, to which she made no objection. Her smooth blonde hair, her immaculate complexion and her gold-rimmed spectacles irritated him beyond belief, and he pretended not to know why. The truth, which he refused to admit, was that, while being perfectly polite, she would not grant him the deference he regarded as due to the Bursar of Lavenstock College.

She had put an African violet on top of the filing cabinet, and a neatly typed list of his most important obligations for the week on his desk, including reminders for his attendance at the Safety Policy Committee, and the Senior Administrative Staff meeting, which was starred. Starred. That meant he would have to make time to see Conyngham first, because the subject of the purchase of 16 Kelsey Road was bound to be paramount on the agenda. If that stubborn old woman continued to refuse to sell, it might be necessary for the school to consider the possibility of making the new entrance by demolishing only the two houses – 14 and 12 – which stood together. This was a less satisfactory proposition by a long chalk than the present proposal, to pull down the middle two, of which number 16 was one, and to utilise the end ones as the new porters' lodges. Or even for some very necessary overspill accommodation. Discussing this would inevitably bring up the vexed question of admitting sixth-form girls into the school as boarders. Not that Wetherby, as Bursar, would have any say one way or the other in either matter, but both situations would certainly pose him with more administrative problems.

He gazed into the mirror which faced the glass panel in his door. He'd had this strategically hung so that he could see what went on beyond the door without them being able to see him. One of the girls from the outer office had appeared with two mugs of coffee, and was handing one to Mrs Atkins, leaning against her desk to gossip as she drank her own, which meant that the switchboard had been left unmanned again. Infuriated, he pushed his chair back to go and remonstrate with her, then saw it was not Trish, in one of her eye-catching outfits, but Beverley. For some reason she was dressed up today, not wearing her usual ethnic garb. He subsided into his chair, thinking, not for the first time, that something would have to be done about her. He'd been a fool to play so near home, and not to have realised the extent of her gullibility.

He was a bad judge of women, he had to admit it. He was destined to pick the wrong kind, their physical attraction blinding him to flaws in their character, which only became evident too late. His wife, Hannah: pretty and aimless when he'd met her, but full of high spirits and with an endearing adoration for him. But she'd developed a knack of arguing with him too much, and then, when he'd finally succeeded in breaking her spirit, she was no longer any fun. It had been pretty much the same with other women. Angela Hunnicliffe, for instance. Butter-wouldn't-melt-in-her-mouth Angela, with her mean, acquisitive ways, her transatlantic twang and her devious mind. He was glad to have seen the last of her – she *and* her husband – but when they'd departed for their native shore, they'd both left behind them a legacy of trouble. And now, Beverley Harriman. Who was a different proposition altogether.

Cleo wasn't sorry to leave Wych Cottage when their stint was over. It still didn't smell good, which was only to be expected after being under flood water. Mrs Osborne, in fact, said there were parts which never dried out completely. The idea of living with something like that gave Cleo the willies.

Sue was anxious to get home, so she drove fast all the way into

Lavenstock, concentrating on her driving. She only worked mornings for MO, and she said she had her own house to clean when she got back, to pick up her children from school and cook the evening meal. In addition, it appeared she was wallpapering the main bedroom and wanted to get it finished so that she and her husband could move back in that night. She made Cleo tired just thinking about it all, and even more certain that she'd been right only to sign up her services part time; she wondered how long they'd put up with her, anyway. She leaned back and closed her eyes.

'Tired? You'll soon get used to it – and you did OK,' Sue remarked, but Cleo had the feeling that she was just being kind, and that she hadn't really pulled her weight; yet the thought of getting the sack depressed her with a sense of failure.

'The first fifteen years are the worst,' Tone said from the back. 'After that you get used to it.'

He had his sketch pad out and all the way back Cleo heard the pages rapidly turning over. Tone was beginning to interest her.

They reached the MO premises in record time, signed off and Sue hurried off home to her DIY decorating, cooking, minding her children, and the rest. Tone stood about on the pavement, looking as though he wanted to say something. Finally, he got out, 'Could you do some lunch? There's a good place round the corner.'

'Cheap?' Cleo asked, making sure he understood by this that she was going to pay her way. Her plans for the day hadn't included lunching with anyone, never mind young Tone, but all that hard work had made her ravenous. Perhaps that was why she felt so low: her blood sugar needed a boost.

He nodded. 'Good grub, too.'

'OK, if you'll let me look at what you've been drawing.'

'Why do you want to do that?' he asked in amazement. But eventually he agreed.

The caff to which he led her looked like a greasy spoon outside, but appearances were deceptive. It was as antiseptic as an old-fashioned hospital ward inside. It wasn't much more than a counter with cooking facilities behind, and a few tables, but the plastic tablecloths were spotless and the sauce bottles weren't sticky. A woman of roughly the same proportions as Sue, though twenty years older, was serving behind the counter, otherwise the place was empty. 'Hello, each,' she greeted them. 'Brought your girlfriend today, Tone?'

'This is Cleo, Marge, she's come to work with us. You go sit down, Cleo, I'll get it. What do you fancy?'

'Oh anything, as long as it's food, I'm starving. Burger or something,' she said absently.

While he was waiting at the counter and oniony smells came drifting over, making her mouth water, she flicked through the sketch pad he'd left with her. He was really, at least to Cleo's thinking, really good. He must surely have had some sort of professional training. It was a true artist's sketchbook – odd, quirky details of people, places, things. He seemed to have total recall, he'd remembered all sorts of surprising things about Wych Cottage: she flicked the pages over, seeing the little wooden carvings on the inglenook, the iron-barred bake-oven where someone had once been able to bake enough bread for an army. He'd drawn every detail of the heavy, wonderfully wrought iron latch on the low, crooked door, leading directly on to an almost vertical flight of damp stone steps into the low, still-flooded, unused cold-store at the side of the house, which some-one had once dug out to six feet below ground, generations before freezers and fridges had been invented. You could still have used it for that purpose, Mrs Osborne had said, except that it never completely dried out, despite a big air space high up in the wall. There was also an apple-loft and what she called the cheese room, half-way up the staircase. It still smelled cheesy, or was that imagination?

There was a sketch of Cleo herself, which made her laugh, wondering what Daphne would think of it – on her knees, mopping the floor, with a harassed expression on her face and her bum in the air. And one of Mrs Osborne. Tone had done a funny drawing of her, sitting like the Queen Mum on the window seat with her fluffy white hair and her little feet in their high-heeled shoes drawn to one side.

Cleo stared thoughtfully at the sketch. Tone had exactly caught the determined chin, the sideways perch of her head, the closed smile. What would his reaction have been if he had seen, as she had, that gun tucked away amongst this dear old lady's embroidered tablecloths?

65

Presently, he came back with two enormous burgers and two coffees. The burger smelled hot and savoury and she took a large, hungry bite. She chewed, more slowly and more suspiciously, swallowed hastily, then pushed it away. 'Yuk. There's something wrong with this. It's disgusting. The meat tastes all mushy.'

'That's because it's not meat. It's a lentilburger, you said you didn't mind what.'

Aaargh! She thought she might be sick. If she'd known it was lentils she was eating, OK. But chewing it, thinking it was meat . . . what sort of person was it, could do such a thing?

He said miserably, 'I'm sorry, but you did say . . . I'll get you something else.'

She was sort of getting used to his face now and she saw from its expression that she might have really hurt him. 'No, it's me that should be sorry – I did say anything. Tell you what, you come home with me and I'll heat us some soup or something,' she heard herself saying, and smiled at him to show she really meant it. It was nobody's fault but her own, yet she somehow couldn't fancy eating anything else, not for a while, at any rate.

One thing that could be said for him, he wasn't the sort to take offence. 'Right.' He grabbed a fistful of paper napkins out of the holder on the table and wrapped both burgers up, not intending to let anything go to waste.

Marge raised her eyebrows at their hurried exit. 'Anything wrong?'

'No, just something we suddenly remembered.'

Tone told her as they walked home that he lived in one of the blocks of high-rise flats quite near her own road, an infill that faced some of the bigger houses. It was OK, he said, now that the rest of the family had left home and there was just him and his mum. Quieter, like. She gave him a swift glance, but didn't ask him what that meant.

Later, after some soup, tooth-achingly sweet, vinegary and luridly coloured, which the label alleged was tomato, and of which no fewer than eight cans had been left in the cupboard by Angel Honeybun (which must have said something about her), Cleo said, 'What are you doing working for MO with a talent like yours, Tone? You could get a really interesting job if you wanted to.'

'I've no qualifications.'

'Who needs qualifications when you can draw like that?'

'Everybody needs qualifications these days.'

'Then why not get some? You could do, easily.' Look who was talking, but it was different when it was someone else, wasn't it?

'Nah,' he said dismissively, and something in the way he said it told her to leave the subject alone.

After Tone had demolished both, now cold, lentilburgers, when they were still sitting at the table in the kitchen, Cleo suggested they took their coffee mugs into the other room to sit more comfortably.

'Wow!' he exclaimed when they went in, staring around. 'You have a thing about Art Deco?'

'Not me. It's just as my Aunt Phoebe left it.'

'You can make whatever changes you want,' Daphne had said, 'but I'm afraid you're stuck with the furniture . . .'

'I don't mind the furniture, Mum, but maybe a coat of paint on the walls?'

Throughout the house, Phoebe's beige, textured wallpapers, with their indeterminate patterns, had now faded, so that the walls had taken on the colour and consistency of porridge. 'I'm thinking of painting the walls,' she told Tone now. 'And that fireplace! It's driving me mad. I keep trying to balance things on it but they slip off, because of its curve. I wondered about a shelf just above it. Dad got some ready-made ones with brackets from B & Q the other week.'

There was a stunned silence from Tone when she told him this. Then he said, reprovingly as a museum curator, 'That'd be sacrilege. You don't want to go ruining everything with things like that.' He thought for a while. 'I could do you some murals.'

'Some *what*?'

'Murals. No, hang on and listen – could be great.' He warmed to his theme. 'Deco stuff to go with the gear, you could choose what before we started.' He saw her face. 'OK,' he went on, though obviously disappointed. 'Sylvan scenes and all that, if you *really* want. Though I was thinking more on the lines of *trompe l'oeil*, you know? Deceive the eye, make the room seem bigger.'

'I know what *trompe l'oeil* means. But no,' she said firmly, 'just paint. And what d'you mean, we?'

'I'll help you. Better still, do it for you. No sweat.'

'Well . . .' she began weakly. 'That's really nice of you, but, sorry. I couldn't pay you.'

'I wouldn't want paying,' he said stiffly. 'Not for a mate.'

Oh dear, had she hurt him again? But no, 'You just buy the paint,' he said. 'Though this paper'd be a bit dodgy to paint on. Needs stripping off before we start. I could begin straight away.'

This was all going a long way beyond the few cans of emulsion paint she'd been thinking of.

'Tone, it's an old house, it'll probably need replastering under the paper.'

'Then I could do you some frescoes – paint straight on to the wet plaster, they'll last for ever. They used to do that in the olden days.'

'Frescoes?'

'Go for it. *Semper sursum!*'

'*Semper* what?' She gave him an odd look.

'*Sursum*. Latin for Onward Christian soldiers, more or less.' He could see she was weakening. 'Go on, live dangerously.'

'No French maids?'

'I could do you something a lot better than that,' he said with a grin.

'We-ell . . . Oh, all right.'

Maybe she owed him for the mistake over that lentilburger.

8

'These crime figures . . .'

Words of doom, coming from Mayo's secretary, Delia Brown, she who ruled him like an old-fashioned but benevolent nanny. She stood militantly between him and the bank of foliage plants that some office design consultant, brought in to tart up the working environment, had deemed necessary for someone of his rank. Her figure, small as it was, blocked out even more of the light, forcing him to put down his pen and pay attention.

'These crime figures from Inspector Kite,' she repeated firmly, tapping the sheaf of papers in her hand, 'they have to be checked and be ready for me to print out by the end of the week.'

'I'll see to it,' he promised hastily.

'Right-oh.' Her eyes held him to his promise, telling him he couldn't bamboozle her. She knew very well how he hated administration above all things, and juggling with crime figures more than any of it. He suppressed a sigh. He'd do his best to keep his promise: he knew it was her efficiency that helped to keep his head above the sea of relentless paperwork: his subordinates' reports became comprehensible under her hands, papers magically stacked themselves in order of importance to be dealt with, he wasn't even allowed to *see* anything that was irrelevant. She fielded his telephone calls and only put through those which she considered necessary. She had a limitless memory for facts, figures and people. Martin Kite called her Mighty Mouse, with some justification. Mayo noted now, with amusement, that she was exactly the same height as the young rubber plant behind her, less than shoulder height with him, but then, few could match his height and bulk.

'On your desk by tomorrow morning,' he said, but she raised her eyebrows.

'Don't make rash promises until you've been through this!' she warned, smiling slightly, putting his appointments diary, open at the day's date, on his desk. Even from where he stood, he could see that today left little room for manoeuvre – except for what Delia called a 'window' around lunchtime, which he didn't point out in case she found something to fill it with.

'Inspector Kite in yet?'

'He's somewhere around – I'll send him in, shall I?'

'Please. And Delia – I'll do my best with this lot, hmm?' He gave her his warmest smile.

She nodded and went out quickly, before he could notice how pink her cheeks were. She'd have died if he had noticed. The chief reason she defended him against all comers was because he made her heart flutter under her neat jumper and gold chain as nobody else ever had done since she'd had a crush, thirty years ago, on the biology master at school. Mayo went back to his files, not as unaware of the effect he had on her as she would have liked to think, but it embarrassed him, so he pretended not to notice, which suited both of them.

At ten, he spent half an hour with Kite, who'd requested a meeting to run through the complicated evidence he was required to give in court later that week, a case at last successfully brought to prosecution. A young peer of the realm had been using his recently inherited stately home for activities not usually regarded as compatible with *noblesse oblige*. Kite had led a spectacular dawn raid, rousing not only his Lordship, but several tired businessmen and their companions, from narcotics-induced slumber. Lord Spenderhill was hopefully due to go down for a long time for supply and possession of illegal substances. Amongst other things.

That dealt with, Mayo braced himself for a meeting with the ACC, who was found to be clutching a copy of the *Advertiser* in one hand and what was left of his hair in the other when Mayo went into his office. 'Seen this?' he barked, pointing to yet another article on the lines of 'What are our police doing about the use of guns in our midst?' It had at least replaced the sniping at the lack of further discoveries about The Mystery Woman. There was little Mayo could say to this and Sheering knew it, but his impotent fury with the paper added to Mayo's own. This latest case was fizzling out like a damp squib. He didn't need this, he told himself, grinding his teeth. If anything was needed to make him even more edgy than he already was, it was being told, if not in so many words, to get his finger out.

Back in his own office, he worked off his soreness and frustration on routine stuff all morning. Delia at least would be pleased with him. At twelve thirty, he decided to skive off, for once, and take advantage of that unprecedented free hour, and to kill two birds with one stone. For a start, it wasn't often he had the chance to enjoy a proper, uninterrupted midday meal these days; formal working lunches were more likely to be his lot, or sandwiches and coffee snatched at his desk. And for another, it would save him cooking when he got home tonight – he didn't think he could face the thought of another frozen Cordon Bleu meal.

He'd initially had the notion that Alex's enforced absence would be an ideal opportunity to take a couple of weeks' leave for a walking holiday, but the backlash of the Fermanagh case had put paid to that and somehow, the idea of going alone, without Alex, didn't appeal. Maybe, then, he'd take himself off to a few concerts, or listen in the evenings to the sort of music that was his personal idea of heaven (the sort mostly without tunes, Alex said) but there was a dearth of decent concerts on at the moment, and at home he found his attention wandering from the music he switched on. He had a clock or three that needed tinkering with, but no patience. Moreover, Alex's weekend break had not turned out to be the unalloyed bliss he had hoped, but had been tetchy and unsatisfactory, for no obvious reason. She was there, but not in spirit, and had left yesterday morning to go back to her course, full of smiles. What did she have to be so cheerful about?

Miraculously, he escaped from the office without being waylaid and took himself across to the Saracen's Head. Once outside, the sharply cold air acted as a tonic to a brain jaded with the stuffy, recycled air he'd been breathing all morning. Dolly, the flower-seller on the corner of Milford Road, was selling golden mimosa. For a moment he hesitated, thinking of buying some for Alex on the way back, before remembering how fragile and transient it was, that its essence of spring would be over long before the weekend.

He walked on, but still thinking of Alex. He was having to admit that he might have been mistaken in his original doubts about the wisdom of what she was doing, this new career she was set on. No one likes to admit they've been wrong, least of all Mayo, but there was no denying the results: a distinct return to the person she'd been before she left the police service. Cheerful, dynamic, with a sparkle in her eyes that said she was happy once more in her own skin. She'd had a tough time of it one way and another over the past few years but, amazingly to him, what he thought of as the boring routine of the CPS offices seemed to be giving her back the energy and vitality that were essentially hers. The work, learning a new discipline, was keeping her on her toes, she said, sharpening her wits, unlike the undemanding last few years, when she'd worked with her sister in her interior decorating business. Mayo considered that had been *very* demanding. *He* wouldn't have lasted five minutes with Lois French, nor she with him. But then, he wasn't her sister, thank God. He could only suppose their entirely opposite natures complemented each other.

Lois hadn't been pleased with Alex's decision to pull out of the business, not least because it was simply beyond her understanding why Alex should find designing interiors for discerning clients less challenging than helping to compile cases for the prosecution of criminals. But Lois was, for all her grumbles, doing very well without her, as Alex had predicted. A new man on the scene went a long way towards restoring Lois's equilibrium. And Pilgrim was very much on the scene. An architect with a recently acquired practice in Lavenstock, he had been prepared to invest money, and to take an interest in the shop that wasn't perhaps solely due to Lois's attractions, but also concerned with its financial potential when he'd finished with it. He was trying to get her to expand, to lease the vacant premises next door.

Mayo found himself a snug seat in a quiet alcove and then lunched somewhat gloomily on a salad, the result of a battle won between his conscience and the delicious aroma of the hotel's renowned steak and kidney puddings, wondering if his decision to take this solitary meal here wasn't a mistake on more than one count. He must be getting old – at one time, he'd have thought nothing of tucking into the steak and kidney, plus chips, but he knew he'd be good for nothing that afternoon if he did. He'd almost given in, telling himself that he wouldn't need to cook that night if he had a substantial meal now, but Alex's eyes were, metaphorically, on him and he'd resisted the temptation.

The salad dutifully eaten, he'd succumbed to the rhubarb and ginger crumble (with custard) almost without knowing it, and was just thinking about ordering coffee when a figure he knew well paused by his table.

'George! What're you doing in here?' The Saracen's was very far from being George Atkins's usual stamping ground. Too rarefied for him by half, the air was in here, he'd always contended.

'Oh, just passing, fancied a pint.'

'Have it on me then.' Mayo summoned the waiter and ordered coffee for himself and a pint of bitter for George. 'How you doing then? How's business?' he asked while they were waiting, thinking the old son of a gun hadn't changed one whit. Pipe drooping from the corner of his mouth, just as seedy-looking. Still unflappable. Eyes shrewd as ever.

'Could be better, you know how it is. Mustn't grumble, though, it's early days, after all.'

'We miss you, George.'

No anodyne politeness, this, but a simple statement of the truth. Mayo couldn't remember how often he still heard people begin to say 'Ask George –' before remembering that George was no longer with them, but had departed hence twelve months previously. The air in the CID office was now slightly more breathable, the cigarette-laden atmosphere relieved of its over-burden of pipe tobacco smoke, but everyone was at sea without his instant, encyclopedic knowledge of Lavenstock and its townspeople, unto the third and fourth generation, which no computer could ever give. He'd been not so much a colleague as an institution.

They chumbled over the CID gossip after the coffee and the beer had arrived – or as much gossip as Mayo was privy to, these days, in his elevated position – and he wondered when George would come to the point and he'd find out just why he'd been tracked down here. George had said often enough that he wouldn't have been seen dead in the Saracen's for Mayo to know it was no accident, this meeting. And he wasn't the sort to make a nuisance of himself, that breed of ex-copper turned private investigator who hung around the station, picking the brains of his old mates about what was going on, he'd have scorned that. A word here and there, maybe, if he happened to bump into anyone, but that was it. The fact that he was here at all put Mayo's senses on red alert. 'How's the family?' he asked. 'The girls?'

'Daphne's still the same. George and the Dragon.' He grinned. 'The girls, they've just left college, and Cleo –'

'She's the budding lawyer?'

'No, that's the other one, Jenna. *She's* doing all right, no problems there. Got herself a First, and a job with a big London law firm, but Cleo . . .'

He shook his head, looking worried, then sank another couple of inches of his pint while Mayo waited. It wasn't like George to air his family worries. Or it hadn't been. Married to the job, and well known for it. Time on his hands now, to do the worrying, perhaps.

'She's left university, too, but she's mucking around, can't make her mind up what she wants to do. Tell you the truth, I'm a bit concerned about her.'

'Oh?' Coming from George, this was an admission.

'She didn't do as well in her exams as she should have, and she's having trouble getting herself sorted. She's got herself this house-cleaning job – which is a laugh, knowing Cleo! That doesn't bother me like it bothers Daph . . . three years at Norwich, and nothing to show for it, you'd think she could do better, she says.' He laughed. 'If she's still doing the same job six months from now, that's when I'll start worrying. At the moment, I think it's just what she needs – good, honest hard work with no need to think too much. Any road, it's partly why I'm glad I've seen you.'

Mayo waited, but George, after a moment, appeared to go off at a tangent.

'This woman who was murdered – found anything about her yet?'

Was he going to be haunted by everyone with questions about the poor woman? 'She might as well have dropped in from outer space, George. We think she was put in the water somewhere at the top end of the Kyneford estate, or just above, and was slowly carried down. It's only when you get below the pig farm the water really starts to move. But that's as far as we've got.'

'That's what I reckoned.'

Mayo waited. George rarely said anything without reason.

'Been anyone else, I'd have taken no notice, but Cleo – she has her head screwed on. And –' he looked down into his beer – 'and they've always been a funny lot, the folks up yonder. I don't know as how I'd trust 'em any further than I could throw 'em.' He took a long draught. 'The name Bysouth mean anything to you?'

'Owner of the pig farm, you mean?'

'That's Jared, he's the one that owns it. One I'm thinking of is his brother, Reuben. Their father was a tub-thumping Welsh chapel-goer, hence their names.'

Mayo trawled his memory, but Reuben Bysouth meant nothing significant. He shook his head.

'On second thoughts, maybe he might've been before your time.'

'You mean he's one of our customers?'

'Was. Used to fence anything that wasn't cemented down, but he's reckoned to have been going straight now, since he started working with Jared. I'll believe that when I see it, though Jared's all right. He's always been a farmer, and when he bought the neighbouring land and farmhouse off the farmer's widow and went into pigs, Reuben and his missis went to live with him. Pig farming and Reuben Bysouth! Appropriate, organic or not.' He grinned and looked at the pipe that had stayed clenched in his fist. Unlit and, Mayo now saw with some disbelief, unfilled.

'Don't tell me you've given up smoking, George?'

'Yes. Daphne's orders.'

There was something to be said for being married to She-who-must-be-obeyed, after all. 'Well, are you saying this Reuben Bysouth might be our man?'

'I'm saying he'd be worth watching. He's a nasty customer, more ways than one. Rough as a bear's arse. He used to slap his wife around something chronic, but he was never nailed for it. You know how it is with these women, they make a complaint and then withdraw it, go back to the old bugger.'

Mayo could see the clock on the wall behind George's head. He had a meeting at two. 'What has Bysouth to do with Cleo?'

'Nothing, I bloody well hope!' George said vehemently, ramming the pipe-holding fist on the table. 'But it's damn funny . . . I don't believe in coincidences.'

'They happen.'

'Yes, well, I think it's not only a coincidence, I think it's a bloody miracle, this old woman who keeps a gun in her drawers, in a manner of speaking, living next door to Reuben Bysouth.'

'Come on, spit it out, George. What are you getting at?'

There'd be a perfectly reasonable explanation, he thought when George had finished. Guns and farmhouses, they went together. No respectable farmer would be without a shotgun, as George well knew, and this was a farmer's widow they were talking about. All the same, if George thought it worth looking into . . . 'I'll give it a spin, send somebody there to poke around,' he promised.

He should have set the enquiry in motion immediately, it was brought home to him later, but the events that awaited him when he got back to the station drove it temporarily out of his mind.

Sam had worked all day in the back garden, without stopping for lunch. Dorrie had disappeared, probably to work on her own garden.

The most you could say, he thought ruefully, resting from his labours at the end of it, was that the garden looked better, despite the determination with which he'd attacked it. Not good, yet, but better. You could at least see where the borders finished and the paths began.

The light was fading, and he decided to pack it in for the day. He was tired, muscles he hadn't used for a long time were aching, but he felt physically good and mentally refreshed. While mechanically clearing and cutting down, his mind working on another level, his thoughts had gained some sort of perspective. The rage that had suddenly overcome him yesterday had channelled into a cold determination to act. And his regrets about the letter he had sent to Hannah Wetherby vanished. They had to meet, sooner or later. Better that it was planned, rather than thrust upon them when neither was ready.

So occupied was he with his thoughts that when he looked up from his digging, he'd been astonished to find himself, not surrounded by glacial vistas, where only moss, lichens and algae survive, but in a temperate English garden, with spring around the corner. And it had lifted his heart. Now, he stood under the bare branches of the apple tree and looked up to where, as a boy, he'd had a favourite, secret reading perch in an angle of the limbs; he was almost tempted to climb it again, as he had once before, no longer a child, just in the impossible hope of getting a glimpse of her, or even seeing as far as the house where she lived. Almost. But no, he could wait. Things had changed since the days when he might have done that, not least himself.

The wind was still around as he cleaned his spade, though not so sneaky, and the soil was drying out at last. There was a damp, loamy smell in the air and, underneath all the debris he'd been clearing, signs that the earth was awakening again. Under a tree, he'd found huge clumps of cyclamen with marbled leaves and tiny, pointed, carmine and white buds nestling in the undisturbed leaf mould. There were late snowdrops there, too, and velvet-petalled polyanthus emerging from their rosettes of crinkled leaves by the path edges. He stacked the tools, sucked the sharp cut on his hand that had begun to ooze blood again and went into the house looking for a fresh Elastoplast and a well-earned beer.

The kitchen appeared to be sinking under the weight of cooking utensils and ingredients which covered every spattered surface, but the air was filled with a savoury aroma that took him straight back to his childhood. 'Mmm. Smells good.'

Dorrie lifted her flushed face and smiled. 'I thought I'd give you something you liked, seeing you didn't have any lunch.'

'I prefer to work up an appetite for my evening meal. I'll do justice to that.'

'You always did.' She was cooking minced lamb and onion for a shepherd's pie, and he sniffed in anticipation. By no means haute cuisine, but one of the simple pleasures of life.

'What have you done to your finger?' she asked, adding grated carrot and herbs to the mince as he ran the cold tap over his hand.

'That damned pampas grass. It has leaves like razors.'

'You haven't been trying to cut a thing that size down! It's been there a thousand years. You should burn it off.'

'Sounds a bit drastic – what if it's killed in the process?'

She sniffed. 'No great loss if it is. It never flowers until November and then the winds blow the plumes straight down.

My father would never get rid of it, though. You go and douse it in petrol and throw a match on it, that's what the old gardeners used to do. Stand clear when you've lit it, that's all.' She sprinkled a mixture of brown breadcrumbs and grated cheese in generous measure on top of the mashed potatoes and mince and popped the dish in the oven of the old black Rayburn. 'Dinner in about half an hour?'

'Fine.' Sam washed his hands, dabbed the cut with disinfectant and stuck on a plaster from a squashed box he found amongst the debris of the oddments drawer.

Dorrie said, 'I came out with a mug of tea at lunchtime, thought you might be persuaded to have a sandwich, but I couldn't see you anywhere.'

Carefully, he sorted out the remaining plasters in the box, one by one in order of size. 'I was probably out in the lane – there's been a lot of activity up at the school and I went to find out what was going on, but I couldn't see anything.' He closed the plaster box and put it back in the drawer. 'Someone's been dumping rubbish in the ditch again and choked it, so I cleaned it out while I was there. Took over an hour,' he added.

An unmade-up and little-used lane ran along the backs of the houses on Kelsey Road, offering access to the back gardens. Between that and the school playing fields ran a drainage ditch which was often blocked with garden rubbish, a constant source of friction between the residents.

'It's too handy, that lane,' Dorrie said, tutting. 'Too much trouble for some people to compost their rubbish, or even put it in a bag for the council to take away. What sort of activity?'

'Police sirens, maybe an ambulance. I couldn't see anything. It's as well I went out, though I wouldn't have noticed the ditch, otherwise,' Sam replied as he opened the fridge and found a can of beer. 'Do you want one of these?'

'I think I'd rather have my usual sherry. No, don't bother, I'll pour it.' She took a pewter beer tankard and a small glass from a cupboard and he remembered that for all her slapdash ways she didn't like him drinking from the can. There was a bottle of sweet sherry on the counter top, thick and brown as cough mixture, and she filled her glass to the brim. 'Cheers. It'll be the ambulances over at the hospital you heard. The sound carries so from over the back.'

78

She stood sipping her sherry, looking out over the rear garden. 'You've done wonders today, Sam. I'm sorry I've let things get to this stage. I don't think I realised just how overgrown it'd all become. The trouble is, it sort of creeps up on you – but don't spend too much time on it. You have your own work to think of.'

She spoke absently, as if the state of the back garden really didn't matter, having turned now to gaze out over the little wild garden which could be seen through the side window in the kitchen. She was looking at the shallow, rocky bank above the pool, where primroses had seeded and cushioned themselves between the mosses, a tender, loving expression on her face.

He wasn't sure whether she even heard him when he replied, 'Don't worry about that. I thought I'd give a week or two to the garden, but then I'll have to start writing up my notes.' He'd anticipated a leisurely spring and summer, getting acclimatised to being back in Britain, working on his scientific researches, preparing them for publication. He wanted that out of the way before he started his new lectureship, and his publishers were expecting the manuscript for the book they'd commissioned by the end of September, a collection of papers and monographs he'd written and which had been previously printed and well received by the journals of various learned societies. In discussions with his editor, especially after they'd seen the photographs he'd taken, they'd become enthusiastic about doing something in lighter vein as well, something they could offer to a more general readership. More than a coffee table book, less indigestible to non-scientists than his other important, serious and scholarly academic work.

Sam was rather excited at the prospect of this himself. He'd often been told that he had a clear and easy style, and he rather liked the idea of his work reaching a wider audience, of being able to write about the awe-inspiring, unimaginable and sometimes terrifying beauties of Antarctica, as well as the scientific facts. But the prospect of going away and leaving Dorrie here on her own, in this house she allegedly hated, was one that made him distinctly uneasy.

'Dorrie?'

She still didn't answer. She was away again, where he couldn't reach her. Since Mrs Totty had made him aware of how much his aunt disliked the house, he'd kept his eyes and ears open and thought it might well be true. But he was still reluctant to concede that it was nothing more than a garden that was holding her here.

9

It was high profile, the case that had come in that afternoon, as any crime happening at Lavenstock College, much less a murder, was bound to be. Demanding top-brass attention, since anybody who was anybody in Lavenstock had links with the school one way or another, be it as school governors or merely parents of day boys. Which was why Mayo had had to inform his officers that he'd been requested – he used the word advisedly – by the ACC, to take charge personally of the enquiries. None of them believed him reluctant to do this, and they'd have been damn right, he thought. It was a decision he'd have made himself, anyway. It never needed much to get him out of the office, no way could you get the feel of a case stuck behind a desk.

And this was another murder, another shooting, making three in as many months. One shooting was rare enough in Lavenstock, even if by accident or suicide. Two was an exception, three unheard of. But the first, at least, the Danny Fermanagh killing – which every downbeat instinct he possessed told him was likely to remain unsolved – had been a matter of expediency, a gangland, drug-related knocking-off. Far removed from the murder of a public school administrator.

'Sit down, Daphne,' he said when it came time to interview her, after the body had been taken away. 'Drink your tea.' He pushed a cup of the universal panacea further towards the Bursar's secretary: though as far as panaceas went, it didn't look very promising, he had to admit. Positively unappealing, in fact. It had been made by the tear-stained, draggle-tailed girl who worked the telephone in the outer office and he suspected its origins. Some flowery, herbal substance, no doubt. But it was hot, and sipping it would help Daphne to relax. She didn't appear unduly shocked, but they were often the worst, after the reaction set in. 'This has been upsetting for you – I'm sorry you had to be the one to find Mr Wetherby,' he said. Though upsetting was an ineffectual word that surely couldn't even begin to describe what the poor woman must have felt.

She'd come back to the office after lunch, unsuspectingly taken some papers in to the Bursar, Charles Wetherby, and found him sprawled over his desk, shot in the back of the head.

But since Daphne Atkins *had* unfortunately found the man in those appalling circumstances, Mayo found himself thanking heaven for a sane and sensible witness. He liked what he knew of her, he believed she'd give him the facts without fear or favour. For years, down at the station, old George had had to put up with a lot of good-natured ragging about his Daph – the Dragon, and of whom he pretended to go in fear and trembling, and perhaps did, a little. There was no doubt she was a formidable lady, and their enduring marriage amazed all but those who knew them well. On the face of it, they seemed incredibly ill matched: slobby old George, everlastingly wreathed in vile tobacco smoke, so immersed in his job he was hardly ever at home, pecking away in the office at the old typewriter from which he refused to be parted, beavering away at his cases, ready at the drop of a hat with information regarding anything that had ever happened in his home town within living memory – and sometimes beyond. And Daphne . . . generally reckoned to have been a saint to put up with old George – but what about George? Perfectionists are bloody hard to live up to as well, Mayo reflected wryly, having mixed feelings of exasperation and tenderness for the same faults in his own partner. Only bearable for any length of time if there's real love to offset their often impossible demands.

Blonde, neat, precise; that was Daphne. Nothing ever seemed to faze her. The perfect wife and mother, the perfect secretary. There were two red spots on her smooth cheeks now, as she sat very upright on her chair, sipping the horrible-looking tea without obvious revulsion, but otherwise giving no sign of how much the shock of finding the body had affected her.

'What time was it when you took the papers in to him?'

'Half-past one, as soon as I got back from lunch. They were all ready – I'd prepared them this morning, and he needed to go through them before the meeting of the Safety Committee later this afternoon – which of course the Headmaster has cancelled now.'

Mayo had already spoken to the Headmaster, Jeremy Easter-brook. He was a man slightly under medium height, fiftyish, and going grey in an appropriately distinguished-looking manner, whose practised smile and warm, professional handshake didn't hide a shrewd glance and an authoritative manner. Wearing an expensively tailored dark grey pinstriped suit, a pale grey shirt, sober tie patterned discreetly in blue and silver, an immaculate haircut, he was the perfect model for the chief executive of a successful company, or a hospital administrator. Which was probably what he was, Mayo thought, an excellent administrator. You didn't have to be a doctor to run a hospital, or a teacher to run a school. Timpson-Ludgate, the pathologist, however, who had a son in the Upper School, had not been slow to inform him that Jeremy Easterbrook *was* regarded as a brilliant teacher, in the old-fashioned way. 'Teaches sixth-form history, and keeps 'em at it. Nothing like it, a bit of discipline. More of it and you and I would be out of a job, though, ha-ha?'

Mayo smiled dutifully. He was all for discipline, to a point. But not if it meant noses to grindstones, for its own sake.

Nothing like this had ever before happened in the school's 140-year history, Easterbrook had made clear right at the beginning of their conversation, as if it were somehow reprehensible of Wetherby to have broken with such a tradition. He didn't add that the school had not been thrown into a panic by the terrible happening, nor did he need to. It was very obvious that the teaching routine, at least, was going on as usual, for which Mayo was duly grateful. Since many of the Lower School form-room windows overlooked the quadrangle and the Bursar's office in the corner, he doubted whether much of what was being taught that afternoon would be absorbed, but it had kept a couple of hundred bright, inquisitive-minded boys out of the hair of the police doctor, the pathologist, the white-overalled technicians, photographers and his own officers while they did their work. The boys would have to be told about the murder sooner or later, and were doubtless agog at all the activity. But for the moment they would have to restrain the curiosity aroused by the arrival of police cars, the sealing off of the Bursar's office and so on.

Before taking his leave of Easterbrook, Mayo said, 'I'd better have some idea what Mr Wetherby's duties as Bursar were.' He had already been given the details of how long he had worked at the school, his age, that he was married with a grown-up son, and had lived with his wife in a house owned by the school a

83

couple of miles away, just off Tilbourne Road, adjacent to the hospital.

'He reported to the school Secretary, who is Head of Administration, but he was in charge of the financial arrangements of the school as well as overseeing its general domestic management, and for communication and public relations, that sort of thing. Make no mistake about it,' added the Headmaster smoothly, steepling his well-manicured hands, 'he was an excellent administrator – I can think of no one more fitted for the post of Bursar. The loss to the school will be indescribable.'

He hadn't liked the man. The cool, scrupulously fair, utterly impersonal appraisal didn't disguise that, nor hide the fact that the Head seemed slightly more affronted by Wetherby being killed on school premises than by his having lost his life.

'He seems to have had a wide remit.'

'Maybe so, but he had a staff of people working under him who took over various responsibilities, and we also have an Assistant Bursar.'

'Who I assume will be taking over Mr Wetherby's duties?'

'For the moment,' said Easterbrook, after a pause. 'His name's Riach, John Riach, he'll give you all the help you need. Meanwhile –' he rose from behind his desk to indicate the interview was at an end – 'I have a sixth-form seminar due in a few moments. If I can be of further use, don't hesitate to ask.'

In one way it was awkward that he knew Daphne, Mayo thought, albeit not very well, having met her only through the few police social events George had been persuaded to attend, along with his wife. But she was, after all, married to a policeman, and knew the necessity for questioning. Which was why Mayo felt able to say, without dissembling, even though he knew that it wasn't exactly going to help her banish the ghastly memory of the moment, 'I'd like you to try and tell me, if you will, exactly what you saw when you went in.'

He hadn't underestimated her. She said steadily, 'I saw he was dead, straight away. No one could still have been alive with his face shot away like that.'

'You were able to see his face, then?'

Even then she didn't flinch, though she hesitated fractionally.

'Yes. He'd slumped forward over the desk and his head had fallen sideways. And then I saw there was something stuffed into his mouth. It appeared to be paper of some sort. It – that was somehow more horrible than – all the rest of it.'

He could almost feel her ordering herself to breathe deeply, not to think of the carnage that had confronted her, which must be there, imprinted on her retina, even if she closed her eyes. 'Yes, it was,' he agreed, reflecting on the sort of person who could shoot someone in cold blood and then, while the blood was doubtless still pouring from what was left of his mouth, stuff a crumpled ball of paper into it.

Daphne had tapped on the door and waited, and when Wetherby didn't bark out his usual 'Come!' she'd gone in, thinking the office would be empty, and stepped straight on to the set of a horror film.

At first, she'd thought that he was, unthinkably for Wetherby, asleep, but the notion was almost immediately dispelled by the metallic smell of blood which hit the back of her throat, making her gag, at the same time as she saw the blood seeping all over the desk . . .

'For obvious reasons, we haven't been able to read what was on the paper yet, it's gone down to the lab to be treated for prints and so on, but it appears to have been torn from several stapled-together sheets which he seems to have been reading at the time.' Mayo showed Daphne the sheaf of papers, now encased in transparent plastic, from which the top sheet was missing.

'Oh yes,' she said, after a quick glance. 'That's a report he'd written. It was something else which was on the agenda for this afternoon. There were negotiations pending for the purchase of a house in Kelsey Road. The school's already bought three along there, and they want that one as well. It's unfortunate that the owner's not for selling. We recently wrote to her again, making her a better offer, but we had a reply only this morning from her nephew, writing on her behalf, that there was no possibility of her agreeing. The house belongs to Dorrie Lockett.'

He knew Dorrie, if only by sight and reputation. Everyone in Lavenstock knew Dorrie – but he hadn't heard of the proposed purchase of her house.

He saw Daphne was hesitating. 'I suppose I'd better tell you. Someone else will, if I don't. She came here about midday, demanding to see the Bursar, waving his last letter. I don't think she could have known that her nephew had already written. Mr Wetherby saw her in his office. I don't know what passed between them, though I can make a guess. There were raised voices, and eventually she stormed out.'

She looked almost sorry she'd spoken. 'Of course, it was nothing. She's a dear, really, and *I'd* be furious if someone tried to turf me out of my house. It's a maddening situation for the school, of course.'

There was always one, it seemed, in such circumstances: someone who sat there, refusing to move, chained themselves to a tree, barricaded themselves indoors and had to be forcibly evicted: he had, on occasions, been a reluctant part of the removal process himself. But he was, with certain exceptions, nearly always on the side of the protestors. The suffering of the few for the convenience of the many had never been his philosophy.

'Why does the school want these houses?'

He listened with quiet attention while Daphne explained the situation to him: at present, the one and only entrance to the school was on Tilbourne Road, which had been all right when the school was built, but with the amount of traffic now passing along there, was highly inconvenient for all concerned, especially when anyone wanted to make a right turn into the gates. He nodded, knowing this to his cost, having been held up along that road more times than he could count, for that very reason. He could well appreciate the necessity for another entrance. The school grounds, however, said Daphne, formed a rough triangle, its three sides being the traffic-laden Tilbourne Road; Vanson Hill, the road on which the hospital was situated; and on the third side Kelsey Road, where it was hoped to build the proposed new entrance.

'And what about the present one?'

'Oh, that'll come down, along with all the buildings on this side, to make space for the new science block.'

From where he sat, Mayo could see out through the window and across the quadrangle. A carefully tended lawn, smooth as green velvet, with brick paths intersecting it, a small lily-pond in the centre, and venerable-looking buildings all round. A testament to Victorian durability, the buildings looked gracious and solid, set to last another century and a half, at least. He was taken aback at the idea of knocking any of them down, despite knowing that computers and laboratory equipment were more important for contemporary studies at the beginning of this new millennium than a few out-of-date buildings, however age-distinguished and hallowed by precedent.

'Demolish them? That won't go down very well with the town worthies.'

'The town worthies don't have to work here,' Daphne said shortly. 'If they did, they'd realise what an old rabbit warren it is, what a ratty state this side of the quad at least is in.'

Lavenstock was proud of nurturing within its bosom an institution which, if not among the top flight of public schools, could boast of numbering among its alumni a First World War poet, a famous fashion photographer, a reactionary right-wing MP, a New Labour cabinet minister, and a TV chef. As long as the ratepayers didn't have to contribute to its upkeep, they liked the general ambience created by the old buildings, which conferred on Lavenstock a prestigious dignity that helped to dispel a Black Country image most felt was unwarranted: the town did, after all, merely touch fingertips with that unlovely sprawl.

But if the buildings comprising the rest of the north-facing side of the quad were anything like the offices he'd already seen, Mayo was forced to acknowledge the school had problems. Daphne's office, where they were sitting, was a Dickensian affair, still sporting, incredibly, an old sloping desk and a high stool, though they'd been pushed into a corner to make room for a modern desk, a fax machine and state-of-the-art computer facilities. The room was low-ceilinged and dark, despite panels in the door having been removed and glass substituted. The windows overlooking the quad were leaded and looked picturesque but rattled in their dark wood frames, the floor was of oak boards a foot wide but worn into depressions in various places by the passage of numberless feet. Steel filing cabinets stood against the panelled dado where the walls above had a problem with peeling plaster. Crude industrial shelving screwed to it held dusty piles of files. The outer office, where the two juniors worked, was similarly uninspired. And, it had to be said, Wetherby's own office wasn't much better.

'Apart from anything else,' Daphne went on, 'a new entrance

would be better from a security point of view. Mr Wetherby was always going on about it, since he was responsible for security arrangements.'

Reflecting on this irony, Mayo recollected a door situated in the far wall of Wetherby's office which had seemed to him to have been the killer's most likely mode of entry. It had, however, been locked when they arrived, and Daphne swore it was kept locked at all times. But she had no idea where the key was, or even if one still existed. It was never opened under any circumstances, because it led on to a windowless corridor which eventually emerged in one of the two identical lodges flanking the main Tilbourne Road entrance. All the same, it was an easy enough method of unauthorised entry for anyone inclined, since it had been ascertained that only one of the lodges had a porter, and the other was used for dumping parcels and casual deliveries, and was often left unlocked. Both had similar blank corridors leading off, running behind what formed offices for the various administrative functions of the school, the only doors being right at the very end of each corridor wing, the route from the unmanned lodge emerging into the Bursar's offices, the other into the stationery stores.

Was it indeed through that allegedly locked door the killer had come? Or through the usual door, via the quad and the outer office? In the Bursar's office, a large, steel-framed mirror hung several feet further along the wall which faced his desk. Looking up from his work, he would have been able to see, in reflection, through the glass-panelled door, right into the outer office. So also would anyone standing outside the door have been clearly visible to him. His killer could have been known to Wetherby then, to the extent that he'd been free to walk behind him and fire the fatal shot, the bullet entering just behind the right ear.

Mayo had one more question to ask before he left: 'Can you think of anyone who might have had some grudge against Mr Wetherby, anyone likely to have done this?' A simple question, the answer to which was often glaringly apparent to all who knew the victim; in most murders, the obvious suspect was quite likely to be the correct one.

Daphne gave the same answer to his question as nearly everyone did, at first, 'Not to want to kill him, no, surely not that!' Then she added, 'Not even Dorrie Lockett. She might have been furious with him, but I can't imagine her storming back with a gun and shooting him!'

'You mean he was well liked?' But her initial reaction had told him what she'd meant. He helped her out by adding, 'What sort of man was he, then?'

She thought for a moment or two before answering. 'He was very efficient, and he expected the same from everyone else, otherwise you got a lecture. He could be very sarcastic, quite cutting, in fact, and he liked the sound of his own voice – though he wasn't the only one around here that applies to!' She added fairly, 'Most people thought him charming.'

'Most people?'

'Yes, well, that didn't include me,' she said truthfully after a moment. 'He was really just too – too full of himself. You know the sort. Good-looking, smooth, persuasive . . .' She took a deep breath. 'But it wasn't only that. If you want the truth, I thought there was something – creepy about him. No, I don't mean obviously weird. I don't know what it was, but it made my skin crawl. How somebody as nice as Mrs Wetherby could stand him, I don't know. Poor woman.'

'Yes, poor woman.' She'd already been told. Abigail Moon was busy setting up the enquiry at the moment, then he would go along with her, probably this evening, to see Mrs Wetherby again. Rotten job, one he hated, but one he made himself do. 'Is she likely to be able to cope?'

'I really don't know,' Daphne said slowly.

Damn silly question, really. One which nobody could answer with certainty. Shock took people differently. Apparently strong people went to pieces, those you'd expect to succumb found unexpected sources of courage, or stoicism.

'I don't know her very well,' Daphne went on. 'I don't think anyone does, except perhaps maybe John Riach, and that only because he worked closely with Mr Wetherby.'

'Riach? He's the Assistant Bursar, isn't he?'

She nodded. 'She took part in school affairs, always came to any function with the Bursar – and she always helps to make wonderful costumes for the school drama group – in fact, she once told me she makes all her own clothes, though you'd never guess. Quite artistic, really, I believe. But she doesn't join in the community, not like the other school wives. I sometimes wonder if she isn't rather shy.'

He watched her finish her tea. He thought there was more she might have said, had she been so inclined, but she put her cup back in the saucer with a little sigh, and said nothing. He looked at the weak, greyish mixture in his own cup and ventured a sip. Apart from the fact that it was now cold, he'd been right to suspect it. He pushed it away, deciding he'd rather die some other way.

10

Joe Totterbridge never used the telephone if he could possibly avoid it. He made Eileen do it for him instead. Even though he couldn't do that today, he still had no inclination to bestir himself. But the alternative was worse, it would mean going all the way up to Kelsey Road to tell Dorrie Lockett, and he wasn't used to walking all round the universe, like Eileen was. His heart would probably give out, toiling up that hill. For a moment he contemplated just ignoring his promise to his wife – Dorrie Lockett would know something was wrong soon enough when Eileen didn't turn up tomorrow. But then she'd likely telephone for an explanation, probably disturb him just when he was watching breakfast TV.

He'd just have to do it, after he'd had a beer and a sandwich. If he could find where Eileen kept the corned beef . . .

'Eileen's not coming for a bit,' Dorrie heard him shout down the phone when she left the supper table to answer it.

'Why, what's wrong, Joe?' She had to hold the phone away from her ear as she listened to the answer. Unaccustomed to telephoning, Joe remained unshaken in his belief that it was necessary to bellow in order to be heard so far away.

'Her's in hospital, they took her in last night. Her hip give out and her slipped and fell and banged her head on the cooker. Knocked herself out, her did.'

'Good heavens, she's all right now, I hope?'

'Oh ar, her come round OK, but they're not letting her out, seeing as how they've got her in there at last,' Joe said, as if his wife were some wild animal which had been evading capture for weeks.

'You mean they're going to do her hip while she's in?'

'Ar. Not afore time, neither.' His voice quavered with self-pity. 'Though how I'm expected to manage without her I don't know.'

'Oh, you'll cope well enough, Joe, a resourceful man like you. Poor Eileen! But she's been waiting long enough for that opera-tion. Tell her I'll be straight along to see her, and not even to *think* about coming back.'

'Oh, her'll be back soon enough, orright,' Joe said hastily. 'We couldn't hardly make ends meet without her bit of money.'

'Joe Totterbridge,' said Dorrie with conviction, when she'd returned to her supper and given Sam the news, 'is a moron. He seems to think Eileen will be back on her knees scrubbing floors next week. Personally, I can't see her wanting to come back ever, not to clean, I mean, though I hope she'll still come as a friend.' Her momentary forthrightness suddenly deserted her, to be replaced by a lost, forsaken look. She pushed aside what was left of her shepherd's pie. 'Whatever will I do without her? We've known each other over fifty years.'

'Mrs Totty'll never desert you, perish the thought! She'll be back, if it's only for a gossip. I'll drive you up to the hospital whenever you want to visit. But meanwhile, what are you going to do about getting some replacement help?'

'Replacement?' Dorrie looked alarmed. 'Oh, we can surely manage! Well, I mean – can't we – well, tackle this sort of thing between us for the time being?' She looked hopefully at Sam.

'Mmm.' Sam had no more idea how to tackle that sort of thing than Dorrie, and even less enthusiasm for it, but neither did he relish the prospect of living in Dorrie-engendered chaos. He'd no objection to getting the garden into shape, but there he drew the line. There was his book to think of, too, as she'd reminded him. 'Pass me the Yellow Pages.'

He was dead.

They would be coming to interview her and they would expect her to be distraught, the grieving wife. Whereas Hannah felt nothing, yet, not even the sense of freedom she should at least have been allowed to feel. She should feel elated, and would, later. But meanwhile, she couldn't play the part, certainly not alone.

The young woman police officer who said she'd been trained in bereavement counselling, coming with John Riach to tell her what had happened, had accepted her dry-eyed reception of the news without surprise. It was shock, she told Hannah, she would cry later, and advised her not to resist it. But she hadn't cried. Couldn't.

WPC Matthews, a big, clumsy, well-meaning young woman who said her name was Tracey, had offered to stay the night with her. However, the thought of a stranger in her home horrified Hannah, even someone as kind and understanding as Tracey was, despite appearances to the contrary.

She picked up the phone and, without having to look up the number, tapped it out from memory.

For nearly three years, two of them spent in the wastes of Antarctica – cold, white, empty, boring and windy, surrounded by miles of frozen sea – Sam had kept a picture of Hannah in his mind. He had no photographs, had needed none, to remind him. Slender, pliant, with soft, thick dark hair to her shoulders. Moving like a dancer, with a languid grace, a soft, slow smile that moved from her lips to light her big, brown eyes.

But now . . . when Sam saw her, he was utterly shocked, wrenched with pity. She looked at least ten years older and, yes – bereft was the word. Yet he knew this was unlikely to be because of her husband. She was, by accident or design, wearing black. Long-sleeved and high-necked as were all her clothes, which he knew she made herself, and one of her soft, chiffon scarves. Her thick creamy skin looked dull and had lost its elasticity. Naturally slender, she was as painfully thin now as an anorexic model.

She closed the door behind him and without words, he opened his arms. She went into them as if coming home, and he kissed her, breathing in the expensive scent he remembered so well. Her body moulded itself to him, feeling light and insubstantial, her arms tightened, her mouth opened hungrily under his, but he drew away gently, feeling strangely reluctant. 'Not yet, Hannah.'

'Not *yet*?'

'He's barely cold.'

She shrank as if he'd doused her with icy water. 'You think we should show *respect* for him?'

'I think we should be careful, that's all.' He reached out his hand and gently undid the delicate, filmy material draped around her neck. 'My God, it hadn't stopped, had it?'

Her hand flew to her throat, fluttered like a bird over the livid bruise, then dropped to her side. 'It has now,' she said flatly, retrieving the ends of the scarf and retying it.

His pulses beat. 'Why wouldn't you leave him, Hannah? There was no reason for you to stay, with Paul grown up.'

'I don't know. Where would I have gone? How could I have lived? And remember, I am still a Catholic.' She looked away from him. 'Or maybe I couldn't quite forget he was my child's father, after all, that I had loved him, once.'

Astonished as he was by the insight of this last, he thought sadly that the first reasons were more likely to have applied, as far as Hannah was concerned. Wetherby had provided her with a comfortable, even luxurious, home. He had money, over and above what he earned, both of which, Sam had to admit, were very important to Hannah, and whatever else his faults, he had been generous. But perhaps more to the point, she had never had any personal ambitions, unlike other women of her age who had careers, or at any rate aspirations to have one after their families were off their hands. Hannah had never done a day's paid work outside the home in her life. He'd thought about this a lot while he was away, and understood a good deal more about her now than he had then.

'The police will be here any moment. Will you stay with me? I don't know how to face them. Am I supposed to show grief? I can't feel it.'

The door bell rang. Colour flew to her face, then receded, leaving her deathly pale. 'I'm not ready for this,' she cried in a panic. 'Please help me – and Sam, don't say anything about – don't say anything, please?'

He had never had any intentions of referring to their one-time relationship. The fewer people who knew, the better. He was going to have enough trouble as it was, trying to break it to Hannah that, especially in view of what had happened, all must be over between them.

After all, they weren't what Hannah had expected, or at least the woman, Inspector Moon, wasn't. They weren't frightening, or accusing. Moon had a brisk manner, controlled in a way that suggested to Hannah she'd had to work at it, that she was naturally more spontaneous. Unlike Hannah herself, she looked very clear as to what she wanted from life, as if her expectations were high and she'd every intention of seeing them fulfilled. She frightened Hannah rather more than the quiet, authoritative man who was her superior. She was well dressed, in an olive-brown trouser suit, a colour chosen expressly to set off that lovely, thick, coppery, expensively styled hair. Beautiful teeth, noticed Hannah, who was always aware of that in other people, afraid it would be noticed when she smiled that she'd had to have one of her own front ones replaced.

Hannah introduced Sam, and Sam asked if they minded if he stayed, while at the same time entrenching his big frame solidly and immovably into his chair. 'Not if Mrs Wetherby doesn't.' Inspector Moon's bright hazel eyes travelled from one to the other, taking in his determined chin and reddish blond hair, contrasting him with Hannah's thin, dark tenseness. He was looking steadfastly at the carpet, as if determined not to interfere.

They didn't stay long, in the event. There was really nothing she could tell them, Hannah said tightly. Of course she couldn't think of anyone her husband regarded as an enemy, but then, he wasn't a man to show his emotions and he wouldn't have confided in her even if he'd had any. She'd last seen him at breakfast. He sometimes came home to lunch, but today, he'd wanted to work on some papers for a meeting that afternoon and had decided to have a sandwich sent in to his office. She'd been at home here, all day, making costumes for the school's production of *The Beggar's Opera*. 'The girl who's playing Polly Peachum came during her lunch hour for a fitting. Oh, and John popped in, John Riach, he's the Assistant Bursar.'

Sam lifted his head and stared at her.

'He walked across for some papers Charles had forgotten. He stayed and had a sandwich with me. Until Rosie came at one. Her fitting took about twenty minutes, I suppose. I was alone after that until John came back with your policewoman to – to tell me.'

Suddenly, she exclaimed, hand to her mouth, 'Paul! Oh God,

I'll have to tell Paul. How could I *possibly* have forgotten that?'

'Who's Paul, Mrs Wetherby?'

'My son. He's a cadet in the Marines.' Her eyes filled with tears, but she blinked them rapidly away; her hand flew again to the knot of her scarf, then as if suddenly aware of the action, she withdrew it and twisted her hands tightly together on her lap.

'We'll get through to his commanding officer, if you like. It'll be a comfort to you to have him home.'

'I don't see how that'll be possible. He's on some sort of training exercise in Belize at the moment.'

'That won't matter. They'll give him compassionate leave.' The superintendent spoke for the first time, and though the words were sympathetic, the quiet decisiveness of his voice suddenly made Hannah reverse her opinion of him. Perhaps he was the one she should be wary of.

'No, I don't want him here, not yet! There's nothing he can do at the moment. I'd rather wait for the funeral. When – when will that be?'

'It may be some time.' The inspector explained the procedures – that there would have to be an inquest, which would be adjourned for the police to make further enquiries, that the coroner would not release the body for burial or cremation until they were completed.

'There's no need for him to come home,' Hannah repeated. 'I'll contact his CO. Maybe they'll let me speak to Paul. I'd like to tell him myself.'

Well, it was her decision.

Mayo was looking at a big, dark grey car parked on the drive outside the window. 'Is that your Saab outside, Mr Leadbetter?'

'No, I walked here. I'm staying with my aunt in Kelsey Road. I walked round when Mrs Wetherby telephoned with the news.'

'It's Charles's car,' Hannah said. 'Your people said it could be brought back, so John Riach drove it round.' She teased a fine thread on the hem of the scarf, which was patterned in soft greys and lilacs. Pretty but not a good choice, without enough colour against the black, draining her face of what little natural colour she possessed, Abigail thought judicially.

Mayo was still looking at the Saab. 'Did you share the car with your husband, Mrs Wetherby?'

Her eyebrows lifted. 'Me, drive Charles's car? That's the last thing he would have allowed! Anyway, I don't drive. I walk into town, or take a taxi.'

'We're all chauvinists at heart, we men,' said Mayo, who didn't particularly care who drove his car, especially on long journeys. 'Kelsey Road, you said, Mr Leadbetter? You'll be Miss Lockett's nephew, returned from the Antarctic?'

'As a matter of fact, yes. How did you know?'

'Oh, news travels fast in Lavenstock.' Dorrie Lockett, he was thinking. The lady who was causing problems with the school's new entrance. The nephew who'd written the letter. Probably insignificant, unrelated facts, but he filed them in his memory for future reference. He added, 'For the record, where were you at twenty past one?'

'Working in my aunt's garden. It's become a jungle while I've been away and I'm trying to clear it.'

'You wouldn't have heard the shot from there?'

He shook his head. 'Too far away. It's a ten-minute walk at least from the school.'

'Of course.' Mayo suddenly asked Hannah, 'Do you – or did your husband – have a gun, Mrs Wetherby?'

'A *gun?*' She almost laughed, as if the idea was absurd. 'Of course not!'

Sam Leadbetter intervened. 'What are you implying?'

'Sam.' It was Hannah who was being protective now. She put a hand on his arm, and then stated, almost as if convincing herself, 'You're saying Charles shot himself, aren't you, Mr Mayo?'

'I'm afraid that's not possible. Not when he was shot in the back of the head.'

A silence fell. 'So he did have an enemy, after all,' she said at last.

'So it would seem. Or someone who needed him out of the way.' He watched her take this without a flicker of emotion. 'And what about you, Mr Leadbetter? Do you have a gun?'

'No,' Sam said shortly.

Mayo paused before getting into the car as they left, looking back at the house. A brick-built 1950s detached, one of about a dozen similar ones on the steep, once-quiet Vanson Hill, off Tilbourne Road. Reasonably quiet, at least, before the hospital further down had been extended. Square and unadorned, post-war austerity style, built at a time when satisfying housing shortages was a first requirement, and imagination wasn't, they'd nevertheless been desirable residences then, and still were, since most of them had good-sized gardens at the back, which allowed for extensions and improvements. They were set well back from the road at the front, the gardens endowed with now mature trees which gave them a spurious graciousness. The prices they fetched when one came on the market were astronomical, in view of their original cost. The Wetherbys had been lucky; the school had presumably bought this one years ago.

He sat beside Abigail and she put the key in the ignition and waited. He seemed preoccupied and she knew better than to interrupt at such times.

He was thinking of the room they had just left. For an artistic woman, said to be so apt with her needle, Hannah Wetherby had done little to enhance what was an exceptionally dull room, despite its being stuffed with expensive objects, unrelated and haphazard, as if a high price tag automatically guaranteed taste. Money had been spent, as if this were the prime objective, rather than comfort, or attractiveness, and it showed. Compulsive shopping? Compensating activity, who could tell?

'Let's go,' he said at last.

Abigail said nothing until she'd nudged the car out into the main road and into the stream of traffic. 'She's very nervous. Did you notice her fiddling all the time with that scarf she was wearing? And the long sleeves, the high neck?'

'It's a cold day.'

'I'll bet she wears them in summer, too.' He looked at her. 'I got used to noticing that sort of thing when I was with the DVU.'

'You think Wetherby knocked her about?'

'It's not confined to the beer-swilling working classes you know!'

'Yes, Abigail, I'm aware of that.' Her unthinking, too-sharp retort earned her a raised-eyebrow glance, a warning not to go too far, not to take his tolerance too much for granted.

She made an apologetic gesture, and sighed. 'Yes, well. We all know about that, don't we?'

The first thing Abigail had noticed about Hannah Wetherby had been the wariness, like an animal who has learned not to trust human beings. The trapped look in her eyes that was all too familiar, one she'd learned to recognise from her stint with the Domestic Violence Unit, a few years ago.

Why some men found it necessary to hit, or even torture, their wives, why women stayed with them until they were half-killed, or ran away then went back for more, was something to which Abigail, with her robust self-sufficiency, had never found an answer. It was one of the reasons she'd been glad to leave the unit behind, upset at the lack of understanding she'd felt in herself, at being unable to empathise with that sort of mentality. It demanded more of her than she was able to give: she could offer sympathy, and practical advice, but she could no more imagine what made these women endure a life of unremitting pain, violence and degradation than she could have endured it herself for one minute. If any man with whom she was in a relationship had raised his hand to her, just once, she'd have left him for good. She felt bad about her failure to comprehend, not only as a police officer, but as a human being, as another woman. They deserved more from her than she was able to give.

Sometimes, of course, women did rebel. Picked up the bread knife and used it when a man slammed his fist, or his boot, into their stomach, or broke their jaw, or worse, much worse. Occasionally, they simply walked out. Or took a whole bottleful of sleeping pills and never woke up. Everyone has their cut-off point, for one reason or another. Even Hannah Wetherby? She'd denied that anybody at all could have hated her husband enough to shoot him dead. But for a moment there, Abigail had glimpsed something beneath the surface.

She knew Mayo was thinking along the same lines, when he said, 'She had a lot to lose by leaving him. Easy lifestyle. Nice house, status. Money.'

And a lot to gain by having him dead. No more physical abuse, for one thing. And if there was money coming, an added reason. And she'd be free for a life with someone else.

'Is there something going on there, do you think?' he added, picking up her own thoughts again. 'With Leadbetter?'

'I'd be surprised if there wasn't. You could cut the vibes between them with a knife.'

'Then we can assume they knew each other before he went away, unless it's a relationship that's developed bloody fast over the last few days.'

'More likely one that's flared up again since he came home – and Wetherby just got in the way.'

'I wondered when we'd get round to that, the age-old motive rearing its ugly head. Sex. Or money. Ten to one there's private money there, too. Unless the Bursar of Lavenstock College is paid more than I think he is, she's hardly likely to have murdered him for his pension. Though the real question is whether she hated him enough to kill him at all.'

'Wouldn't you feel like killing someone who'd been knocking you around for years?'

'Probably. But I might have restrained myself. Besides, we don't *know* that he had.'

Abigail's look said it all.

'And probably verbal abuse, too,' she added after a moment. 'If it's true that he had a nasty tongue. That can be just as bad, or worse, in a different way.'

They drove in silence for a while, until Mayo said, 'And what about Riach? Did I detect some nuance there, too? Is she the sort of woman who'd play one against the other?'

If she was, that posed another question: was Wetherby entirely to blame for what had patently, in spite of the caution Mayo had just voiced about assuming physical cruelty, been an unhappy marriage?

'None of them have an alibi worth considering. Covering for each other doesn't constitute that, in my book – nor does it account for the time. But unless she's lying about how long that fitting took, she didn't have time to get to the school. On the other hand, Riach had plenty of time to get there, and as yet no alibi. And Leadbetter has none at all.'

'If you're guilty, you go to some trouble to provide one.'

'Well, just now was hardly the time to press the point, but we'd better see to it we talk to Riach, and the other two again, separately. They're the best suspects we have so far.'

Abigail said, after a moment, 'How about if she went from the back of the house and cut diagonally across the playing fields? That would cut the time down to ten minutes maximum, I'd say.'

'Can you get into the playing fields that way?'

'I walked across the rugger pitch and had a look. There's a gate with a lock leading directly into a passageway between their back garden and the next door's,' said Abigail, stealing a march on him yet again.

11

If anyone had told Cleo that Daphne would be proved right and that very soon she'd be admitting that working for Maid to Order was a mistake of the first water, she wouldn't have listened. But after that first day, she'd known guiltily how true it was, it was definitely out of her league. Not that it was a league she any longer wanted to be in. Getting the brasses to come up a treat without leaving a trace of polish in the crevices, chasing innocent spiders out of corners, vacuuming under the rugs – talk about life being too short to stuff a mushroom! She'd have packed it in there and then, only she'd promised Val to stay on until the staff-shortage crisis was over.

The one bright spot on the horizon was that she hadn't committed herself to anything long term. Meanwhile, she was to be fitted in when any team was short of an extra body, which at the moment seemed to be most of every day. Tone, who worked for Maids on an ad hoc basis, had made himself unavailable to them for the time being, presumably to concentrate on her decorating. She felt guilty about that, too.

It wasn't the hard work that she objected to so much as the mind-numbing boredom. Mostly, it wasn't hard work anyway, just repetitive, tedious chores. The clients fell into two distinct types: those who tidied up before the cleaners arrived, so that you wondered what could possibly need to be done; and those whose houses looked as though a bomb had struck and, defeated by the mess they'd created around themselves, called in other people to sort them out. On the whole it was the latter category who used Maid to Order; the tidiers usually had their own regular cleaning women. Cleo couldn't yet expect to be sent to the more covetable jobs such as office or surgery cleaning.

Mrs Osborne had told Val that the team she'd sent had done such a good job at Wych Cottage there would be no need for another visit to finish off, so there'd be no opportunity to take another peep into that drawer – though fat chance remained of the gun still being there. After telling her father of the incident, which had seemed to her the best thing she could do, she'd tried to forget it. She'd had enough of looking into the grubby corners of other people's lives. But obscurely, it worried her. Just as the newspaper item of that woman who had been found dead in the Kyne haunted her. Perhaps it was the juxtaposition of the two things: the dead woman, who'd turned out to have been shot, found so near Wych Cottage, and that rather horrifying glimpse of what she was sure had been a gun, the last object one would have expected Mrs Osborne to possess. She was glad she'd mentioned it to her dad, she knew she ought to tell someone but she'd have felt embarrassed approaching the police over something which might be put down to her imagination. But George hadn't pooh-poohed her concern. It was possible, he pointed out, that the gun was owned quite legitimately by Mrs Osborne, but this in itself seemed unlikely, especially in view of the old lady's consternation when it had been exposed. She could understand Mrs O being persuaded that she might be safer with a weapon in the house against intruders, but unless she knew how to handle it, wasn't it terribly dangerous? Anyway, George had promised to see it was looked into, and she'd had to be satisfied with that.

She was due down at MO at nine. She'd been up since five, eager to write. For days, she'd felt the creative spirit was not so much stirring again as clamouring to be heard. And now, she could hardly wait to start, get her thoughts on paper, get the book up and running. But this morning, she'd worked on it for three hours and the more she did, the less clearly defined her ideas seemed to become, refusing to be transferred from what she saw so clearly in her mind into words on paper. At eight, defeated, she gave it up, wondering despondently if she really had the stamina to be a writer, or if she only liked the idea of being one. With a sigh, she switched off her PC and slipped down to the corner shop for bread and milk for her breakfast.

Walking home, she decided it was time to see how Michelangelo was getting on with painting her ceiling. She hadn't actually seen Tone since the day she'd agreed to let him do the job, though there was evidence of his activities in the smell of paint issuing from under her front room doors – both of which were kept locked, on Tone's insistence. After gaining her approval of the colour he'd suggested for the paint, he'd said he preferred her not to see the intermediate stages, and she'd agreed to his artistic needs. She never wanted anyone to see anything but the finished product, either. But she was getting fed up with living in the kitchen. Not to mention having to leave by the back door and re-enter via the front whenever she wanted to go upstairs.

She found him in the kitchen, making himself a coffee when she returned. 'Finished, apart from the woodwork,' he remarked laconically. 'Want to come and look?'

Finished? Already? Crikey, that was quick! What sort of a cowboy job had he made of it? She followed him and he threw open the front room door. 'Ta-da!'

She was speechless for a while, then finally found her voice. 'Tone, it's brilliant!'

'Glad you appreciate it, ma'am.' His tone was throwaway, but his ears glowed red and his lips twitched at the corners in the effort not to grin like a Cheshire cat.

He hadn't, in the end, had time to strip off all the paper, and it had to be admitted that he'd slapped the paint on, but why worry when the total effect was so amazing? The walls were a subtle apricot, and the whole room was suffused with a golden light, transforming it. But that wasn't all – most of his time had been spent painting, right into one fireplace alcove, a mock window with a view of sky and the tops of trees visible through it. At right angles to this, on either side, he'd screwed to the walls two large pieces of mirror glass he said he'd acquired – no, don't ask! – which trebled the effect of looking out into a garden, pushing out the walls of the little room and adding even more light. It didn't seem to matter now that the other, real window, looked out on to the high rise flats.

When the furniture was back in place, the silver-paper Spanish tango dancers on their black velvet swaying together above the fireplace, and Phoebe's skein of ducks flying ever-optimistically upwards on the opposite wall . . . well, at a stretch, you could nearly imagine it was meant to be like that. She might almost come to believe it in time.

Meanwhile, a table for her word processor, provision to play the sort of music she liked without being nagged . . . Belatedly, she thought of what Daphne called 'the finishing touches'. A trip down to the market for material for new curtains, cushions for the chairs and settee? 'What colours should I choose, Tone?' she asked humbly, wondering how on earth she'd live up to all this, keep it neat and tidy. 'I'd be afraid of spoiling anything, getting the wrong thing.'

'I'll come with you and make sure you don't.' The livid scar twisted his face up as he grinned, but she could sense his jubilation at her appreciation and once more she wondered about Tone. That *trompe l'oeil* window was the work of someone with more to give to life than cleaning people's houses – or even doing a quick-fix decorating job on them.

And there was something else she'd noticed about Tone. His broad Black Country accent occasionally slipped. It was almost as though he were – not putting it on, it was too natural for that – but as though he'd once been accustomed to using received pronunciation as well, and now wasn't quite sure of himself in either form.

Cleo found she was working with Sue again, and she'd no complaints about that. She liked Sue, who always had a smile on her pretty, dimpled face, never got into a flap, and managed to get through incredible amounts of work. Cleo thought she might even be learning something from her.

Val had today fitted in number 16 Kelsey Road, at short notice, in place of Mrs Osborne and as a special favour to the owner, whose cleaning lady was in hospital.

While Sue rang the bell, Cleo peered over a hedge and saw a totally unexpected sight: a sunken area running the length of the house, back to front, secret and enclosed. Clouds reflected in a pool bubbling with frogspawn, at its verge reeds and last year's prickly teasel that had persisted through the winter. The flickering sunlight revealed a splash of gold, a corner studded with aconites, the emerging spears of bluebell leaves, a kind of greening over of the whole plot. Beside the rocky steps were hellebores – bell-shaped lime-green flowers tipped with plum-purple – and here and there the broad arrow leaves of lords and ladies were pushing through. A spiky blackthorn hedge was just about to burst into flower, and a cherry plum grew in one corner.

Cleo was enchanted. A wild flower garden, here in Kelsey Road, where in every other garden, not even a buttercup was allowed to flourish! It couldn't just have happened, it must have been planted. She looked with quickened interest at the house, a faded Victorian charmer with a neglected air, its paintwork peeling and the Virginia creeper on the façade grown out of hand: the bare tendrils clung tenaciously to the brickwork, you could see them curling over the spouting, ready to thrust under the roof tiles and prise them off. She couldn't help wondering what the owner would be like, not to mention the interior.

But despite its size, the house wasn't going to pose any problems, even Cleo could see that immediately. The small, plump, eccentric-looking person who in fact turned out to be Miss Lockett herself told them vaguely that many of the rooms were shut off, and the few in use were kept clean and in good order by her regular lady, at present in hospital for a hip replacement. It was soon obvious that she spoke the truth. As Sue pointed out, it wasn't going to take the time allocated to have the place spick and span. Miss Lockett merely smiled very sweetly and said good, then that would give them time for a cup of coffee before they started, perhaps a slice of chocolate cake and a chat, so that they could get to know one another. She liked to know all about people she met, she said, who they were and where they came from, and within minutes had managed to obtain this information, despite appearing, not to put too fine a point on it, like a woozy-minded Miss Havisham on a bad day, her hair falling down, and dressed as she was in a collection of garments which would have been more at home heaped on a church jumble sale stall. She smiled vaguely and showed them into the warm, comfortable kitchen and when the coffee was made, asked Cleo if she'd mind slipping outside to ask Sam, who was working in the garden, if he'd like one, too.

Cleo walked up the path in a back garden that made the unstructured wild garden at the side of the house seem organised, though there seemed to have been recent attempts to tidy it up. She approached the gardener, a large young man in corduroys and stout boots who had seemingly been digging over a patch of ground elder. A pile of the thick fleshy roots sat obscenely on the path beside him.

Sam swore luridly as yet another root he was tracing back to its

106

source snapped off. He stamped his fork down into the moist earth, his boot shoving it down so hard the tines disappeared. He leaned on the handle, breathing hard. He'd picked the wrong job on which to vent his worry and frustration. Should have had more sense – rooting out ground elder was a slow, fiddling job, requiring the patience of a saint, and patience was something in short supply with him this morning. Not when the events of yesterday were tumbling over and over in his mind, any clear thought about the situation obscured by doubts, like frost smoke above the Antarctic ice.

Could he ever be sure of Hannah?

He was sure of nothing since his return, and meeting her again.

In his book, you played it straight. Life, or whatever. If it didn't work out, you either put up with it, or packed it in, or did something decisive, even ruthless, if necessary, and refused to have regrets. As he had done, when it became obvious their ill-matched affair was going nowhere. He had wanted to rescue her then, the young Lochinvar riding out of the west, and he had an uncomfortable feeling now that she had never really wanted to be rescued. And that bothered him.

There was something dark about it that Sam didn't under-stand, or want to understand. She could have escaped, if she had wanted. That she hadn't even tried, had stayed with the bastard until somebody had removed him for her, disturbed him more than Wetherby's murder, which seemed almost incidental. At the back of his mind, unacknowledged because Sam was Sam, and not in any sort of way imaginative, was the thought that this sort of attitude was – well, sick . . . Oh, *screw it!*

'Are you Sam?'

He turned to see a small girl of about seventeen with a scarlet MO emblazoned on the front of her black sweatshirt standing beside him, little and dark and quick, her hair raggedly cut like a street urchin's, apparently with a knife and fork. Big, greenish-blue eyes in a small, serious face. She was frowning and momen-tarily he wondered if she'd overheard him cussing and was offended. If so, she was the first girl he'd come across of that age who was likely to be shocked at bad language – most of them could teach drunken sailors a thing or two about swearing. He

107

apologised with as much grace as he could muster all the same.

'That's OK,' Cleo said, passing on the message from Miss Lockett.

'You're from the agency.'

'Right. And you'd better take your wellies off before you come into the kitchen, otherwise Miss Lockett'll be paying for us to be here all day. Does she always invite the hired help to share coffee and chocolate cake?'

'My Aunt Dorrie,' he said solemnly, 'never does what you expect.'

Aunt!

'Whoops, sorry – I just assumed . . .'

'Sam Leadbetter. Sorry I can't shake hands, mine are filthy.'

'Cleo Atkins.'

Her glance took in the cashmere sweater Hannah had once bought him as a present, motheaten in places though it now was, the rather nice gold watch on his wrist. 'I should've known. You don't look much like a gardener.'

'What's a gardener supposed to look like? You don't look much like a charlady, either.'

'Neither do I act like one, I'm afraid. I'm only a temp, thank heaven fasting, as my mother would say. Which is probably what everyone else feels too.'

'Why are you doing it then?' he asked, amused.

'Money,' she said succinctly. 'I'm writing a book, but I can't live on air . . .' She stopped and looked down at her feet. Why had she told him that? She could count on the fingers of one hand the people who knew of her ambition. All the same, she noted that she had said 'I am writing', not 'I'm hoping to write' and felt cheered.

'A writer?' Sam's interest was kindled, and he looked at her with more interest, though he realised immediately she couldn't mean his sort of writing – dull, factual stuff. She was, he saw now, older than he'd thought by about five years. 'Well, there must be other jobs than cleaning –'

She groaned. 'Oh, don't! You sound just like my mother. She works in the Bursar's office over there –' she waved a hand vaguely in the direction of the school – 'and thinks everyone should have the same sort of well-defined job, even though it's a terrible office to work in and the Bursar's a ratbag.'

He didn't smile. A stiff silence had taken hold of him. He looked suddenly years older. They had reached the stone seat by the corner of the house, where a pair of size twelve sneakers rested. He sat down and began to remove his gumboots.

'Have I said something I shouldn't?'

He put the boots neatly side by side, slipped on the sneakers and stood up. 'Haven't you heard the Bursar was shot dead yesterday? Didn't your mother tell you?'

He was sorry he'd been so blunt when he saw her face crumple, her eyes widen. 'No, I didn't know. I don't live at home now, I didn't see Mum yesterday. And I haven't seen the papers, either. Was she – was she *there*?'

'Not when it happened. But I'm afraid she was the one who found him.'

'Oh, no!' Questions raced through her mind, all beginning with the word why. Why hadn't they let her know? Why hadn't she rung home the previous night, as she'd intended to do? Why hadn't she heard about the murder?

The answers were all there, take your choice. Because they didn't want to worry her. Because she hadn't yet had Phoebe's phone reconnected and she hadn't had change for a phone box on the way to the cinema last night and they wouldn't have had a clue where to get hold of her: she'd been to see a supposedly significant Japanese film about recently dead souls, the subtitles of which had turned out to be even more obscure than the plot. Afterwards she still hadn't known what all the fuss was about. And also because she'd had to rush through her breakfast after spending so much time admiring her newly decorated front room and hadn't even switched on the radio.

'I shall have to go and see if she's OK.' Poor Mum, even she would have a hard time coping with something like that.

'Of course. Would you like me to run you over there?'

Yes, she would, was her first thought. Brilliant. He'd be a wonderful man in a crisis, like having a seven-foot baseball player just behind you if you fell over. But no, even at a time like this, Daphne wouldn't appreciate anyone feeling she needed a shoulder to cry on, just because she'd found a dead body. Even

109

though – especially as – it was someone she hadn't much liked.

'That's really nice of you,' she told Sam, 'but if I could just use your phone . . .'

'Sure.'

A passage led off the kitchen into the echoing, Victorian tiled hallway at the end. He indicated the telephone, a heavy, ancient black one where you had to dial instead of pressing buttons, and left her to it.

She let it ring twenty times, though after the fourth or fifth ring she knew there'd be no answer. Daphne was always prompt at answering the phone. She rang her father's office and it was Muriel who picked up the call.

'Oh, Cleo! Have you heard? You have? Well, your dad's had to go out, but he's been trying to get you. You should have your phone reconnected, or get a mobile, you know, he says he's going to buy you one, first thing he does.'

'I know, I've been thinking the same thing. Is Mum all right, Muriel?'

'She's gone in to work, if that's what you mean.'

'She's *what*?'

'Well, you know Daphne. She wouldn't let a little thing like murder stop her – nor would she listen to your father, though I know he doesn't approve of her going in today,' Muriel said, the hint of malice in her voice showing she didn't either. The two women were not by nature designed to feel affinity. 'He said he'd be back here around ten for a few minutes, if you want to see him. He's very busy. We've suddenly had a whole stack of work come in.'

'I'd better come straight down, then, I'm only at Kelsey Road,' Cleo told her, before she'd considered her obligations, though she needn't have worried about that. Sue had already made a start with the vacuum cleaner, and Sam having explained the situation to her, insisted that she could cope with what needed to be done on her own.

'Of course you can,' Dorrie clucked. 'Just leave what you can't manage, my dear, a bit of dust never hurt anyone. You go to your mother, Cleo, and tell her how sorry I am, especially for her, for he was a horrid man, as well I know.' She paused. 'I've met your mother, you know. I slipped in the snow last winter, going down

110

the hill, sat right down on my coccyx and simply *couldn't* get up. Not a soul came to help me up, except your mother. So kind! I'd thrown a snowball right across the street at one man and shouted yoo-hoo for help, but he took no notice. Your mother brought me home in her car and made me a cup of tea and a hot bottle, rang for the doctor and waited while he got here. No permanent damage done, thank goodness.'

Highly diverted, despite her indignation at Dorrie's plight, by a picture of her sitting in the snow throwing snowballs until rescued by Daphne, Cleo almost smiled. But yes, that did sound very like her mother.

12

Earlier the same morning, the men and women delegated to the enquiry were variously dispersed about the dedicated incident room at Milford Road Divisional Headquarters, waiting for Mayo. Waiting for Godot, it was beginning to seem like. He was late, which was unusual. Hating to be kept waiting himself, it was one of his virtues not to keep others waiting. People had found seats or perched on desks, windowsills, leaned against the walls. The air was thick with chat, banter and cigarette smoke, this last a permanent gripe for the non-smokers, who considered it an infringement of their rights which forced them into passive smoking. Abigail threw open a window before Mayo came in, hoping to forestall any abrasive comments from him. Looked at her watch, again.

'Finish that Caramello, Scotty, give us all a chance to hear what the super has to say when he gets here,' ordered Kite irritably. He wished Mayo would get a move on. He was torn between the desire not to miss out on anything connected with these two major enquiries, and his appearance as an official witness for the prosecution in the case against Lord Spenderhill at Birmingham Crown Court, where he was due to start giving evidence in an hour or two. The hearing was expected to last some time, so the investigation here might even be over before he'd had a chance to get stuck into it. Story of his life.

Unperturbed by the reprimand, DC Barry Scott, the station slob, amiably screwed the Caramello wrapper and threw it more or less at a waste bin, missing, while noisily sucking the last of the toffee from his teeth and washing it down with a loud slurp of coffee. Kite gave him a look, though chocolate bars were less offensive than some of the more pungent snacks he consumed, and much less so than his personal problem. Despite the look, the belch which followed was barely suppressed. Jenny Platt pointedly picked up the wrapper between finger and thumb and binned it.

'You can be disgusting,' she told him.

112

'You should see me when I really try.'

'Try? That'll be the day!'

'Watch it, Scotty!' Farrar warned, meaning watch it in more ways than one. There was no room for passengers on Mayo's team and Scotty had been pushing it for some time. Grown idle as well as incompetent, he was already a marked man. Few would be sorry to see him go.

Farrar's intervention gained him Kite's approval. He hadn't been among the advocates for Farrar being made up to acting sergeant, but since Carmody, the big Scouse sergeant, had landed himself for a long spell in hospital by being pushed spectacularly down three storeys of a fire escape, thereby leaving a desperate gap on the team, Farrar's long sought-after promotion had been inevitable. And as his senior officer, Kite felt bound to support him, in public at any rate. Occasionally, he sensed that the lad was at least trying. And Kite had a lot of time for anyone who tried.

Where the hell was Mayo?

A look passed between Kite and Abigail; she nodded and decided to start without him. Immediately she began, the room became quiet, and she had the attention of everyone there. She had just outlined the case, then turned to the board behind her, where the usual montage of facts, names, dates, times, crime-scene photographs was assembled, when Mayo came in, unsmiling and apologising for keeping everyone waiting. He waved a hand for Abigail to continue, took a seat to one side and sat listening, one hand cupping his elbow, the other covering his mouth.

Near the top of the board was written the name of the victim, Charles Howard Wetherby, aged forty-four, and pinned underneath was a large photograph of him taken at some school function, very much alive, plus several less attractive ones taken after he was dead. Stills of the room where he was killed, diagrams plotting the position the killer must have taken, the distance he stood from the body, the pattern of blood splashes, a diagram of the estimated trajectory of the bullet, plus a computer-generated map on the wall showing the layout of the school and tracing all the possible means of entry into it, and entry into the Bursar's office . . . all this surrounding the bland face of the man who was now dead.

113

'I trust you've now all read your information sheets,' Abigail went on, 'so you don't need to be told that Doc Ison estimates the time of death as not more than ten minutes or so before he was called, which was at one thirty.'

At 12.08 precisely Trish, one of the two girls in the outer office, had set the recorded message giving the times the office would next be open, and departed with the other girl, Beverley; they'd been clock-watching because they'd wanted to catch the stall on the open market where they could buy reject designer knitwear, before everything was sold out. A minute later, Mrs Atkins had popped her head round the door and told Wetherby she was going to lunch. She'd then driven home for a quick snack and to prepare vegetables for the evening meal, and returned at half-past one. She had taken some papers into his office and found Wetherby dead.

'Other people we need to speak to are these.' Abigail indicated on the board the names of Wetherby's colleagues on the administration and teaching staffs, with special attention to the name of John Riach, and additionally, Sam Leadbetter. After a moment's thought, she picked up the marker and added Dorrie Lockett's name to the board. 'Most of you are familiar with this lady. She's on the list because she went to the Bursar's office around noon, too, seemingly to give him a piece of her mind.' This generated some amusement among the troops, and she warned, 'But before you get any ideas, he was seen alive after she left.'

'All the same,' Kite intervened thoughtfully, 'until she got too old to cope with that sort of hassle, she used to work at Villiers House.' He was referring to one of the women's refuges in the town. 'And I once saw her go for a drunken Irishman twice her size who was looking for his wife there. He didn't know what had hit him.'

'That's a thought to bear in mind, unlikely suspect though she might seem,' Abigail said. 'Dorrie saw her home under threat - or at least herself as being persecuted. She knows enough about abused women to hate their abusers – plus, she's a law unto herself.' Privately, she thought Dorrie Lockett actually shooting Wetherby seemed, even so, an unlikely scenario.

'So, there are the basic facts we have to work with,' she concluded. 'What we now need to find out is what his relations were like with his family, his colleagues, if he had any other known associates. Especially if any of them owns a gun or knows how to use one. As you know, a cartridge case was found at the scene. Ballistics say the weapon was a 9mm automatic, something like a Beretta, or a Walther PKK. Plus anything else you can pick up. You know the drill. Sergeant Farrar will issue the allocations. Mr Mayo?'

He seemed worried, she thought, as he stood up to speak. Not outwardly apparent to anyone who knew him less well than she did, perhaps, but this murder, coming almost on top of the other, was putting a strain on everyone, and Mayo most of all. Extra resources had been forthcoming, but not nearly enough. There would necessarily have to be some doubling up and this would put additional demands on men and women already disappointed by the lack of any success in getting anywhere at all with the previous murder. Nor were they likely to get any further, until they found out who the dead woman had been, yet no one had so far come forward to claim her as a missing relative, friend or partner. The inevitable conclusion was that she had been a stranger to the area, brought here from elsewhere – which made the question of the place where she'd been found an even more puzzling one.

Mayo said, 'All I want to say is that we need a result on this case, and I'm sure you're all aware of why. But not at all costs. We need a safe conviction, but let me emphasise that I want it handled properly. None of us want *this* investigation to drag on – but don't sacrifice thoroughness for speed.'

Having exhorted everyone to get cracking and waste no more time, thanking them in advance for what he knew would be their best efforts, Mayo closed the meeting. 'Give it your best, lads.' Before leaving for his own office, he then spoke to his two inspectors, explaining why he'd been delayed.

'I've just spent the last half-hour with the ACC, drawing up a statement for the press. There'll be a conference tomorrow morning,' he told them abruptly. 'He's not too happy, as you might imagine, with this latest shooting.' Which must be the understatement of all time, Abigail thought, looking at him with sympathy. Sheering, the ACC, was not a patient man, perhaps understandably, being ultimately accountable for what had now become three outstanding, unsolved murders on his patch.

An hour later, every man and woman having been made aware of their particular area of responsibility, the incident room had emptied. Kite brought two cups of coffee for himself and Abigail and perched companionably on her desk. The scratchiness between them after his return to plain clothes on his promotion to inspector had reached a fairly amiable truce. Kite wasn't the introspective type and he didn't care to probe too deeply on the reasons. It might have had something to do with the fact that Abigail's departure was a more or less foregone conclusion.

They'd barely drunk their coffee before Mayo buzzed. 'My office, both you and Martin, pronto,' he barked when Abigail answered.

It wasn't like Mayo to be so peremptory, not without apparent reason. 'Jump to it, Martin. His Nibs is suddenly either in a mood or a big hurry.'

Mayo motioned them to two chairs in front of his desk when they entered, and without saying anything further, slid across the surface what Abigail saw immediately was the pathologist's report, which must have just come in. It ended up midway between the two of them. 'You first,' Kite said generously.

Abigail read it, guessing now at the source of Mayo's abruptness. Tension could take you like that, when you hardly dared to believe in something that indicated a break might suddenly be possible.

The report was straightforward. A general description of the body. Results of the internal examination, with details of the condition and weights of the various organs, showing that he had been a man in previous good health. And most importantly followed the results of the external examination, giving a detailed description of the cerebral wound caused by the entry of the bullet, fired at close range from a small-calibre handgun. In-driven fragments of bone had resulted in irreversible damage to the brain, causing immediate death.

But the rider accompanying the report was why Mayo had sent for them: the bullet which had been extracted from Wetherby's brain had been identified as of the same make, model and calibre as the bullet which had killed the woman found in the River Kyne.

Timpson-Ludgate had made no further comment, except to say that it had already been sent to the ballistics people for further examination and comparison with the first one. Every bullet retained the markings of the barrel it was fired from, every barrel had singular irregularities peculiar to itself and none other, therefore if it could be shown that the striations on the bullets were identical, it could safely be assumed they were fired from the same gun . . .

'And I don't need any funny remarks about first finding your gun,' Mayo said, forestalling Kite before he'd time to open his mouth. He lapsed into a thoughtful silence, from which he eventually roused himself, reaching for the telephone and requesting Delia to put him through to someone called Geoff Blake in Forensic Ballistics.

The resulting conversation, after an interchange of greetings, made as little sense as one-sided conversations usually did, except that it was very apparent a favour was being called in, and that Mayo would appreciate the results of the tests and comparisons of the two bullets extracted from the two victims being on his desk as soon as possible. It didn't actually sound like a request for a favour: from here, it sounded half-way towards an order, but presumably Geoff Blake didn't see it like that. He said something which evidently restored Mayo's equilibrium and made him laugh as he put the phone down.

He pushed himself away from the desk and paced about a bit with his hands in his pockets. 'The press are going to have a bloody field day with this – three unexplained shootings in as many months!'

'You don't believe –' Abigail began.

'No, I don't believe the Fermanagh business had anything to do with these last – but no way are these two cases going to follow that into the same limbo – not if I've anything to do with it. Forget Fermanagh, concentrate on this.' He slapped a hand down on the path report. 'We might start by having a look at something that cropped up yesterday.' He told them about his conversation with George Atkins.

'If George thinks there's something fishy the chances are he's right,' Kite said when he'd finished, and Mayo nodded. Like himself, George believed in what he called his copper's nose. Neither acknowledged hunches or intuition – except the sort gained through a lifetime's experience. They weighed a notion,

117

balanced what they knew of the facts against the possibilities, and came up with ideas.

'And Reuben Bysouth's reputation doesn't exactly smell of violets,' Kite added. 'I remember him from when I first joined the force. If this old woman is as friendly with him as she seems to be, I suggest she'd bear watching, too.'

'Right, but they're not necessarily *friends*,' Abigail pointed out. 'Though you might need to call your neighbours that if they're the only ones for miles. If she needed help when she was being flooded out, who else would she turn to?'

'Fair enough. And George says Jared's straight enough, at any rate . . . all the same, we'd better have a word with this Mrs Osborne, but check beforehand to see if she's licensed to own a gun,' Mayo advised, annoyingly stating the obvious.

'If it *was* a gun Cleo Atkins saw,' Kite said.

'Oh, George thinks it was. He says Cleo wouldn't make a mistake about a thing like that.'

'Wouldn't she?' Kite looked doubtful. 'OK, but a gun wouldn't be all that surprising. The old girl used to be a farmer's wife and she'll be used to having them around the place. Living out there at the back of beyond, maybe she thinks it a good idea to keep one handy.'

'In a drawer?' Abigail asked, frowning.

'The ground floor had just been flooded, furniture and other stuff carted upstairs, I don't suppose anybody bothered too much about what was put where, that's why she'd got excited about it. Maybe it's a relic of her husband's – which she knows she isn't entitled to keep, without a shotgun licence. Especially since it wasn't locked up, as it should have been.'

'We're not talking shotguns, though. It's a pistol we're looking for – and if it was in the drawer, we're not going to find it, now, are we, not after somebody's seen it?'

'Check, all the same,' Mayo said tersely, bringing the discussion back to the point. 'If only to eliminate . . . especially with this latest development. We're looking for a gun that maybe killed both victims – which means whoever used it knew, or was targeting, them both. So it's important – and so is any possible connection Wetherby may have had with Kyneford. It wasn't chance the woman was found where she was. Given the choice, there must be hundreds of better places to dump a body than

118

where it was left. And don't forget to check on the Bysouths at the pig farm. Grand job for one of you – a ride out, lovely breezy day like this, what more can you ask?'

Kite, looking unusually spruce in his best dark suit, donned especially to impress the jury later that afternoon, looked pointedly at his watch and grinned beatifically.

Abigail groaned. 'Why do I always draw the short straw? Reuben Bysouth sounds a real sweetheart, another who's been belting his wife around. I can't wait. Never mind. I'll take Jenny with me, but later this morning. I'd like to have a word with Cleo Atkins before I give myself the pleasure, and I have people to see at the school first, as well.'

'Leave the Assistant Bursar to me,' Mayo said. 'Riach, isn't it, John Riach?'

He could never properly focus his mind on a case until he'd seen all the important witnesses at least once. Riach no doubt fell into this category, since he had worked alongside Wetherby for many years, and could almost certainly tell him as much about the Bursar as anyone. The more you knew about the victim, the closer you got to the killer was a basic rule to work by, but as yet no one had been able, or willing, to tell him just what sort of man Wetherby had been. While he didn't seem to have been actively disliked – his wife and Sam Leadbetter apart, perhaps – nobody seemed to have cared for him overmuch. Certainly no one seemed particularly distressed at his demise. He'd led an apparently ordinary and uneventful life, no different in substance from many another man who kept the real state of his marriage and his domestic affairs to himself. So why had he been shot through the head? Murder didn't normally happen without cause.

Cleo had decided, after all, that there wasn't much point in rushing down to see her father, now that she knew why he'd wanted to speak to her. It would only upset Val's arrangements for MO and interrupt the unexpected run of work at her father's office: if Daphne had gone in to work, it was unlikely that the discovery of her boss's body had upset her too much. She rang George instead at ten, when Muriel had said he would be in, and he told her with a resigned sigh that going in to work was probably the best thing for Daphne . . . she'd no doubt taken charge and was organising everybody there, it would be good therapy as far as she was concerned.

'Come round and have some supper tonight,' Cleo suggested, 'It'll have to be a takeaway but I can't wait for Mum to see what the front room looks like now.'

George said they'd be delighted. He'd cause for a celebration of his own, he said. He'd landed an assignment to act on behalf of a leading insurance company to investigate some dodgy car accident claims, work enough to keep him busy for months – and what was more, he'd found Sara Ruby.

'You have? Great!'

'It was pretty much as I thought.' Predictably, there'd been a quarrel that Mrs Ruby had omitted to mention to him, over Sara's choice of boyfriend, and Sara had flounced off to live with the said young man. George hadn't been able to persuade her to return home, but at least she'd promised to ring her parents and reassure them she was all right.

After Kelsey Road, Cleo and Sue were expected at a house where the mother of four children under five had recently given birth to another. Cleo had been sent there with Sue the day before, to make a start, and wasn't looking forward to a repeat performance, but it wasn't a task she could opt out of: she was, she'd gathered, the last desperate end of Val's resources as far as Mrs Bristow was concerned, the only one of the MO personnel apart from Sue who hadn't refused to enter the house again after their first time. Cleo couldn't blame them. The house was a tip, the children – twin boys, a girl of three and a toddler who wasn't potty-trained – were like wild animals, while the mother remained serene and calm in the middle of it all, feeding her new baby while reading or marking student sociology papers for the Open University, sublimely unaware or uncaring of the mayhem going on around her. Mucking out the monkey house at the zoo, with the monkeys in it, would've been preferable.

It had to be around here, it was somewhere on the rough end of Victoria Road, Abigail had been told. She had parked her car in a side street and was now searching for George Atkins's office, which, knowing George, she half expected to be some sort of dump above a launderette or a betting shop. She was pleasantly surprised to see the freshness of the newly painted exterior standing out amid the dismal surrounding shops. The interior decor continued the welcoming theme, gave promise of careful attention to detail, though all this was somewhat marred by the familiar sight of a cluttered desk and a battered typewriter glimpsed through an open door which, however, told her she'd found the right place. George couldn't be far away.

'May I help you?' A small, elderly woman with iron-grey hair had pushed her knitting quickly, though not quite quickly enough, into an open drawer and picked up a Bic, looking attentive. A dachshund, curled in a basket under the knee-hole of her desk, sniffed around Abigail's shoes with interest and growled softly when she moved them away. 'Quiet, Hermione!'

'I've really come to see George – Mr Atkins. I'm one of his old colleagues, Abigail Moon.'

'Oh, I've heard him speak of you – but I'm sorry, he's out. He should be back any minute, though,' she added, looking at her watch. 'I'm Muriel Seton. Do have a seat. Tea or coffee?'

'Well, thanks, tea please, if he's really not going to be long . . .' Abigail was spitting feathers, but adding to her guilt-load by drinking yet another of the coffees she ought to cut down on was something she didn't need.

'Earl Grey, Lapsang, peppermint, or rosehip and straw-berry?'

'Oh – er – just ordinary tea will do, I'm not fussy,' Abigail said, bemused by the choice. 'No milk or sugar.'

'I see you know how tea should be drunk. Ordinary tea? It had better be George's Indian, then.'

Muriel Seton disappeared through a door into a back room and Abigail bent to stroke Hermione, changing her mind when she saw the little dog's lip curling alarmingly. What was the point of pets when they were so disagreeable? She didn't object to dogs but she'd never been inclined to get one herself, notwith-standing her lifestyle, which didn't adapt itself to the idea. If ever she'd been tempted, the monster black dog that lived at the end of her lane and terrorised everyone who approached her home, including herself, would have stopped her.

'Well,' said Hermione's owner, coming back with a tray laid with Royal Albert china and apostle spoons in the saucers. A *traycloth*, for goodness' sake! She put it down on her desk with an expression that said, We May Be Small, But We Don't Let Our Standards Slip. 'I see they've had a murder up at the school, then?' she commented as she poured.

Abigail sighed. She was expected to pay for her tea, after all. She nodded and avoided further comment by saying, 'Actually, it's not George I want to see, not specially, I just thought he could tell me where I might find his daughter.'

'Oh, I can give you her home address, but better still, if you want to speak to her quickly, you can get in touch with those contract cleaners she's working for. Val Storey will tell you where you can get hold of her.' Her mouth turned down at the corners in disapproval, whether of the cleaners or the job itself wasn't clear.

Just as Sue was about to start up the van after she and Cleo had finished at Kelsey Road, a car drew up behind them and a woman with red hair jumped out of the passenger seat and ran towards the van.

'Hold on a minute, I'd like a word, please. Are you Cleo Atkins?' she asked, peering around Sue's rotund form to where Cleo sat. 'Oh, good, I'm Abigail Moon, Lavenstock CID.'

'Well, we're just on our way somewhere else, and we're on a tight schedule,' Sue replied sharply, putting the van into gear, immediately jumping to the conclusion that Cleo would want to avoid having that word.

'Wait! Cleo, I used to work with your dad and Muriel Seton put me on to Mrs Storey, who told us you'd be here. I only want a quick few minutes. How about you getting in the car with us and we'll follow your friend to wherever you're going next? You can talk to me on the way.'

'We-ell . . . OK. It's all right, Sue, I haven't done anything wrong,' Cleo told Sue, hoping she hadn't, but not having a clue what this was all about. 'I'll see you when we get to Mrs Bristow's.'

'Sure?'

Cleo nodded and climbed into the back seat of the car, as instructed by Inspector Moon, who introduced her to the other woman detective, Jenny Platt, the one doing the driving. 'Nice to meet you, Cleo,' said Jenny. 'Where to?'

'It's Corby Avenue. Number 5, the one with the clapped-out Mini and all the kidditoys in the front garden.' And, she thought but didn't add, the smeary windows, which she'd tried without much success to clean yesterday of all the muck left by sticky fingers and snotty noses pressed against them. 'What do you want?'

'George has told us you saw a gun at Wych Cottage, Cleo,' said Abigail Moon. 'Can you describe it to me?'

'Well, it was just a gun.' Cleo was taken aback, wondering why her seeing it should suddenly have assumed such importance as to warrant her being questioned by CID officers. 'I only mentioned it to Dad because it was such a funny place to see it and an odd thing for someone like Mrs Osborne to have.'

'Just a gun. The sort with a long barrel?'

Cleo gave her a steady look. 'It wasn't a shotgun. I don't know much about guns, but I can recognise the difference between a shotgun and – and the other kind.'

'A handgun,' Moon supplied. 'A revolver or a pistol.'

'I suppose that's what they are, but I wouldn't be able to recognise either.'

'Could it have been a replica?'

'If I can't tell one from the other, I wouldn't know that, would I? Anyway, I thought that was the whole point of a replica? That it looks exactly like the real thing.' Realising she was beginning to sound belligerent, she added, 'I only got a glimpse, but anyway, I don't know how you'd tell.'

'With difficulty,' Abigail said. 'Only on close inspection. Even professionals can be fooled otherwise.'

'Then that's maybe just what it was, just something to scare away intruders. I'd be inclined to have one myself if I lived out there.'

Abigail nodded. 'Especially as she's a dealer.'

'*What*?'

'Antique furniture, porcelain and so on. We've done our homework on Mrs Osborne.'

'Oh.' So that's what Mrs Osborne had meant when she said she'd occupied her life with other things than being a farmer's wife. 'For a moment there, I thought –' She laughed. 'I'm not sure I'd be all that surprised, even so.'

'What makes you say that?' Abigail asked sharply.

'It was a *joke*. She might look like the Queen Mum, but she isn't your typical sweet old lady.'

'That was your impression?' Abigail asked, looking thoughtfully at Cleo. 'Was that why you mentioned seeing the gun to your father?'

Cleo thought about it. 'Not really. I just meant that she's *shrewd*. She's still got all her marbles – and her reaction surprised me, as much as anything, otherwise I'd probably just have forgotten it.' She added worriedly, 'She's not going to get into trouble, is she? She was very nice to us.'

'Oh, there'll be some satisfactory explanation, I'm sure.'

'So you're going to ask her about it?'

'Probably.'

Cleo said suddenly, 'It's to do with that woman they found in the river, isn't it? You *can't* think Mrs Osborne did that!'

Abigail smiled. 'There's nothing to say she did. But little old ladies don't usually have dangerous things like handguns lying around. She should be warned about that, even if it's only for her own protection.'

'Maybe so. But I'm beginning to wish I'd never said anything!'

'Don't worry, we won't mention your name – we won't let her know we even know she has a gun, unless it's necessary. But thanks for your time, Cleo.'

'Oh, don't mention it,' Cleo said. 'Any time you want me to snoop on my friends . . . Is that all?'

'Yes, you've been very helpful – but look, don't get the wrong idea –'

'All right, I'm sorry, I know. You're only doing your job.'

'This the house?' enquired Jenny from the front seat, as they turned into Corby Avenue, a neat street of semis with shining paintwork and spring gardens being coaxed into bloom. Clusters of nursery-reared polyanthus in day-glo colours were helping on the crocuses. Universal pansies abounded. A forsythia or two was already flowering. Number 5 was conspicuous for having none of these. Jenny looked at the Mini that had been rubbed down and prepared for a long-forgotten respray, and now sat abandoned on a weed-sown drive, at the overgrown grass plot, strewn with primary-coloured plastic toys. The windows were smeary again and the grey net curtains sagged on their wires. 'What *can* it be like inside?'

'Don't ask,' said Cleo. 'The mother's a PhD and the life of ordinary mortals passes her by.'

John Riach cast his eyes around the office he'd set his sights on seven years ago, knowing it should rightfully have been his then, and now, at last, was. Only temporarily, he reminded himself with his usual caution, but permanent tenure of the school bursarship was now in the palm of his hand, and if he couldn't grasp it this time, he wasn't the man he believed himself to be. The last obstacle had been removed. Charles Wetherby had been eliminated from the scene. And John Riach was here, every detail of the job at his efficient fingertips, the right man in the right place. He wouldn't be passed over this time, as he had been before. They wouldn't be able to look on him as ineffectual any longer, someone who faded into the background.

He'd always been too easily overlooked, despite his undoubted abilities, something which he blamed on his small stature. He was slight, under middle height, always conscious of this when he was in the presence of taller men, especially men like Wetherby. Lack of height was in his genes, an inheritance from his father who, like many other short men, offset this by aggression, a well-known compensating factor. Aggression all too often vented on his son. Riach had taught himself not to give his enemies this sort of handle to use against him, not even to think it. His resentment stayed curled up inside him like a sleeping snake, while outwardly he appeared pleasant, self-effacing, reliable, all the qualities needed for a second fiddle.

He pulled the chair closer to the desk. A new chair was first thing on the agenda. This one had suited Wetherby's long frame but its high back dwarfed its present occupant, giving out quite the wrong signals. The rest of the room wasn't to his liking, either, but its life-expectancy was doomed anyway: it was only a matter of time before the new offices would be built.

Taking off his rimless glasses, he polished them on the maroon silk handkerchief in his breast pocket, refolded the handkerchief and placed it with the points just showing, adjusted his cuffs and the discreet gold and enamelled cuff-links and placed his well-kept hands in front of him on the blotter.

Everything that had once been Charles Wetherby's would now be his. The increased salary which would be useful but wasn't paramount, the increase in power which was. The house that went with the job . . . the wife?

A surge of adrenalin hit him.

Riach had schooled himself not to give an inkling of how much he wanted to step into Wetherby's shoes, and believed his colleagues were still unaware of the burning desire he kept so well hidden. Just as he'd disguised the extent of his feelings for Hannah. He'd known they were dangerous and he'd taught himself to keep them well under control, at least in public.

But now, with an unaccustomed stab of excitement, he allowed his thoughts to dwell lingeringly on her, something he could at last legitimately do. A small smile touched the corners of his mouth. Yes, Hannah. She wouldn't, he thought, be – ungrateful. After all, he had, if nothing else, smoothed her path . . .

He closed his eyes and imagined her as he'd first seen her, when she came with Wetherby to the school on his appointment as Bursar. Dark, slim, and with those lovely eyes, a mirror to her grave and gentle manner, so much in contrast with Wetherby's arrogant self-importance. It was the thought of her, the daily chance that he might see her and talk to her, that had stopped him from seeking another job when Wetherby had been given the position that he, John Riach, as Assistant Bursar, had pinned his hopes on when the former Bursar had retired. Despite his furious disappointment, he had stayed on in a subservient posi-tion, hoping – though for what, he hadn't rightly known.

Hannah had always felt warmly towards him, he was sure of that. Outwardly, she'd never shown him any more than friend-ship, but then she wouldn't, would she? Women like Hannah kept to their marriage vows, no matter what, and he respected her for that. Her life with Wetherby had been miserable. Not that she'd ever said anything – though she'd been on the point of doing so the other day, he was sure – but Riach had quick intuitions, especially where she was concerned, and what he

126

didn't actually observe for himself, he sensed from the atmosphere that surrounded the couple. And from the unemotional way she'd received the news that Wetherby was dead.

He had volunteered to accompany the young policewoman, Tracey Matthews, who'd been detailed to do the job, and they'd been only too glad to accept his offer. It always helped, they said, when friends or relatives were there to play a supportive role, for the bereaved to have a shoulder to cry on. Except that Hannah hadn't cried, had she? Not a tear. He was exultant. Everything pointed to the fact that the wheel was, at last, spinning his way.

He glanced at his watch. There was much to do. Amongst all the other duties and administrative details that had been piled on his shoulders since Wetherby had died, he had to make sure that the police investigation wasn't getting in the way of the smooth running of the school. There were tasks concerning that which were likely to take him all afternoon. After that, at six, he had an appointment with the Head in his study, where he'd receive confirmation of the decision of the board of governors, and no doubt a congratulatory glass of sherry on becoming Bursar of Lavenstock College.

13

The wind was in the right direction, blowing away from the pig farm, which was perhaps as well, given the strength of the aroma without benefit of a breeze.

'Whew!' Jenny wrinkled her short nose. 'And they try to tell us pigs are really clean animals!'

Where were the sties? There wasn't a sign of anything that Abigail would have called a sty, nor were there any pigs or piglets, for that matter. Instead, there was a series of low, domed sheds set in acres of oozy mud, which ran right up to the farmhouse. Was this what organic pig-rearing meant? If each hut represented even one pig – and she'd no idea whether this was so or not – she reckoned there was quite an investment there. Had the floods reached this far? Hard even to begin to envisage what a disaster that would have been. Though it looked as though the farm might have escaped the worst: from the dip in the lane where Wych Cottage stood, the land rose towards the farmhouse in what might almost stand for a slope in these parts. The water level had by now gone down dramatically, but a keen wind still rippled the standing water in the lower fields.

They stood outside the car, which Jenny had drawn into a convenient widening of the narrow lane, half-way between Wych Cottage and the farmhouse. 'Let's try the cottage first, while our feet are still clean,' Abigail suggested. 'We don't want Mrs Osborne coming down on us like a ton of bricks before we start, accusing us of dirtying her clean floors. She might be hiding behind the door with that gun.'

Ten minutes later, sitting in front of the blazing fire in the cosy sitting-room, supplied with cups of fragrant Earl Grey and thin, crisp lemon biscuits, it was hard to see Iris Osborne, with her fluffy white hair and twin-set, as a gun-toting old harridan. 'I told the other policemen I hadn't seen anything of that poor woman,' she'd greeted them when they'd introduced themselves as police officers.

'That's not principally why we're here,' Jenny said mendaciously, explaining that in view of a recent tragic case where a farmer had shot dead an intruder, they were making a check on all firearms, something routinely done in outlying districts where people might be expected to have them. Checking whether they were safely locked up, how many they had, whether they were licensed. Dangerous things, guns, if they fell into the wrong hands.

Oh, she had no need of a licence, Mrs Osborne assured them, since she didn't own a gun of any kind – well, only an airgun that had belonged to her husband, for scaring pigeons, and you didn't need a licence for that, did you? In any event, she didn't even know how to load it, or where the pellets were, still less use it. If she wondered why a detective inspector and a constable were occupied with such a mundane task in the middle of a well-publicised murder investigation, she didn't ask.

'Only an airgun? That's all right then. As long as you don't have any other sort,' Abigail smiled. 'You don't? No, of course, I can see you wouldn't have! Not even one of those toys people buy to frighten intruders? Well, you're quite right not to. If the intruder was armed, it might spark him off to use his first.'

Mrs Osborne gave a gasp of horror, a hand to her pearl-adorned bosom. 'What a terrible thought! But do come in and have a cup of tea, while you're here. It's a lovely day but there's a really cold wind out there and you look frozen. Come in, I'm sure you're allowed five minutes for a tea break!'

So here they were, in front of a roaring fire, being regaled with stories of how the cottage had suffered in the floods, with Iris Osborne really savouring the drama of the situation, now that it was all over. There'd been nothing like it in living memory, she informed them dramatically, water rushing down the lane like a mad thing, swirling around the house, the lane outside impass-able on foot.

'I can still hear it sucking and slopping away!' She blanched at that, her distress very real even under the drama. The flood had *poured* in, she went on, it was unbelievable, the main rooms had been under eighteen inches of water, and the cold-store along-side the house, dug at a lower level, still wasn't back to normal. 'And oh, the smell! You wouldn't believe it – nor the amount of mud it left behind. I had to get a cleaning firm in to help, even after the boys from the farm had got rid of the worst. And then

Reuben sent Vera down to give it a final polish – so now, we're almost as good as new – or will be when I get my chairs back. I'm afraid the covers on three of them were ruined! Nothing for it but to have them re-upholstered. That's why it looks a little bare in here at present.'

'The boys?' Abigail asked, when she could get a word in. The poor soul couldn't see many people to talk to, she was thinking. Thinking also that three more chairs in here would be three too many. The room was tiny – charmingly furnished with antiques and a great deal of pretty china, but the ceiling was too low, the windows too small, the panelling too dark to allow for the amount of furniture already there.

'The boys?' Mrs Osborne repeated, and laughed. 'Well, that's what they seem like to me, though they're in their forties, both of them. Jared Bysouth bought the farm from me after my husband died, and though I've never been very happy about the *pigs*, I've learnt to ignore farmyard smells over the years, and I must say he and his brother, Reuben, are always willing to help me out when I need a strong arm – or a Land Rover to get me out, as happened in the floods.'

'Don't you find it lonely out here?' Abigail asked.

'I haven't time for that, dear! I keep myself busy. All this –' she gestured to the old furniture with its patina of age and the deep shine that came from years of polish and elbow-grease, at the delicate porcelain – 'it's really my showroom. I buy and sell antiques, you see – in a small way, although, if I *do* say it myself, I've quite a reputation in seventeenth-century porcelain. It brings in a bit of pin-money.'

'Really? How do you get customers?' Jenny asked, tactfully showing the surprise Mrs Osborne evidently expected. No need for her to know they'd already made it in their way to find out about her business.

'Word of mouth, mostly. And I advertise in magazines and trade papers. Quite a lot of my business is done by mail order. Using my home as a showroom cuts down on overheads, and it does mean I never get bored with my decor!'

'Well, I must say that's very enterprising.'

Mrs Osborne laughed. 'Oh, I've never been one to let the grass grow under my feet. You should ask my daughter.'

*   *   *

'And I bet she isn't one to make a penny where she can make a pound, either,' Abigail said as they walked back to the car. 'She's one of a type. All charm and little old lady sweetness, while underneath . . . Did you see the look she gave me when I asked about having a replica? Went through me like a road drill.'

'I know. Reckon she was telling fibs?'

'Maybe not. I'll have another word with Cleo – she seemed certain enough but she admits she only got a very quick glance and it *might* have been an airgun she saw. Which still won't be much use to us when it's a handgun we're looking for. Though whatever she says, I wouldn't put it past Mrs Osborne to keep some sort of weapon handy – and be prepared to use it – to protect her property.'

'You can't say it isn't worth protecting,' Jenny said, looking back at the cottage as they reached the car. 'All that lovely furniture and china.'

'Not to mention the house itself. Charming, isn't it?' Abigail followed Jenny's glance to what was almost a cliché of a country cottage. 'Especially in summer, I suppose. Roses round the door, even. All the same, I'll bet that one's Albertine. The rose with the wickedest thorns I know.'

'Yes, but I wouldn't fancy living out here. And the place still smelt funny and damp, didn't it?' Jenny said with a shudder. 'It's not my idea of the *dolce vita*.'

'Nor is this,' said Abigail as they reached the gate of the grim, flat-faced, three-storey farmhouse that would have made Cold Comfort Farm seem welcoming.

There was no answer to their ring on the front door, which they'd chosen because it was the only entry with any sort of path. But nobody ever used front doors in farmhouses, it was probably hermetically sealed. They picked their way round to the back through the farmyard muck, thankful for the protection of the winter boots they'd both taken the precaution of wearing.

It was a farmhouse of the old-fashioned kind, enclosed by barns and outbuildings, maybe part of the piggeries, and a yard filled with various pieces of unspecified, dangerous-looking machinery. To one side stood a hen pen with several coops and a few chickens pecking desultorily at trodden grass. A neglected kitchen garden flanked it and a huge, mean-looking dog of dubious ancestry flung itself dementedly at the wire netting of a dog run. The back door of the farmhouse opened right into the yard but there was no answer to their knock. Abigail was trying the knob when a man with a black and white border collie at his heels came round the corner. The other dog, behind the wire, immediately sank down, head on its front paws, watching.

'Mr Bysouth?'

'Reuben Bysouth. What do you want?'

He was rough, all right, as they'd been warned. Tight jeans, belted under his belly. Long, unwashed, curly black hair tied back into a high ponytail with what looked like a bootlace. It didn't take a genius, either, to guess that his dark chin wasn't intentional designer stubble but simply the result of not bothering to have shaved for two or three days at least. One of his front teeth was missing and the rest wouldn't bear close inspection. His sweatshirt was greasy with food stains.

You learned not to show either surprise or disgust at anything or anyone when you were in the Force – if you were wise – but Abigail saw the fastidious Jenny gazing at him with the same sort of horrid fascination she herself felt. He reminded her of one of the sluggy things that had laid hundreds of its progeny in the leaf axils of her angelica, before eating it alive.

'DI Moon and DC Platt,' she told him. 'We're here on a firearms check.'

'We've had all you lot round once – haven't you got more to do than waste other folks's time as well as your own?' he asked with a surly look.

She wasn't going to let him rattle her. 'We're not here for the same reason. Will you please show us your guns, and your licences? You or your brother. It won't take more than a few minutes.'

He seemed about to refuse, then changed his mind. 'My brother's out.' He opened the back door, which led into a one-time scullery that now appeared to be used as a farm office as well as a dumping ground for old boots, waterproofs, unspecified machinery parts, some of them rusty. Papers of various kinds were held untidily in bulldog clips and jammed on to spikes. There was an old metal filing cabinet and, sitting incongruously on a formica-topped table with splayed legs, a small PC.

He fished in a drawer for a key, unlocked a cupboard and showed them the three double-barrelled, twelve-bore shotguns inside. 'See, all locked up, just as they should be. Satisfied?'

'And your licences, please.'

He went into an adjoining room, shutting the door behind him, but not before Abigail had a glimpse of a well-tended kitchen, a brightly burning fire in a wide inglenook, surrounded by gleaming horse-brasses, had caught a smell of lavender furniture polish mingling with savoury cooking odours. One of the Bysouths at least was not averse to comfort and cleanliness, it seemed.

Reuben came back within a minute or two with the necessary papers. Two of them were licensed to Jared Bysouth, one to Reuben Bysouth. 'Thank you, sir, everything appears to be in order.'

'What did I tell you? Waste of everybody's bloody time.' He opened the door and they stepped out into the yard. The mongrel behind the chain-link fencing set up a frenzied barking and Bysouth snarled at it to shut up, which it did immediately. The silent collie slunk alongside its master, keeping a shifty, sideways glance on the two women, while Reuben stepped close on their heels, a manœuvre which gave them no alternative but to walk towards the gate. But Abigail had no intention of being hustled. She stopped suddenly and turned, so that she almost collided face to face with Bysouth, not a happy experience.

'Watch what you're doing, can't you?' he growled.

Abigail ignored the gentlemanly manners. 'Before we go, I'd just like to check on one or two other points. You told the officers who asked you previously that you didn't know anything of the woman who was found in the river, just down there –'

'Course I didn't bloody know anything about her, I'd have said if I did, wouldn't I?'

'Memory can be a funny thing, sometimes we remember things afterwards that we've seen or heard, but not registered at the time.'

'Well, I don't.'

Out of the corner of her eye, Abigail caught a glimpse of a woman with pale, gingerish hair and a bulky figure encased in a floral pinny, coming from round the corner of one of the outbuildings. The heavy bucket dragging down her right side, the cautious way she crept along, her feet making hardly a sound, the downbent head, eyes averted, might have made her almost a caricature of a drudge, a cowed and abused woman, had not the picture been so real.

'Then perhaps we can speak to Mrs Bysouth – she might have remembered something you don't.'

'She's not here.'

The lie was patent. 'Who was that woman who just went into the house?'

'I didn't see any woman,' Bysouth returned. 'Probably the cleaner.'

He stared her down. And short of forcing their way into the farmhouse and searching for Vera Bysouth, there was nothing they could do, as well he knew.

On their return, they found the incident room in a state of mild excitement. While they'd been out, at last a break – of sorts – had happened.

A delivery man, just back from holiday, having seen for the first time the appeal in the local paper for information on the dead woman, had come into the station and offered what he thought might be some useful intelligence.

Several times, he said, during the week before his holiday, while he'd been delivering feedstuffs to the farm, he'd noticed a blue Fiat, with a woman in the driving seat, parked in the same spot where Jenny had parked the car. He'd wondered what she was doing. It wasn't the sort of area frequented by picnickers and sightseers.

Nowhere to sit except scrubby, sodden fields full of reeds and nothing to see except more of the same – and anyway, it was hardly picnic weather, was it? Plus, it had been earlyish in the morning each time he'd seen her. He'd thought she might have been some sort of artist, drawing or photographing the flooded landscape.

Unfortunately, that was all he could tell them. He hadn't noticed the number of the car, or even much about the occupant, except that it was a woman, he'd been too concerned with negotiating his truck down the narrow lane.

Caution dictated that no automatic assumption should be made that the car had belonged to the dead woman, but no one seemed to be doubting that it had, that its driver had ended up in the Kyne. And what about the car, had anyone else seen it – where was it now? More door-stepping might provide some of the answers, and the first of those to be questioned were the folks at Kyneford. 'The Bysouths?' asked Jenny.

'And someone else,' said Abigail. 'Mrs Osborne.'

'I'm going to find a few minutes to visit Ted during my lunchtime,' she told Jenny. 'I need to stock my fridge up as well, so I'll kill two birds with one stone and get him something nice to eat while I'm at it.'

'He'll appreciate that after two weeks of hospital food. Give him my love and tell him to watch it, with those nurses,' Jenny said. 'I'll pop in when I can.'

'I will.' Abigail laughed. She and the middle-aged, laconic sergeant had been partners for a very long time, and she found the picture of Carmody chasing the nurses, even had he been in the best of health, entertaining. Possible, of course, anything was possible, but she thought he'd be too afraid of what his Maureen would do if she caught him, for one thing.

She wandered around the shelves at Tesco's, shopping for one, since Ben – don't think about it! – was unlikely to be there to share her meals for a while. What she did buy still looked depressingly meagre and spinsterish at the bottom of the trolley, especially following the woman in front of her, who seemed to have been shopping for England. How many cats did she have, for goodness' sake, twenty-five tins of Kit-e-Kat, and three bags of kibble? Not to mention how many children. Dozens of packets of crisps, cornflake boxes the size of suitcases and enough sliced white bread to feed starving Africa. Abigail's own supplies for a week barely filled one plastic bag when she'd emptied her trolley, even with the huge box of chocolate gingers she knew Carmody doted on and a bunch of grapes. She hadn't been able to find anything else she thought he might fancy that didn't need cooking, except fruit and chocolates.

On the way out, pausing to adjust her slipping shoulder bag, she caught a glimpse, through the potted plants that screened off the coffee shop, of a woman with pale auburn hair. She paused and looked again. Yes, it was!

She was sitting alone, in front of a cup of coffee and the largest cream pastry Abigail had ever seen, an expression of absolute bliss on her face as she dug in her fork and transferred the load to her mouth.

Reluctant to interrupt such communion between a woman and her comfort, Abigail knew she might never get another chance to speak to her. She slipped into the coffee area through the space between a huge indoor tree and a *Fatsia japonica*. Plonking her plastic bag on the floor, she slid into the free chair opposite the woman, who looked up with a guilty start, at the same time trying with a futile, involuntary gesture to shield the plate containing the cream cake. And then her face became suffused, a burning ugly red sweeping in a tide from her neck to her hairline.

'Mrs Bysouth? Mrs Vera Bysouth?' Abigail pushed her warrant card across. 'I'm Abigail Moon, Lavenstock CID.'

'I know who you are,' the woman whispered, as if afraid of even raising her voice. 'I saw you earlier on at the farm.'

'I'd like to talk to you for a minute or two. Let me get you another coffee, you've almost finished that.'

'No – I really must be going.' She began to gather her bags together.

'You can't leave that delicious cake.'

Vera Bysouth looked at the pastry, wavered, and was lost. 'Well . . .'

'Won't be a sec,' Abigail said, hoping the service would be quick, so that Mrs Bysouth wouldn't have time to change her mind and disappear. She was lucky, and in a few minutes was back with two coffees and a wrapped sandwich for her own lunch. She was famished, but not even in the interest of solidarity and gaining evidence could she have faced one of those sickly confections sitting on the plate opposite, which Vera Bysouth shouldn't have been eating either, in view of her pasty complexion, and a figure that was flabby, if not fat. Along with the auburn hair, she possessed such pale lashes and brows, such light eyes that she might almost have been an albino. Even her lips were colourless.

'Thank you – Inspector, isn't it?' she breathed, accepting the coffee.

'Abigail.'

The woman opposite her opened two packets of sugar and stirred them into her coffee. Her voice was very nearly inaudible, and her frightened glance slid from side to side as she whispered, 'I can't tell you anything.'

I haven't asked, yet, thought Abigail. Vera picked up her fork again. 'My one treat,' she explained, softly apologetic, though she didn't look as though she was enjoying it now. Shame to have spoiled the moment for her, but you couldn't pass up an opportunity like this. 'I know I shouldn't,' she went on, jabbing with the fork, 'but it's the only time I get to myself, once a week.' She ate the last morsel of the pastry and pushed away the half-finished coffee. 'Look, I have to go now, get the shopping done, he expects me back by half-past two.' He. Not Reuben, not my husband. He.

'Please don't go just yet. Give me a minute or two of your time. It's about that poor woman who was drowned. Somebody, somewhere, must be wondering what's happened to her, and we have to find out who she was and let them know. We've very recently learnt that what was probably her car was parked several times in the passing space in the lane below your farm –'

'No! You're wrong!'

Abigail gave her a steady look. 'I don't think so. Your husband may have been busy about the farm, and not noticed it –' and she could believe that if she wished! – 'but I think the spot is probably quite visible from the farm windows, and you may have seen it there.'

'No,' Vera insisted, but didn't raise her voice at all. As if keeping her voice down was another way of obliterating her personality, making herself even more invisible. The hushed whispering was irritating, Abigail had to strain to hear her. But perhaps the poor woman had come to be afraid even of the sound of her own voice.

A waitress, clearing the next table, smiled in a friendly manner, unaware of their tension. Automatically, Vera smiled back. A weary, defeated smile, but a smile, all the same. She'd once been pretty, perhaps very pretty. Why didn't she make more of herself, darken her eyebrows and lashes, put a bit of colour on her face? Stupid question. If she had the ability to think that way, she'd be able to break through the inertia and resolve her hopeless situation.

'If you know anything, you really should tell me.'

'No, I don't,' Vera insisted wanly. For don't, read can't. If what Abigail had been told of Bysouth's previous history was true, his wife was obviously still terrified of him, of being hit if she spoke out of turn, but she was probably even more terrified of losing him. It was something Abigail had seen, time and time again, during her stint with Domestic Violence, an attitude against which you battled, but could do little. But she had to try.

'Mrs Bysouth, Vera, I know this is a painful subject for you, but you have in the past come to us when you've been in trouble –'

'It's not like that now! You don't realise! He's different.'

That, too, Abigail had heard. Ad nauseam. And knew how little it meant. 'We can help. You don't *have* to stay with him, you know.'

'You don't understand, do you? He – all right, yes, he's inclined to lose his temper a bit, especially when he's had a drink or two, but he's not always like that . . . he can be a real charmer, you know.'

Abigail nearly choked on a mouthful of coffee. Reuben. Well, you had to believe her. If she said so.

Vera stood up, gathered her things together. 'I have to go. And you mustn't tell him I've spoken to you – you must promise!' Her voice was still barely above a whisper, even in her extreme distress.

'Not a thing you should say to a lady, but you look tired,' Ted announced bluntly. He wasn't looking good himself yet, or anything like it, but a whole lot better than he had, considering he'd been pushed three storeys down a fire escape when struggling with the toerag he was apprehending. His leg was still in traction, but some of the bruises on his face were healing.

'Well, I'm no lady, so I don't mind. But tired isn't in it. Knackered, more like it.'

'Case going badly?'

It wasn't that. For the first time in her life, she was sleeping badly, worried about Ben. Worried about the promotion board, too, though she wasn't going public on that. She was beginning to feel superstitious, talking about it, even to Ted Carmody, whom she'd trust with her life. Especially Ted. The big Liverpudlian, a stolid, salt of the earth detective sergeant, had been her mentor when she'd first come here to Lavenstock and could read her like a book.

She smiled. 'Cases, Ted, cases, in the plural. You've heard there's been another one? And neither of them exactly spinning along . . . But never mind that, you know what they've said: no shop talk or they'll ban all police personnel from the ward.'

'Bollocks.'

'Don't be difficult. Here you are. Only grapes and chocs, but they might take your mind off the hospital food. Oh, and Deeley's sent you a couple of westerns.'

'The food's not all that bad. Bloody marvellous after Maureen's – but don't tell her that.' He'd asked his wife for a photo of her to keep on his locker, and Maureen had been so surprised by this evidence of tenderness in her laconic spouse she'd brought three. One childood one of their two daughters and their son, another a holiday snap, Carmody towering above his chirpy little wife, and one of herself when she was seventeen. Not much resemblance to her now, but it showed why Carmody had fallen in love with her. 'Anyway,' he said, 'my stitches.'

'Do they hurt?'

'Only when I eat.'

Along with his fractured femur, he'd suffered a broken collarbone and several cuts to his face, which hadn't improved his long, doleful countenance, but he'd been assured the scars were only temporary. 'Come on, blossom,' he pleaded, 'bring me up to speed on this latest, that'll make me feel better than chocolate gingers. Bored bloody rigid in here, I am. Homicide at Lavenstock College, and I have to miss it – I don't believe it!'

'You'd better.' Seeing he wasn't going to be deflected, she put it briefly together for him, and then told him of the latest developments, the possibility of the same gun having been used in the two cases, and Cleo Atkins's sighting of a gun in Mrs Osborne's house. 'She only caught a glimpse – she may well have been mistaken, but the whole set-up around there's a bit peculiar: that woman was found in the river just below Kyneford, and a woman who might fit her description was seen parked in the lane between the farm and the cottage several times the same week.' She stopped, seeing the odd expression on his face. 'What have I said?'

'There's no such thing as coincidence, right? Bloody wrong, and this proves it!' He achieved a smug expression, despite his stitches, boredom forgotten.

'What coincidence? What proves it?'

'Well, there's this lovely old girl in here, name of Eileen Totterbridge, works for Dorrie Lockett. Seventy-odd and spry as a cricket –'

'Dorrie Lockett? You mean Sam Leadbetter's aunt? Sorry, go on.'

'She had a hip replacement only two days ago, and she's taking 'em at their word when they say she has to exercise it.'

'I know,' Abigail said. 'My aunt's just had one. They get them to walk around in a few days. She won't be in long.'

'That's just the point. This one's already on her feet. Any road, they wheeled my bed down to X-ray this morning and while she was waiting for her turn in the unit, she came up and started chatting. A right old rattle-can she is, jaws never stop, but she's OK. I've been down to X-ray before and I know how long it can take, so I'd taken the *Advertiser* with me. She sees Wetherby's photo on the front page and we get talking about the murder – and it turns out she works for Mrs Wetherby as well as Dorrie Lockett. But soon as she knew I was a policeman she shut up like a clam. As they do,' he added with resignation. 'But you get her talking and you might learn a lot. Worth a try, any rate.'

'Thanks, Ted. I'll pop along and see her now,' Abigail said, looking at her watch, standing up as the sound of a trolley was heard in the corridor. 'Mustn't get told off for tiring you out. Look after yourself. Don't do anything I wouldn't do.'

'Fat chance of that in here. More to the point, you look after yourself, love. And remember, if you can't be good, at least enjoy it.'

When Abigail called to see Eileen Totterbridge on her way out, she found her bed empty, and when she asked to see her, the ward sister informed her that she had just been taken home.

After leaving Abigail, Vera Bysouth had pushed the heavily laden shopping trolley over to the van which she'd parked, as she always did, right over at the far side of the car-park. It was so far away from the entrance there were nearly always plenty of empty spaces, so the van was less likely to get damaged: if she went home with so much as another scratch on the already battered paintwork, he'd know, and he'd kill her.

She faced with dull acceptance that one day it might come to that. She'd been used as a punchbag so often, she took it as a matter of course now: she'd had more black eyes than she could count, she'd been hit and kicked in the stomach when she was pregnant, lost the child and could never have any more . . . once, he'd hit her on the side of the head with such force that she'd staggered right across the kitchen and fallen unconscious. The fact that he'd happened to have a heavy iron frying pan in his hand at the time had made it worse; she had terrible headaches now, and she'd been deaf in that ear ever since.

But all that was nothing to what he'd do if she talked. Somehow, she hadn't been able to make that woman detective understand. She'd spoken as if it was simple, just to leave him. Given her a number to ring if she decided the time had come when she'd had enough. A safe house where she could stay. Vera smiled bitterly. She knew all about safe houses. She'd tried that several times, but he always found her.

But things *were* a bit better now, since they'd gone to live at the farm. Jared was roughly kind to her, and Reuben never hit her when he was around. And there were times, in between . . . also, the farm was a nicer home than any they'd had before in their married lives. Jared's wife had always kept it beautiful before she died, and Vera took great pride in maintaining the tradition.

Yet she knew she had a duty to tell what she'd seen. She crossed her arms over the steering wheel and for a moment laid her head down on them. How wonderful it would be just to let go – for an hour or two. For ever.

Then she heard the parish church clock chime. Its lovely

141

musical cadences sounded right across the town, and she realised with horror that it was two o'clock. Switching on the ignition, she prayed there would be no traffic snarl-up on the bypass.

It was felt by the board of governors, said the Headmaster, carefully using the passive voice to distance himself from personal responsibility for the decision, that the position of Bursar of Lavenstock College should be nationally advertised, in the spirit of fair and open competition, you understand. Mustn't be accused of nepotism. Of course, your application, after all your years of experience here, will be extremely favourably considered, there is every prospect you will be successful. But have you never thought of moving on to a higher post in university administration? No? Well, one mustn't stagnate, however happy one is . . . A sherry, my dear Riach, before you go?

John Riach walked back to his office, concentrating on keeping his shoulders back, a swing in his stride, just in case he should meet anyone. He prayed that he wouldn't encounter even one of the boys before reaching the safety of his own set of rooms, a small, private dominion, high above the quadrangle, to which he invited no one. Small, but quite adequate for one. Furnished with taste, even a little restrained luxury, it offered the warm, deep comfort of privacy, soft sofas and cushioned chairs, glowing lamps, music, and thick carpets. He thought he might need to throw himself down on the Indian rug and howl like a dog.

His mood was not improved when he saw Hannah in the distance, heading towards the house he'd just left, with Sam Leadbetter beside her, his hand proprietorially under her elbow. For a moment, he almost regretted the tentative suggestion he had put forward to the Head in the social skirmishing before they had come down to the nitty-gritty of their meeting. A nice gesture, wouldn't it be, Headmaster? To let Mrs Wetherby, a sitting tenant, have first refusal to buy the house? The school's policy now being not to provide houses for staff?

He didn't think he could bear it if Hannah did buy the house, and Sam Leadbetter, not he, moved in with her.

14

Daphne said nice things about the newly decorated room, though Cleo thought they might have been said more in the spirit of encouragement than actual admiration, given Daphne's own tastes. She'd even kindly refrained from pointing out that the work hadn't really been bottomed, though it was obvious to anybody. The *trompe l'oeil* window, however, received the Atkins seal of approval.

They'd eaten takeaway pizza, and a salad Cleo had successfully made. George had brought along a bottle of red wine, and Daphne one of her famous lemon tarts as dessert, and now they were drinking coffee in the front room.

Daphne said, 'You don't want to sit in here when you're on your own with the curtains not pulled, Cleo. Anybody can see in.'

'But I love to be able to see the lights.' Beyond the darkened window they twinkled and spread like the Milky Way, a band of stars stretching down and across the town, lighting the night sky and fading into the distance.

'Those curtains of Phoebe's have passed their sell-by date,' Daphne announced, ignoring this. 'I'll make you a present of the fabric for some new ones, some new cushion covers, and make them up for you.'

It was no use arguing with her. 'Well, thanks, but haven't you enough to do?'

'Rubbish. I can finish them in a couple of evenings. *Who* did you say did the decorating for you?'

'I didn't, but his name's Tone. Well, Tony, actually. Tony Gilchrist.'

Daphne put her cup down very precisely on the saucer. '*Tony Gilchrist?*'

'Don't say you know him?'

'Not to say know, not someone like that!' Daphne pressed her lips together.

'Oh come on, you can't leave me in suspense! What do you

mean, *someone like that?'* Though of course, Cleo knew very well what Daphne meant.

Her mother peeled the foil very carefully from one of the chocolate mints on the coffee table. She put it into her mouth and ate it slowly. 'I'm surprised he's had anything to do with you, knowing who you are,' she said. 'And if you've any sense, you'll have nothing more to do with *him.'*

'Not until I know a good reason why.'

Cleo looked to George for support, but George was evidently determined to let Daphne get on with it. Daphne smoothed her skirt. She looked as smart this evening as she did when visiting classy friends, as if this venture of Cleo's into normality should be encouraged. Or perhaps she just needed to cheer herself up after the traumas of the last few days. Her outfit was new, consisting of a long, straight black skirt, a cream silk T-shirt and a silk jacket in post office red.

What could she have meant about Tone? A sort of sinking feeling, beginning around Cleo's midriff, warned her that her mother might have a point. She'd always known there was something about Tone that didn't ring true, however much she liked him. And then it came to her, that conversation which she'd buried, consciously or not, until now.

He'd turned up at MO again, and she'd spoken to him about the murder of the Bursar as they'd walked home together. 'Yes, well, it's easy enough to get into his office via that corridor from the porter's lodge,' he'd said absently.

A little, humming silence ensued while Cleo digested this. Eventually, it got through to him. He realised what he'd said, but the silence went on.

'Tone?' she'd said, at last. 'Tone? How do you know about that?'

After a moment, he recovered himself. 'Once did a bit of work there, didn't I?' He grinned. 'When I was going through me window-cleaning period, like. After I left school. We was carrying some ladders and they let us through that way, didn't they?'

It sounded implausible. You could have cut his accent with a knife.

George said suddenly, 'Daph, Cleo should know about this, it's not fair to keep it from her.'

144

'How well *do* you know him, Cleo?' There was more than a hint of apprehension in Daphne's question.

'Oh, it's nothing like *that!*' Cleo said impatiently. 'He's a friend, that's all, just somebody I work with! He's only eighteen!' Then she heard herself say suddenly, quite beyond her own volition, 'What's the school motto, Mum?'

She had no idea why the question had come to her, or from what unsuspected depths. Unless it had arisen from intuitive suspicions she'd had for a while which were now crystallising into certainty. But it encompassed a lot that had puzzled her: Tone's sudden stillness when she'd told him that her mother worked for the Bursar at the school; that curious variation in his accent. She'd known all along he'd either been deliberately putting on the Black Country, or deliberately suppressing the middle-class one. That the standard of his education was much higher than he liked to pretend. As when he'd used that Latin quotation . . .

'The school motto?' Daphne repeated, momentarily diverted.

'Is it *Semper sursum?*'

'Why, yes, it is. Ever upwards. Ever on high. Or something like that.' Daphne stared, then bit her lip. 'You know, don't you?'

'Know what?'

'You know Tony Gilchrist was a pupil at Lavenstock College.'

'It seems I might have guessed.'

'He was a scholarship boy. Very bright, really, until he was sacked – expelled.'

'Oh!' Cleo was stumped, momentarily lost for words.

Daphne rolled the gold foil she was playing with into a tiny, hard pellet, and took another mint. She *never* ate more than one chocolate.

'It's hard for boys like him,' she said, struggling to be fair. 'Coming from that sort of background. I'm not sure it does them any favours in the long run, either, they end up being neither one thing nor another. Their parents haven't got the wherewithal to back them up, not like the other boys' parents have, and the result is they feel different, fishes out of water. Some of them do manage to integrate and lose their rough edges . . . and since most of them are very bright, they go on to university. But some get a chip on their shoulder, and can't rid themselves. Like Tony Gilchrist.'

145

George decided it was time to join in. 'Those Gilchrists are bad news, Glory. Live in the council flats behind here. He has two brothers who've done time – one's still in, if my memory serves me.'

'Yes, well,' Daphne said, 'that didn't help him very much when it all happened.'

Despite the feeling that her insides were being stirred with a stick, Cleo managed to ask, 'What was he supposed to have *done*, then?'

Daphne picked up another mint, but this time put it back.

'Come on, out with it, Daph.'

George sounded impatient, and Daphne looked pleadingly at him. 'You tell her.'

He shook his head. 'It'll come better from you, love.'

'Well, the truth is, Cleo,' she began reluctantly, 'he took the Bursar's car for a joyride and smashed it up. It was a write-off.'

'Is that all?'

'All? Good heavens, don't you think it's enough?'

'Yes, of course, it's awful. But it's not –' She broke off. She didn't really know what it wasn't, only what it was. Youthful high spirits? Done for a dare?

'It wasn't like that,' Daphne said, reading her thoughts. 'He really hated Charles Wetherby. Everybody knew he'd done it on purpose.'

'You are joking, aren't you? Nobody totals a car on *purpose*. He might have written himself off, as well!'

'He very nearly did, Cleo. He was lucky to be alive.'

Yes, he'd been left with physical scars that would be with him for the rest of his life. And an attitude. Which probably included a lifelong hatred of the Bursar, too . . . How deep would such hatred go? 'What are you saying? Your police pals surely aren't suspecting him of shooting that man, Dad? That's *bloody* unfair!'

'Cleo.'

'It is, Mum, it's –'

It was at this point that the telephone rang.

After supper, Mayo sat with his curtains undrawn, too, the

lamps reflected in the darkened windows, the trees in the garden darker shapes against a sky that was never quite black, that always held something of the light from the urban sprawl below. Under Moses's opportunistic gaze, he had eaten the last, thank God, of those solitary, oven-ready meals. Salmon – *en croûte* this time, admittedly very tasty. But the cat was unlucky – Mayo was hungry and besides, he'd forgotten to shut Moses out of the sitting-room that morning and had arrived home to find a sub-dued Bert huddled on the topmost perch in his cage, several feathers on the floor and the cat looking smug. 'Hard luck!' he told him as he rinsed his plate and didn't forget to put it in the dishwasher. 'It's Whiskas tonight, mate, and thank your lucky stars for that.'

Alex was due home the next day and life would return to normal, or what passed for normal during a murder enquiry. But whenever he *was* available, she'd be here, providing, apart from other more obvious home comforts, opportunities for intelligent, objective discussion with someone not directly involved in the case. This talking things over with someone who knew where he was coming from had turned into a habit that Mayo – and perhaps Alex, who missed the police more than she'd ever admit – was finding addictive, too.

Tonight, however, he'd have to do without her. He sipped his Laphroaig in the post-Elgar, melancholic silence the composer invariably induced in him – that majestic music, grandly Edwardian, but triste, which, however, had chimed in with his pensive mood tonight.

The cat settled, heavily forgiving, on his right foot, as he switched to Radio 3 for more music. Schoenberg. Atonal music that well repaid the close attention it needed. But after a while he turned it off. John Riach's face kept coming between him and his concentration. John Riach as he'd talked to him in the Bursar's office that morning: a man permanently on the defensive, Mayo guessed, a buttoned-up individual who rarely gave direct answers to questions but nevertheless had provided more inter-esting information than anyone else who'd been interviewed so far.

Why? Mayo had asked himself, meaning what was he being so uptight about? And then had seen why, as soon as Hannah Wetherby's name was mentioned. He watched Riach even more

147

closely after that. Apart from carrying some sort of torch for Wetherby's wife, it was evident that Riach had also disliked the man himself pretty conclusively, perhaps for the same reason. Every defensive answer he gave provided more proof of this.

He sat stiffly upright on the straight office chair that had replaced Wetherby's large, status-symbol, intended-to-impress one, sticking firmly with Hannah Wetherby's statement that they had been having a sandwich together from twelve fifteen to one. To specific questions regarding Wetherby, he gave scrupulously fair answers, while managing to convey that the deceased Bursar's reputation as an excellent administrator hadn't been entirely unconnected with having Riach as his deputy. And that still rankled, Mayo could see, despite the fact that he was presumably now all set to take Wetherby's place.

Mayo decided to press this advantage. 'Tell me, what sort of man was Wetherby?'

Riach examined his well-kept fingernails. 'He wasn't always popular. He didn't go out of his way to make himself so. He was a stickler for rules and regulations and that doesn't always go down very well with young people, as you can imagine.'

'Did he have much to do with the boys, then?'

'Not really, but there were occasions . . .' He seemed about to expand but what followed sounded unconnected. 'He was also inclined to take too much on himself.'

'In what way?'

After a momentary hesitation, he said, 'There's some controversy about a new entrance to the school.'

Mayo decided that he didn't need to mention he already knew about that, since Riach looked poised to tell him anyway, and he might learn something new. Then he thought of something else. 'He was writing a report on that when he died.'

Riach's face was a mask, his thin nostrils drawn together. He said carefully, not quite able to hide some smouldering resentment, despite his flat, unemotional tone, 'So I understand.'

'You know that the top sheet of this report was stuffed into his mouth?'

'Someone with a macabre sense of humour, obviously.'

Rules you out, then, old chum, Mayo thought, guessing there wasn't much humour there, macabre or otherwise. He studied the other man, and wondered. He saw distaste, dislike, and

148

looked for fear, but didn't find it. He said, 'How exactly did this new entrance concern the Bursar?'

Riach seemed to relax a little. 'We don't have strictly defined limits in so far as duties go. Geoffrey Conyngham is school Secretary and Chief Administrator, and he'd agreed to let Charles deal with the negotiations for buying the property in order to resite the main entrance to the school on Kelsey Road. If you'll bear with me a moment, I'll show you.' He crossed to a cupboard and took out a large, rolled-up plan of the school grounds which he spread out across his desk, weighting it at the top corners with a paperweight and a puncher. He held the third, and Mayo the fourth corner. 'He'd completed the purchase of three of the four houses, there. There was just one more he thought we needed. This is the one, here, number 16, belonging to Miss Dorrie Lockett. And when I say *this* is the proposed entrance, or would be if Miss Lockett would agree to sell, you'll see what I mean.'

'Yes, I do see. Bang in the middle – and she's not inclined to let you buy it?'

'If Charles had handled her better in the first place, yes, perhaps. But she adamantly refuses to – now aided and abetted by her nephew, Sam Leadbetter, I might say.'

'I've already made his acquaintance.'

'No doubt. He's doing a good job at providing a consoling shoulder for Mrs Wetherby to cry on.' The acid comment escaped him without him seeming aware of it. His lips thinned. The rider that his should have been the shoulder was left unsaid. But it was there, hanging almost visibly in the air. Riach might, Mayo thought, be a very good hater.

He watched him carefully begin to roll up the plan, then change his mind, hesitating for a moment before speaking. 'Miss Lockett's refusal might not be so important, not now. Originally, some time ago, the idea was that the new entrance to the school, albeit a less pretentious one, should be sited here, below the hospital,' he said, pointing to the school boundary along Vanson Hill, 'rather than demolish the Kelsey Road houses which could well be used as dormitory overspill. Wetherby was adamantly against the idea, he was wedded to the notion of a grand entrance. I'm afraid he could never brook the slightest opposi-tion, and it was his baby, as they say. He managed to sway the

149

vote – just – in his favour. But now . . . well, it's not too late to go back to the original plan.'

'Which one were you in favour of?'

'Oh, it's no secret that I voted for Vanson Hill, and that I think it's vandalism to pull this side of the quad down rather than spruce up the interiors, which it shouldn't be beyond the wit of man to do.' He waved his hand at the dingy walls and outdated furniture. Mayo, reminded of his own outrage at the idea of the old buildings being pulled down, had some sympathy with Riach's feelings, though he couldn't feel any warmer towards him. 'The science blocks could always go up on the Kelsey Road side,' he was saying. 'But my opinion isn't likely to count one way or the other. Charles was very . . . persuasive.'

Mayo had met 'persuasive' people like that. Not a few of them in his own organisation. And also people like Riach himself, who beavered away secretly behind the scenes. He thought Riach was now deliberately playing himself down, and made a mental note not to overlook the fact that the disagreement over the entrance might conceivably have blown up into a major row.

He steered Riach back towards Wetherby's personal life, and it gradually emerged (though not by accident – Mayo was already aware that Riach was not a man to let anything slip) that Wetherby had been a womaniser. Well, three women, when it came down to it, but that had evidently been three too many for Riach to stomach. And quite enough for Mayo, to be going on with.

'We'll need to talk to them,' Mayo said. 'Can you give me details?'

'I can't tell you anything about Marie Holden, except that she was a peripatetic music teacher who worked here for a while, but no doubt the Secretary's office will know how to get in touch. Angela Hunnicliffe's an American whose husband has been working here at the school for about twelve months, but he left and they both returned to the States a week or two back. Beverley Harriman actually works here in the office – that's her with the long black hair all over the place and the long skirt.'

She seemed an odd type for Wetherby to have taken up, but when he suggested this to Riach, he was met with a shrug. 'He liked adoration.'

'And she was working here on the day Mr Wetherby was killed.'

150

'Yes, but I wouldn't lay too much store by that. She's not the violent type. Unless she accidentally killed him with a cup of her herbal tea.'

It took Mayo a moment to realise Riach was making a joke. Riach himself looked surprised, and rather embarrassed. His narrow, high-cheekboned face flushed slightly. He took off his rimless specs and polished them with a silk handkerchief he took from his top pocket.

'And that's about it,' he said, refolding and replacing the handkerchief with the deft precision that characterised all his movements.

'Yes, that'll do for now,' Mayo said, standing up and looking out over the quadrangle where several boys were passing through, dressed for rugby. 'Sports feature largely in the curriculum, I gather,' he remarked. 'What about after-school activities – music, chess . . . boxing, army cadet corps?'

'Music and chess, yes,' Riach answered, knowing exactly what Mayo was getting at. 'Practising for blood sports is not encouraged.'

'And you don't possess any firearms yourself?'

He smiled faintly. 'Guns are objects of violence, and I'm not a violent man.'

It wasn't an answer, but Mayo had decided to let it ride for the moment.

The interview with Marie Holden had revealed nothing that might throw light on Wetherby's murder. She knew very little of his personal circumstances, she told Jenny Platt, her affair with him had been brief, and she was terrified it might come to her husband's ears. The day Wetherby had been murdered, she and her husband had been on the Isle of Wight, visiting Osborne House with their children, looking at the grizzly sight of Prince Albert's photograph on the pillow next to Queen Victoria's, where it had slept next to his widow every night after he died.

Angela Hunnicliffe was similarly out of the picture, having left the country before Wetherby was shot. Which left only Beverley Harriman – for the moment. Those three were the ones Riach had known about – but if three, so quickly, one after the other, or possibly even running simultaneously, it was eminently possible there might be more.

That was what Abigail had concluded, after having spoken to Beverley, a gullible girl dazzled by the attentions of an older, attractive man, a girl who, in Abigail's sharp and sometimes censorious opinion, was not very bright. She'd had the opportunity to kill Wetherby: after going down to the market with Trish to visit the stall which sold designer knitwear at discount prices, they'd parted and she said she'd then cycled to the Green Man over at Lattimer where she'd agreed to meet Wetherby for a pub lunch, something she'd failed to admit when she'd first been questioned. He had never turned up. She'd returned to the office tear-stained and twenty minutes late to find the place in an uproar and Wetherby dead. Nevertheless, there was only her own word to say where she'd been after she left Trish: she said she'd waited for Wetherby in the car-park of the Green Man but no one remembered seeing her there. There had been ample time after leaving Trish for her to have slipped back to Lavenstock College. She had the motive: it wasn't the first time Wetherby had stood her up, said Trish shortly.

'But you surely don't imagine she came back here and shot him?' she then demanded scornfully. 'She was a fool over him, and he was a louse, but she *was* in love with him – or imagined she was. Besides which, she's not the type to do anything like that, our Bev. Otherwise, she'd have given him the push long since, like I told her to.'

Trish was a very different proposition from Beverley, in her early twenties but already hard-faced, fashionably dressed and made up like a china doll. But despite the scorn, there was an element of exasperated kindness when she spoke of Beverley; she seemed fond of her, in a patronising way, though Abigail guessed it was only the close proximity of working together that had made them friends.

'I think Trish is right, though,' she had said to Mayo. 'Beverley wouldn't have done it. Apart from having nothing to gain by killing him, I can't see her as the sort to take revenge with a pistol. She's one of those who'd forgive him and let him do it again. A tree-hugger, I shouldn't wonder.'

'Funny, that's more or less what Riach said.'

*   *   *

152

When the phone rang into the silence which followed the revelations about Tone, Cleo jumped a mile. She hadn't yet got used to it being reconnected by British Telecom. Muriel, by dint of suddenly acquired efficiency and who knew what powers of persuasion, had miraculously managed to persuade them to act immediately.

'Hello?'

'At last! Is that you, angel?' asked a male voice.

'This is 54278,' Cleo said, rather stiffly, cross at being interrupted at such a crucial point by some love-lorn caller who'd obviously got the wrong number.

'Then I'd like to speak with Angel, Angela, please,' the man said, with what she now discerned as a transatlantic accent.

'Mrs Hunnicliffe doesn't live here any more. She's gone back to America.'

'What's that you're saying? Who is this? To whom am I speaking?' the caller demanded, with admirable American correctness.

'Cleo Atkins.'

'Atkins? Daphne, is that you?'

'No, it's *Cleo*,' she said, feeling this conversation was rapidly sliding out of control. 'Daphne's my mother and I'm living here now. She's here if you want to speak to her.'

'No, no. Where's Angel, then?'

'I've told you, she's with her husband, in America.'

'No, she isn't. *I'm* her husband. Brad Hunnicliffe here,' he introduced himself belatedly.

There followed a measurable pause, which Hunnicliffe broke by saying, 'I apologise for disturbing you, it must be late over there, but I'm very worried about her. She was supposed to fly back here to the States, couple of weeks after I did, and stay with her sister in Boston for a few days. My father hasn't been too good and I've been staying with him in Connecticut since I got here. Angel and I were due to meet up at Logan airport today to take the flight for San Francisco. She never turned up and I've found she never arrived at her sister's, either. What's going on?'

'I've no idea, but I think you'd better speak to my father. He's here, too. He was the one who dealt with Mrs Hunnicliffe.'

'I'd surely appreciate that.'

153

Yes, said George, Mrs Hunnicliffe had certainly left Lavenstock as arranged. Everything was paid up and she'd left the house all in order (apart from a Clarice Cliff candlestick, thought Cleo, suddenly remembering she'd never spoken to her mother about it) and returned the keys by the date she said she would. He took out his notebook and began making notes. Yes, if Mr Hunnicliffe wished, he'd certainly start making enquiries immediately . . .

Keys! thought Cleo.

By the time the conversation had finished, she had the bunch of keys in her hand, back door key, front one and a smaller one which was probably the one to the locked cupboard upstairs, which she'd never had cause to open.

'Go on, Dad, open it,' she said in a choked voice a minute later, suddenly feeling extremely glad of Daphne's hand on her shoulder as all three of them stared at the blank cupboard doors.

George turned the key. It was empty but for five pieces of matching blue luggage, locked, strapped and labelled with Angela Hunnicliffe's name, destination Boston, and flight number. Sitting ready on top of one of them was an airline folder containing the flight documents and her ticket, dated Friday 3rd March, with her passport also tucked inside.

Cleo slowly let out her breath, let her heart resume its normal beat. Too much imagination, that was her trouble! She and her father looked at each other, the same unspoken thought in both their minds.

'I think,' said George, 'Brad Hunnicliffe had better get himself back on the first flight over here.'

15

The spring sunshine, signalling the beginning of the end of winter, had overtaken the best efforts of the central heating programme at Milford Road, and Mayo's office was several degrees too hot for comfort, despite the open windows. He ran a finger round the inside of his collar and wondered how the man sitting opposite could bear it.

Bradshaw K. Hunnicliffe Jr, drawn and jet-lagged, an American equipped for English weather in a long, heavy raincoat of British origin, had thrown it open as his only admission of the heat but refused to be parted from it. He sat staring at a cup of cold, untasted coffee. His face was blank with stunned incomprehension, refusing to believe that anyone could have wanted to harm *his* wife, his lovely wife, much less kill her.

'She can't be dead, not Angel!' He had seen her body, positively identified her, yet he had said this three times in the last fifteen minutes.

Mayo sympathised. Hunnicliffe was understandably shocked and under strain, he had just suffered the terrible ordeal of looking into his dead wife's face, but however much Mayo felt for the man, there it was, he had run out of platitudes with which to console him. They were getting nowhere like this. 'I know how painful it must be for you, Mr Hunnicliffe, and I'm very sorry to press the point, but I'm afraid there's more. Your wife's death isn't the only murder we're investigating. Charles Wetherby was also shot last week.' He paused to let that sink in, but when the other man barely responded, except with a nod, as if the fact were quite irrelevant, he added a rider that he hoped would prod him. 'Most likely with the same gun, I'm afraid.'

'Wetherby? The Bursar?' Hunnicliffe still hadn't made the connection, which should by now have been evident to anyone. Either that, or he was refusing to face the inescapable conclusion. In denial, as current jargon would no doubt have it. But Mayo was having none of that claptrap, he preferred his own interpretation. He saw Hunnicliffe as a typical academic, with a mind

155

raised above the mundane, or the practical. Bright intelligent eyes behind wire-framed spectacles, hair receding at the temples, dark-complexioned. A thin man with a habit of clasping his hands over a small, incongruous pot-belly, like a swami in contemplation. He was said to be brilliant at his subject, he had written several textbooks dealing with such wonders as particle physics, he was reputedly a good teacher, but he was not proving good at coping with or understanding the crises of life, large or small.

Mayo clicked his pen several times. 'I see I must make it plainer, Mr Hunnicliffe. We have reason to believe your wife and Mr Wetherby had at one time been having an affair. And directly or indirectly, it has led to their murders.'

First, a refusal to believe. Now – outrage. The bright eyes suddenly shot sparks from behind the glasses. 'You bring me across the Atlantic and tell me my wife has been murdered – then you tell me she was having an affair under my nose! Mr Mayo, my wife was not that kind of woman – not ever!'

'When she was found she wasn't wearing a wedding ring.'

'She never wore one. She regarded it as a badge of subservience, or some such feminist bullshit.' Impatience flashed briefly across his face, then he recovered himself. 'Nevertheless, we had a wonderful, meaningful marriage.' He sounded as though he believed every word of it. But in the end he was the first to look away.

Delia had that morning brought in a big bunch of tight green daffodil buds and stuck them in a vase on top of the bookcase near the window. They had unfolded their petals almost immediately in the warmth and flickering sunshine now caught their bright gold, sent coins of light dancing on the ceiling. Hunnicliffe stared fixedly at the flowers, refusing to meet Mayo's eyes, but in the face of his silence was forced at last to speak. A huge sigh escaped him, seeming to be fetched up from the bottom of his heart. 'Oh, my God,' he said tiredly, 'if the first is true, then why not the other? If it's true she's dead, then . . . They're both equally unbelievable.'

'I'm very sorry, Mr Hunnicliffe.'

'I guess.'

156

'Are you willing to answer a few questions? We need to know the answers if we're going to nail whoever did this.'

'Go ahead. If you must.'

While Mayo was talking to Hunnicliffe, Abigail was told that a Mr Bysouth was at the front desk, wanting to speak to her. She went downstairs without much enthusiasm for a second encounter, and found a stranger waiting. It took a second or two, before he introduced himself, to register that this was Reuben Bysouth's brother, Jared. They had clearly come from the same mould, but Jared was an older, fitter, altogether more acceptable version than Reuben. A big, outdoors man with close-cropped hair, a stern, weatherbeaten face, a firm handclasp and a steady look, his movements were slow and unhurried. 'Can I speak to you in private?'

She took him into an interview room. He politely declined tea or coffee and came straight to the point. 'I've come here on behalf of my sister-in-law, Vera. She told me you'd spoken to her.'

'She's all right?' Abigail asked quickly.

'She is now,' the farmer replied grimly. He clasped the edge of the table with both big hands and leaned back, his arms stretched out in an attitude usually considered confrontational. As soon as he began to speak, however, she realised the body language was simply that of a man who meant to drive home his points without any misunderstanding. 'I've sent that brother of mine packing,' he announced bluntly.

'Packing? What happened?'

'What happened? He thought I was away, not expected back, that's what happened. I was just in time to stop him knocking the hell out of Vera. I think you know what I'm on about.' He met Abigail's gaze squarely. 'I blame myself, I should have realised what's been going on. To tell you the truth, I *did* suspect it, but not the half of it, he was always careful to hit her where it didn't show. Once or twice I tried to get her to talk to me, but she never would. Not until now.'

'That's the difficulty, Mr Bysouth. Women like Vera, they blame themselves, come to think they must have deserved it, somehow.'

Slowly, he nodded. 'Trouble is, I suppose, she still has some feeling for him, though how she can have . . . And how he can do that to her, after what we saw our father do, as kids, beats cockfighting . . . *That* sanctimonious, hypocritical bastard used to lambast our mother till she was black and blue, until one day, when I was fourteen and as big as he was, I hit *him*. He never did it again.'

Good for Jared. He'd not easily be roused, a man like him, but watch out when he was.

'It wasn't an act of charity on my part to take them in, you know. I needed an extra pair of hands on the farm, and after Joyce – my wife – died, the house and the cooking were all to blazes. I knew Vera would get stuck in there, sort things out, and so she has.'

'So Reuben's gone? Gone where?'

'Ireland, he says, but I don't much care where. He reckons he has a mate there been begging him to join him for months. I've been fair with him, given him some money and told him if he ever shows his face again, I'll break his legs. He knows I mean it, he'll not come back. I won't have history repeating itself, not in my house. Life shouldn't be like that.'

'And Vera?'

'Vera can stay with me. She'll be able to settle down, once she gets used to the idea he isn't coming back. She's a good wench, and I'll take care of her.' A tinge of colour crept into his cheeks. 'She's safe with me.'

She believed him. Vera had found a saviour. Her Rock of Gibraltar.

'There's something on her mind and she wants to talk to you,' he said. 'Would you come and see her? She's still mortal shamed of going out. She somehow got between us when I went for him, see, tried to stop me getting hurt, she said, and she's not a pretty sight just now.'

'I was coming to see her anyway.'

Brad Hunnicliffe, now that he'd accepted the unbelievable, had loosened up. He spoke freely, revealing himself as a man who rarely used one word where six would do. He even slipped off his Burberry as he prepared himself for Mayo's questions, and noisily slurped the fresh coffee which had been sent for.

'Let's start with why your wife stayed behind after you left?'

'My move back home came up somewhat unexpectedly.' He droned on for some time, explaining every detail of the circumstances. 'And since I wanted to visit with my father before taking up my new appointment, I left her to wind up all the business over here. Sorting out the lease of the house, getting rid of the car and so on, plus all the necessary bureaucracy, pardon me, we transatlantic visitors have inflicted on us when we visit Europe. Shipping all the English bits and pieces she'd collected . . . she was, I'm afraid, a real sucker for your country house sales and all that – you would not believe the amount of rubbish she'd picked up!'

Mayo sought rapidly for something less controversial to fix on, in case he might be tempted to say what he thought of this unexpected attack on his patriotism. 'Your car . . . what sort of vehicle did you run?'

'It was a used Mondeo Verona I bought from Automart on the Coventry Road when we came over here. Used in that it had only a few thousand miles on the clock, you understand. The agreement was that they would buy it back from me at a reasonable price when I had to return to the States, and they were happy to do this. I told Angela to leave it with them the night before she left and take a taxi to the airport next morning, which I assumed she had arranged to do.'

'What colour was it?'

'The car? Green. Metallic green. Have you found it?' The prospect of having lost the car, and therefore the money it represented, as well as his wife, appeared to increase his consternation and his annoyance considerably. 'I have to say,' he added austerely, 'I would have thought identification before now would not have been too much to expect from you people.'

A metallic green Mondeo, thought Mayo, holding on by ignoring this last. Then why had Angela – for he was sure, now, that it had been Angela who had been parked in the lane – been using a blue Fiat? Unless she'd already sold the Mondeo and had hired the Fiat, a fact easy enough to establish.

159

'No, we haven't found it yet,' he said. Mildly, he felt, in the circumstances. 'Do you recall the registration number?'

'I have it written down somewhere.' Hunnicliffe fumbled in various pockets and eventually came up with a pocket diary from which, after some searching, he produced the information.

'There's a possibility she had already turned it in, of course. We'll get on to Automart, see what they have to say.'

Hunnicliffe put down his cup, clasped his hands across his belly, a gesture Mayo was beginning to find increased his own irritation. He looked as if he expected Mayo to ring Automart immediately, but Mayo had no intention of breaking into the thread of the interview. That could come later.

He said, 'We've made enquiries from Mr George Atkins, the owner of the house you'd been renting, and it appears everything else was left ready for her departure on 3rd March. From the evidence we have so far, we think it likely she met her death on Thursday, and it looks as though she was all set to leave the following morning, Friday. All her things cleared out and packed. There was no food left apart from some milk in the fridge.'

'She never ate breakfast,' Hunnicliffe said absently, then went again into attack mode. 'I have to ask you, Mr Mayo – didn't anyone think it strange when she didn't turn the car in, wasn't there for the taxi, didn't claim her seat on the airplane? Why were no questions asked? And what about the house keys?' He slurped more coffee and set his cup down with a distinct bang on the saucer.

'The keys were pushed through the door of Mr Atkins's office, with a letter. People do fail to turn up for flights they've booked, you know, or forget they've booked a cab. And she may have decided to keep the car for a little longer, for all the garage knew. Taken together, all these things might have been suspicious, but since they were separate happenings, none of them gave out warning signals. Mrs Atkins did say she was surprised to find a pair of pyjamas and a few toilet things still in the house, but she thought they'd been forgotten.' (What Daphne had actually said was that since Angela hadn't even bothered to strip the bed, she could write for them if she wanted them forwarding. Something she was rather shamefaced at having even thought, now.) 'The

160

rest of her luggage, with her passport, if you remember, was locked up.'

'I have to say that was one thing in her favour, she could be relied upon for that, she was always the sort of person to be careful about her possessions. What's happened to her purse, by the way?'

It took Mayo a second or two to realise he meant her handbag. 'I'm afraid that's something we haven't recovered yet.'

Hunnicliffe raised his eyebrows at this further evidence of incompetence. Having decided half an hour ago he didn't like the man, Mayo hadn't seen any reason since to change his opinion. Maybe Angela could be forgiven for playing away from home – although it did seem as though she might have exchanged one pompous prat for another in choosing Wetherby as a substitute.

When he had gone, half an hour later, Mayo was left with the unsettling question: could Hunnicliffe have been quite so unaware of what was going on under his nose? Without a hint, however much his academic head was in the clouds, that his marriage was not as perfect as he'd believed it? It wasn't uncommon, after all, for people not to have an inkling in such circumstances – or to profess they hadn't – even people much more percipient than this American appeared to be.

He picked up the phone and gave instructions to have Brad Hunnicliffe's travel times checked, and to make sure that he had actually been in Connecticut the whole time he declared he had, and hadn't made a trip back to England in between. Although everything obtained from the American had been seemingly negative, Mayo allowed himself to feel a little more optimism. The identification of the murdered woman as Hunnicliffe's wife at least indicated a move forward in the investigation.

Connections were being made, links were forming. Lives which had apparently had nothing to do with each other were seen to have touched in a significant way. He never ceased to marvel at how one person's life could, by remote association, brush against so many more, through every individual's personal network of family, friends, acquaintances, business contacts . . . with the milkman, the window cleaner, the TV repair man, a hundred others . . . And how each of those reached out to yet more. It was the sort of interactive view of life, a mechanistic world view that appealed to him as a policeman and an individual, the world like one of his own clocks.

He doodled as he thought, spun his chair round, gazed out of the window at the Gothic Town Hall, smelled the faint spring scent of the daffodils.

Means, motive and opportunity, and the greatest of these is means. In this case, a gun. We didn't yet, thank God, live in a gun culture society, for all its increasing violence; the number of people likely to own and know how to use guns in a community like this was small, compared with America. Nevertheless, a gun had been used – and not yet found – a gun, moreover, which had in all probability been used to kill two people.

Motive, then. If what Abigail suspected was true (and Mayo had no doubt it was), and Wetherby had been physically abusing his wife, Hannah had every reason to wish herself free of her husband, but it was no use questioning her about his violence towards her, she would only deny it, she wasn't going to provide another motive against herself – not forgetting that other she might have, her possible involvement with Leadbetter. Or with Riach, come to that. Both of *them*, moreover, might have thought they had cause to kill Wetherby for that same reason: indeed, Riach could have had a double motive – to pave the way for Hannah and himself, and to step into Wetherby's shoes. But motive was a slippery notion at the best of times. Find the means first, look for the opportunity, and the motive, however slender it might appear to be to anyone but the perpetrator, would present itself.

Opportunity? None in the case of Hunnicliffe, unless he was lying and had in fact known about Angela's association with Wetherby, and *had* slipped back into England and murdered first his wife, and then her lover. John Riach had had the time, but had covered himself by proving he was drinking coffee with another member of staff between arriving back at the school and half-past one. Sam Leadbetter, on the other hand, had no credible alibi at all for that time. Moreover . . . Mayo thought about that little nugget of information which had been dug up about Leadbetter. He had, it seemed, a capacity for violence. His affair with Hannah, as they'd suspected, had started about four years ago. Gossip gathered from around the school had it that it had been brief – Wetherby had found out, and that had been the end of it. Sam had left Lavenstock, though not before a spectacular fight in which he had broken Wetherby's jaw. Some time later he'd joined the Antarctic expedition – the equivalent, Mayo supposed, of joining the Foreign Legion. He decided it was time he spoke to Leadbetter again, and his allegedly dotty aunt. Bearing in mind that Leadbetter had never, apparently, met Angela.

And this was where it stuck. Why should any of them have killed *Angela?* Indeed, the reasons for her being killed at all were murky – and the biggest puzzle of all was why she had been dumped in the Kyne. Yet her death, and the fact that she *had* been put in the river, he was convinced, were what mattered. There was a loose end to be picked up there, somewhere, the Ariadne thread that would lead them to the centre of the whole mystery.

For a long time, he thought about that, and the gun that Cleo Atkins claimed to have seen. He rang through for Abigail but was told he had just missed her, she was on her way to Covert Farm. He looked at the time. He had a meeting at three. He thought of who was available, and eventually decided he'd have to send Farrar to Kelsey Road. Farrar, who was quick-witted and astute, and even as a humble DC could always be relied upon to do a thorough and responsible job, notwithstanding he was somewhat lacking in the public relations department. However, there was no one else to send, apart from DC Barry Scott, and Farrar had to be better than that. As a new, untried sergeant, Mayo just had to hope that Farrar would be careful not to put his foot in it.

16

Dorrie looked at the clock and said, reaching for the tattered old gardening jacket that hung behind the back door, 'Still time to get an hour or so in, before the light goes. Where's the pepper dust? That blessed tomcat from over the road is paying my garden far too much attention.'

'And I suppose I'd better slip over and see how Hannah is,' Sam said.

Dorrie thrust her feet into her rubber gardening clogs. She looked up through her round specs at her nephew, hesitated and then said softly, 'Suppose nothing, Sam. Help her if you can, but don't go letting yourself in for something you'll regret, just because you're sorry for her.'

'Set your mind at rest. All that was over a long, long time since.'

'Ah, but does she know that?'

As so often happened, Dorrie, under her vague exterior, had her finger right on the button. Hannah still clung to him. He acknowledged this was only natural, in the circumstances . . . who else did she have to turn to? But though he'd told her plainly enough that anything more than friendship wasn't on, he wasn't sure she'd accepted it. And he was still worried about her, and that masochistic tendency she had to attract trouble to herself. In the present situation, that was something which could be disastrous, for both of them.

'Don't think I'm interfering, Sam, I wouldn't do that, but I couldn't bear to see you get hurt again.'

She looked so woebegone he hugged her, his arms encircling, with difficulty, the chubby little form wrapped in layers of clothing, plus the padded jacket. 'Not to worry, I've better control over myself nowadays.'

He dropped a kiss on her head, and when she stood back she asked him, as if he were still seven years old and had been caught bunking off Sunday school, 'You have been telling the truth, haven't you, Sam? Only –' She was interrupted by the loud peal of the front door bell. '*Now* who's that?'

'I'll get it,' Sam said, and a moment later, ushered into the kitchen a tall, well-tailored young man with blow-dried blond hair who looked like a bank clerk and who Sam said was a detective sergeant.

Farrar looked at the bundled form and the gentle face topped by soft, floppy grey hair scrabbled up anyhow on top of her head, its fringe falling over her glasses, and wondered what he was expected to wring out of this dear old thing. Then he remembered what Kite had said about her attacking the big Irishman at the women's refuge and nervously took out his notebook.

She took the wind out of his sails by reversing the order of things, asking him questions before he could begin to question her: how long had he been in the police, was he a native of these parts, where did he live? 'And are you married, Sergeant?'

'Yes, nine years.'

'Really? Have you any children?'

'Not yet,' he said, and blushed. 'But come July . . .'

Dorrie beamed. 'Let's have a glass of sherry to that!' Farrar smiled and said thank you, but not on duty, and forbore to look at the clock – sherry, mid-afternoon! No wonder the old girl acted like she didn't know the time of day – but he began to see what Sandra had been on about all these years when she said people regarded you differently if you had a family.

But since he was in one of his upbeat moods, he was prepared to go easy with old Dorrie, and accepted a cup of tea. Life for him had taken a turn for the better, at last. In his career – and not least, in his relationship with his wife. Sandra, after all the years of hospital tests, temperature-takings and other more unmentionable necessities, had become pregnant, her world had regained its balance, she'd stopped nagging and Farrar's life had become more comfortable all round.

Dorrie said suddenly, disconcerting him, 'So you're here about the Bursar's murder, young man – what do you think we can tell you that we haven't already?'

Farrar finished the last of a delicious homemade cake, his second and the like of which he hadn't seen in years. Butterfly buns, his grandmother used to call them. Little sponge cakes

165

with the tops cut off and wedged like wings into a butter-cream topping, decorated with jam. You were lucky if you got a Mr Kipling cake at 3 Elm Close. Sandra hadn't done any home baking for years, considering it time-wasting, sinful and unhealthy.

'Well,' he said, picking crumbs carefully from the lapel of his beautiful suit, taking his cue from Dorrie Lockett's directness, 'maybe you'd care to tell me exactly what took place between you and Mr Wetherby just before he was murdered.'

'Dorrie?' said Sam. 'What's all this about? You never told me you'd been to see Wetherby!'

'It's all right, Sam, it's nothing. He only wants to ask me –' She broke off, and to Farrar she said, 'I didn't kill that man . . . though I don't say I didn't want to! Or that he didn't deserve it. But if I had, I'd have seen to it he died in a more painful way!'

'*Dorrie*!'

'No use beating about the bush, Sam! We had high words, the Bursar and I, yes, but he was still sitting there, smug as a blessed plaster saint when I left him. Still as determined to press on with that stupid idea of knocking down four perfectly good houses no matter who it hurts! He started threatening me with compulsory purchase orders, and friends on the council and a lot more rubbish. I told him he could talk about friends in high places till he was blue in the face, it wouldn't make any difference, I still have a few friends of my own left, they're not all dead yet, and we'd see what *they* could do! I said he couldn't make me move out of my house if I didn't want to go, nothing he could offer me would persuade me, and that was that. I left before I said too much.'

Sam, studying the gingham cloth covering the kitchen table, tracing its checks with his forefinger, waited until Dorrie had finally finished. When he raised his eyes, his lips were twitching.

Farrar, however, was looking stunned. 'Oh, right, yes, OK. I see.'

'He *was* alive when I left him.'

'Of course, we know that,' Farrar said, recovering. 'There's no question. Several people saw him afterwards.'

'Then why are you plaguing me? I came home straight after-wards and I had to go for a little lie down, I was so upset.'

Maybe she'd done just that, thought Farrar, wondering why she was so bothered about moving from a house that was, after all, a bit of a dump. He looked round the old-fashioned kitchen, comparing it to his and Sandra's, with its fitted units and all the latest technology. You'd have thought a little old lady like her would have jumped at the chance of a good offer that would enable her to buy a nice little home somewhere else, plus a bit in the bank to see her through the rest of her days in comfort. Then he thought, OK, maybe she *had* come straight home after seeing Wetherby, and relayed the incident to her nephew, who'd been so concerned on her behalf he'd gone round to the school to confront Wetherby himself. Another fight, ending with Wetherby being shot in the head? In the *back* of the head, sitting at his desk, he reminded himself, but still he asked, 'What time did you get back here?'

'About twenty past twelve, I suppose. And just in case you're thinking it, I *didn't* go back later and shoot him.'

'Did you see Mr Leadbetter when you came in?'

'No, but I used the front door and went straight up to my bedroom. Sam was working in the garden at the back, weren't you, Sam?'

She looked directly at her nephew, as if willing him to give the right answer. Sam nodded. 'There, and clearing the ditch in the lane behind. When I heard all those police sirens, I went out to find out what was going on. I couldn't see anything of course, so I was none the wiser, but I happened to notice the ditch was blocked and I thought I might as well have a go at it while I was there.'

'But nobody, apart from your aunt, would have known this?'

'My aunt didn't know *what* I'd been doing until I told her that evening. But Mr Ryman was with me, our retired neighbour further along. The noise made him look out of his bedroom window, and when he saw me clearing the ditch, he came down to help me. We worked there together for about an hour – until about quarter to two, I should think.'

'Why didn't you say this before?'

'As far as I'm aware, I did. When I was asked what I was

doing, I told them I was gardening and they seemed satisfied. Nobody asked me to prove it,' he added, knowing he was being bloody-minded, but obeying the same instinct that had been telling him all along to say as little as possible.

With admirable restraint, Farrar said no more. He couldn't help feeling he'd hardly distinguished himself in this interview, but at least he'd found someone who could confirm Leadbetter's alibi.

'Well,' Dorrie said, 'if that's all, young man –'

She was interrupted by a commotion of caterwauling and high-pitched barks from outside. She rushed to the door, followed by Sam, with Farrar bringing up the rear. Outside, they were greeted by a tremendous fight taking place on the stretch of garden at the side of the house, where a miniature dachshund and a big ginger cat were locked in combat. Earth and plants were flying in all directions. A young woman was standing by, shouting, 'Hermione! Come here *at once*!' and holding a dog lead with a collar dangling from the end, commands which the dog totally ignored.

When the girl saw them she cried, 'Oh, Miss Lockett, I'm so sorry! She slipped her collar – and now she won't come back!'

At that moment, the combatants, falling on each other with tooth and claw, dislodged a large rock, which rolled down the slope and fell into the pond with a great splash. Both animals leaped aside to avoid it, and the cat seized its chance and shot away, while Sam grabbed Hermione by the scruff of the neck. Dorrie gave a soft, heartbroken moan and ran towards where the rock had been, uttering something which sounded like, 'Oh no! My baby!'

After she had heard that the woman the papers had dubbed The Mystery Woman was in fact Angela Hunnicliffe, Cleo hadn't thought she could face up to the gruesome fact of staying in the house where she'd lived. But something had happened the next day which made her decide to tough it out, to remember that Phoebe's little house had held enough happiness and contentment to overcome any bad vibes she might imagine. She wasn't going to be there long now anyway, she hoped, crossing her fingers. Not if the most amazing, the most exciting thing she could imagine came true.

Although this should, in theory, have made her concentrate even more on her writing, it had the opposite effect, even though her work at MO was petering out and she had plenty of spare time. She would have welcomed even the chance to work for Mrs Bristow and her demon family, but Val hadn't sent for her.

In the end, she went out to look for a present for Tone, since he'd refused to accept payment for the work he'd done on the house, but she couldn't find anything that seemed remotely appropriate, except artists' materials, and felt she didn't know enough about them to risk it. Even George, not renowned for his imagination, must have better ideas. She called into the office on her way home. He hadn't.

'Where's Muriel?' she asked, bending down to stroke Hermione, who was taking advantage of her mistress's absence to roam at will around the office, but thinking better of it when Hermione's lip curled back warningly.

'She came in this morning with a face the size of a football. She'd broken a tooth over the weekend and she was in agony. I packed her off to the dentist.'

'Poor Muriel!' Cleo had a horror of someone poking about in her mouth equalled only to that of being leaped on by a mad axe murderer.

'Only thing to do. He gave her emergency treatment and sent her away with painkillers and advice to go home and sleep it off for a few hours. I told her she could leave the dog and I'd deliver her on the way home. She wouldn't have got any rest otherwise.'

'I've what's left of the afternoon free and I know how busy you are. Anything I can do?'

'Not really – except to get this damn dog from under my feet for a while. My impulses got the better of me, letting her stay here. She needs a run, would you . . .?' He didn't need to add that he'd just as soon be seen walking the streets of Lavenstock naked than with a miniature dachshund on the end of a lead.

'Tell you what – I'll give her a long walk, tire her out and by then it'll be time to deposit her at home with Muriel, how's that?'

The long walk took her up Kelsey Road, either by design or by subconscious processes. When she got to number 16, she paused for another glimpse of that magical little wild garden. But the hedge that shielded it from the road was too high. She walked up the sloping path beside it to where the hedge almost levelled out near the house and she could finally peer over.

And that was when it had happened. Hermione had seen the ginger tom scratching at the soil, and had slipped her collar, leaped the foot-high hedge and pandemonium had broken out.

By now, it was all over and Hermione, back in her collar, was twisting the lead round Cleo's legs in an effort to get away again, her every instinct telling her to get back to the hole left by the displacement of the rock, and dig: her ancestors had, after all, hunted badgers. But there was Dorrie, bending down and lifting something from the earth where it had been buried behind the large boulder. A sort of domed metal coffer it appeared to be, green with age and damp, not apparently heavy, about the size of a large shoebox.

Cleo told herself she couldn't have heard properly, above the din Hermione was making, those despairing words she thought Miss Lockett had cried out.

Dorrie swallowed a mouthful of the sherry she'd asked Sam to pour for her, refusing to accept his advice that brandy would be better. The thick, sweet liquid seemed to soothe her, and she kept her fingers curled round the stem of the glass, the other hand resting on the lid of the coffer, which now sat on newspapers on the kitchen table.

Farrar sat stiffly on a kitchen chair with his back to the window, uncharacteristically shaken, trying hard not to show it. Sam and Cleo sat on either side of Dorrie at the table.

'I don't suppose it matters now, after all,' she said.

'What doesn't matter, Miss Lockett?' asked Farrar, far too sharply, pulling himself together but earning himself unfriendly looks from the other two.

'Whether I leave this house or not,' Dorrie answered. 'I couldn't go before, you see, not while my baby was lying here, but now that her resting place has been disturbed, it doesn't matter, does it?'

The hairs rose on the back of Cleo's neck. She couldn't mean baby – as in *baby*. Could she? No, that was ridiculous! She swallowed and reached out to put her arm around Dorrie's shoulders. 'Won't you let us put that box back where it was, Miss Lockett, as though it had never been disturbed?' she asked gently.

'You can't do that!' Farrar intervened, outraged. He reminded himself he was an officer of the law, it was his duty to take charge of the situation, at least until he'd satisfied himself what was in the box, and that he hadn't really heard what he thought he'd heard when that stone rolled down the bank.

For a moment, it seemed as though Dorrie had failed to hear what Cleo said, or wasn't going to respond, but then, with a scarcely heard sigh, she smiled at the girl and shook her head. 'No, dear. It's time someone else knew, in any case. I want this box laid to rest with me, you see,' she said. She put her other hand on the lid of the box.

Sam had felt colder surrounded by a million tons of frozen ice, but not much. Cleo sat transfixed, and Farrar was almost as still. The box looked evil, Sam thought, gave off an aura of corruption, or was that only his imagination? Copper, or bronze, worth a fortune probably. Where in heaven's name had it come from? he wondered, trying to think of anything but what was in it. Most probably simply found amongst the extraordinary accumulation of stuff, junk and otherwise, that had gathered dust for years in this old house.

At first, the lid wouldn't respond, and as he watched her try, it was all Sam could do not to stop her. 'Dorrie, must you do this?'

She gave him that extraordinarily sweet smile. 'It's all right, my dear,' she said as the lid eventually yielded with a metallic scrape that set the teeth on edge.

There was an involuntary backward movement from everyone, even Farrar, but no one took their eyes from Dorrie as she plunged her hands into the box. Half expecting to see a bundle of dry bones, a small skeleton, the shock was no less when Dorrie lifted out a small figure clothed in long yellowed

171

cotton and pillowed on a delicately crocheted shawl, fine as a cobweb.

A doll. Only a doll.

'I've had her since I was three. I used to call her Marietta.' Dorrie laid the doll tenderly on the table, its face winsome, chubby-cheeked, rosebud-mouthed, with long-lashed, blue glass eyes, its synthetic, glued-on hair gone bald and tufty.

'Dear God,' said Sam.

Dorrie stared at him for a long moment. Finally, she said softly, 'Yes, my dear, that was what I said when I put her there. Dear God, keep my baby safe. They wouldn't let me keep her, you see, my own baby. I was dreadfully ill when she was born, and she died. They took her away before I'd even held her. My father said it was a judgement on me. But he had a stroke soon after, and was bedridden for years, which I thought was a judgement on him.' She touched the doll's smooth, cold, still-pink cheek, her hands caressed the broderie anglaise cotton of the small gown. 'This was to have been my baby's christening robe, it was the only thing I had to remind me of her. I couldn't believe she was really dead, I'd never seen her grave, so I buried my dolly in place of her. That way I could always keep her near me,' she said simply.

It was true what they said about her, she *was* mad, thought Farrar. Not just eccentric, but seriously off her trolley. Though not, thank God, as he had feared, someone who'd committed infanticide. A doll in a box. That was all it was.

And yet, it represented a ruined life, though it was an all too familiar story. Dorrie, an unworldly young woman, taken in by a man already married and with children, who'd disappeared when he found out she was pregnant. Sent away by her father to have the baby in obscurity, away from wagging tongues. Small towns had not been so non-judgemental then, as now. After the difficult birth, after the baby's tragic death and her own slow recovery, there hadn't seemed anything left to do but come back home. And make that garden.

'The wretched man seems to have won, even from the grave,' she said into the silence that followed the ending of her story. No one thought she was talking about her father now.

Farrar, unusually, restrained himself from pointing out that Wetherby was not yet in his grave, a remark he wouldn't have

172

hesitated to make not so long ago, for even he had not been left unmoved by the story. He had already resolved not to say another word about all the fuss and palaver Sandra was making over her pregnancy.

After he'd left, Dorrie carefully smoothed down the yellowed cotton christening robe, and then put the doll back in the box. 'That's that, then,' she said practically, then paused. 'I know people like that detective think I'm crazy, and they're probably right. They'll say I could just as well have kept my baby's clothes in a drawer to remind me, but without a grave I could put flowers on, she'd never have seemed really dead to me, do you see?'

'Yes, of course, I do see,' Cleo said, and thought she did. Dorrie reached out and patted her hand. She picked the box up and walked to the door. 'Come and see me again, Cleo, will you? And bring your mother.'

The door shut behind her and Sam said into the silence that followed, 'She's not crazy, you know. In spite of evidence to the contrary.'

'It's not crazy to my way of thinking. Everyone has their own ways of coping.'

At last, Sam was able to smile. 'You're a nice girl. Will you do as she asks and look in on her occasionally, when I'm gone?'

'I'd love to, but it might be difficult. I may be going away myself shortly, to London.' Surreptitiously, she crossed her fingers. 'But I know someone who would, and that's my mother. I'm sure she'd be delighted.'

The smile that was the reflection of his aunt's lit his face. 'That would be really kind, if she wouldn't mind? London?' He looked enquiringly at her, but she willed herself to say nothing, though she was bursting to tell him. It would be tempting fate to say anything more, yet, and she merely nodded.

'We can see something of each other, then. I shall be teaching at UCL. OK?'

Who could resist that smile, that honest, open friendliness?

'OK by me,' she said.

Farrar had recovered most of his assurance by the time he got back to the nick. He could almost persuade himself that he

173

hadn't for a moment been unnerved by the sight of that box, and the batty old woman.

'I had a word with the old bloke, Frank Ryman, along the street before I left,' he reported back to Mayo. 'I couldn't see him being much use, ditch-clearing, but he seems to have been going through the motions, along with Leadbetter. Fair chuffed, he was. Nobody's asked him to do anything useful for years, not since he was put out to grass, as he says.'

'He confirmed the time?'

'More or less . . . though the words might've been put into his mouth. I reckon Leadbetter had been there before me. What Ryman actually said was,' said Farrar, reading from his note-book, '"I didn't take much account of the time, but Sam says we were there until two, and if he says so, we were. I've known him since he was that high, and he wouldn't lie."'

17

No wonder Vera didn't want to be seen in public was Abigail's first thought when she saw her on her arrival at Covert Farm, late that afternoon. Neither dark glasses nor make-up would hide the purple swelling round her eye, her swollen lip and the dark, ugly bruise along her jawline.

But, battered though Vera's face might be, she was a changed woman. The incubus that had made her life a nightmare for the last twenty years had at last been removed from her and even her voice had gained strength. She looked years younger, and if not happy, at least less browbeaten, no longer wrapped in the subservience of a flowered overall, but wearing a sweater and trousers, with her hair newly washed, revealing pretty golden lights among the auburn.

She had baked scones and prepared tea, and set it on one end of the big, scrubbed working table in the middle of the welcoming room which Abigail had glimpsed on her previous visit, where lamps were lit as the afternoon darkened. Another collie, not the black and white one, but an old dog with a grey muzzle, lay at Jared's feet with one eye open. The kitchen was big, a proper farmhouse one which had developed naturally over the years into a general-purpose living-room, with an old-fashioned stove and shabby old chairs around a blazing fire in an ingle-nook fireplace.

Vera removed a cat from one of the chairs, brushed the hairs off with her hand and offered the seat to Abigail, who perched on the edge, fearful that the warm fire and the sagging comfort of the chair might prove too much for her concentration.

As they sipped their tea Vera, prompted by Abigail, gradually came round to telling her why she wanted to speak to her. 'I've been thinking . . .' She looked to Jared for encouragement. She was the sort of woman who would always need to defer to a man, she would never be independent-minded, either by her own nature or because it had been knocked out of her; but Jared Bysouth was a different proposition altogether from his brother, an honest man who would, as he had promised, look after her.

He nodded now and she swallowed, then went on: 'It was that car you asked after. Yes, I did see it, three times in all. I should have told you the truth before.' Having brought herself to say this, her glance slid away, as if it had all been too much for her.

'What kind of car was it?' Abigail asked and got the answer she half expected.

'I'm not much good with cars. I can't tell you the make but it was blue, and an S registration, or maybe it was R. But I do remember the rest of the numberplate.'

'That's a bonus!'

Vera brightened.

'Well, you see, the letters were my initials, VMB, Vera Margaret Bysouth. I noticed that right away, well, you would, wouldn't you? Then, after seeing it there three times I thought, well, that's a bit funny, and I memorised the numbers as well. 52 . . . Let me think, 529, yes that was it, 529.'

'You didn't assume it might belong to a customer of Mrs Osborne's?' asked Abigail, writing it down.

'Not when she didn't get out of the car! I saw her arrive, and drive off, each time. She stayed about half an hour. You see –'

She broke off and looked to Jared for encouragement. He gave her a small nod. She sighed, and when she resumed, her voice had lost its assurance and was again almost a whisper. 'Whatever else, Reuben's never been one for other women, so what I thought was, she might've been waiting to see him, over – well, some business he didn't want anybody else to know about. But I didn't like to say this to you. I could've been mistaken.'

'She means he was never up to any good, Inspector,' Jared interrupted. 'But if you knew what was best for you, you kept your head down when Reuben was up to his tricks, right Vera?' Excusing Vera by including himself, giving her a smile. Away from the constraints of the police station, here in his own home, he was much more relaxed and at ease.

Encouraged by his support, Vera agreed. 'Jared's right. That's why I didn't mention it to him, I didn't want to cause trouble between him and Reuben. Jared hadn't seen the car himself, he

176

was busy elsewhere about the farm each time. And I suppose Reuben had his reasons for keeping out of the way.'

'Better if you had mentioned it to me, though, Vera. See, I'd warned that brother of mine, right from when he first came to live here, that he'd have to watch his Ps and Qs, he'd have to play it straight, from then on.' He paused. The dog at his feet stirred and snored in its sleep and Jared leaned down and stroked its head. 'You won't have come here without knowing what I mean by that.'

'We're talking of his record.'

He nodded, but added fairly, 'As far as I was aware, he'd kept his promise. I couldn't have sworn he had, of course, but if he'd been up to anything dodgy, he had the sense to keep it from me, otherwise he'd have been out on his ear. I've too much to lose to take any risks. I'm committed to this organic pig-rearing, and this farm's taken me half a lifetime to build up, from just having my own smallholding, and now plus Iris's acres.'

'Well, anyway, I'm glad I got that off my chest,' Vera volunteered suddenly into the silence that followed this, then looked shy. 'I hope it's been helpful.'

'More than you know, now we have the numberplate.' Abigail thought she might try another question, though she wasn't hopeful of the answer. 'I don't suppose you can recall the exact dates you saw the car?'

'Not exactly – each time it was a weekday.'

'Great!' And so it was, for even though Vera couldn't add anything to the delivery man's description of the woman who was driving it, their recollections tallied in every respect. 'But don't worry, it won't take long to trace her.' Abigail shut her notebook and prepared to leave. 'Thank you for the tea, and the scones. By the way, does the name Angela Hunnicliffe mean anything to either of you?'

Jared shrugged his big shoulders. 'Can't say as it does.'

Vera bent over the fire and poked it, threw another few lumps on to the already ferocious blaze. Her face was flushed with the heat when she turned back, shaking her head, her expression equally mystified.

'She was an American, and she's been identified as the woman who was found down there in the Kyne. We think she was put into the river at the time Mrs Osborne's cottage was flooded.'

The old dog, as if sensing a change in the atmosphere, lumbered to its feet and padded to the door, where it stood, turning its head mutely back. Vera went to let it out.

'What you're saying,' Jared said slowly, 'is that she was the woman in the lane? That Reuben killed her, put her in the river and got rid of her car? That's what you're trying to prove?'

'We're not at the stage of proving anything yet, but I have to tell you it's a possibility we can't overlook.'

'He wouldn't! Not even Reuben!' Vera burst out, unwilling, even now, to believe that. 'He's handy with his fists, but he'd never use a gun!'

His brother looked at her. 'He might, Vera, if he was paid enough.'

Vera's eyes fell.

'Did he ever mention a man called Charles Wetherby?' Abigail asked. For if Jared believed Reuben capable of killing Angela for money, then why not Wetherby also? If someone had paid Reuben to kill, no wonder he'd been so willing, when the excuse had presented itself, to make himself scarce. Pity that Jared had no idea of this so-called friend of Reuben's in Ireland, but finding him probably wasn't insurmountable.

'Wetherby?' Jared was shaking his head. 'Not that I ever heard. Isn't that the name of the bloke from Lavenstock College? Him that's been murdered?'

'Yes.' Abigail looked out of the window to where her car was parked in the dip, beside Wych Cottage. 'Would the day Mrs Osborne was flooded out be one of the days the car was there by any chance, Vera?'

'I didn't see it, but I was helping the men that day. It was terrible weather and they were having some bother with the stock.'

'Pigs are very sensitive to atmosphere, easy upset, they are,' Jared explained. 'They were over-excited and it took all three of us to deal with 'em.'

'But you still found time to help Mrs Osborne get her furniture upstairs.' And maybe for Reuben to get rid of that gun, slip it into a drawer until it was safe to retrieve it. 'It must be a comfort to her, having such good neighbours, living out here alone.'

'Oh, I've known old Iris for yonks, we do what we can – not that she needs or asks for much help. And I'd like to meet the intruder that got past her! Anybody trying anything like that and she'd like as not see 'em off with a backside full of shot! I've seen that happen afore now. She's not frightened of anybody, Iris, never was.'

'Air rifles?' Abigail asked carefully. Mindful of several things, of how Mrs Osborne had said she wouldn't even know how to load one, for instance.

'And shotguns. But that was in her younger days. She was reckoned a crack shot, then, with a rabbit or a hare. She doesn't see all that well, nowadays, though she wouldn't admit it, of course.'

But that wouldn't have mattered. Marksmanship would not have been a point at issue when either victim was shot. The killer had been near enough in both cases to have shot at point blank range. He could hardly have missed.

Abigail said absently, while her mind went into overdrive at this new aspect of Mrs Osborne, 'I can't say I think it's a good idea, living alone surrounded by all that valuable stuff.'

'Well, she's a game old bird, but I'll admit she was fair hopping in case any of her precious antiques got damaged when the water came down.'

'So would you be, Jared, if you were depending on it for keeping you in your old age!' Vera said.

'If old Iris never makes another penny and lives to be a hundred, she won't starve. She's got plenty stashed away in her old stocking, you can depend on it – or she should have, the price she wrung out of me for this farm! Don't blame her for that, though. You have to look out for yourself. But she's never been too particular how she makes a bob or two.'

The sun was just below the horizon, the darker part of twilight, with the soft, diffused light of the ending of a beautiful spring day by the time Abigail left the farm. The reeds stood blackly in the flat wet fields and she shivered, feeling a coldness that was not entirely due to having just left the warmth of the farmhouse kitchen. All the same, she felt a sudden unease, a sense of inexplicable urgency that made her decide, as she walked back to her car, that she couldn't pass up the opportunity to call on old Mrs Osborne again while she was here.

But Wych Cottage was in darkness, its windows like blank eyes under the frowning, low-tiled roof, making it a much less attractive proposition than it had seemed on the sunny, bright morning when she'd first seen it. There was no reply when she knocked on the door, and although she stood and waited in the porch for some time, no one came. Like the house itself, the porch was cluttered, stacked with umbrellas and walking sticks and the sort of protective clothing which is a necessity for anyone living in the depths of the country: she counted two waterproofs, a man's tweed hat, a Barbour jacket and a hooded anorak, three pairs of gumboots – one large, two small. Iris obviously believed in being prepared for the worst, even for visitors, and after what had recently happened in the way of weather, who could blame her?

After knocking once more and still receiving no answer, she left the cottage, not without some reluctance. Before she started the car, she switched on the interior light to log both calls in her notebook, and to make certain she hadn't missed anything of vital importance. She was a careful note-taker, never relying too much on memory, since she knew how unreliable this could often be. She was about to close the book when her eye lit on a name she'd previously written down.

Speaking to Eileen Totterbridge hadn't so far been high on her list of priorities, since she hadn't held out much hope of what it might bring forth. But now, remembering that it was Carmody who'd suggested it, she decided she could fit in a call to Mrs Totterbridge on her way back to the station. The sergeant's phlegmatic Scouse temperament didn't lead him to flights of imagination or going off at tangents, he wouldn't have suggested it if he hadn't had good reason to think a bit of backstairs gossip might be productive. Even if she only picked up some snippet of information that might reveal more about Hannah Wetherby's character than had so far become apparent, it could be useful. Hannah was still something of an enigma, and the road where Mrs Totterbridge lived wasn't too far out of Abigail's way back to the station.

After the initial surprise, followed by a general wariness, Eileen Totterbridge reverted to the state of comfortable friendliness

Abigail soon saw was as natural to her as breathing. 'Come in then, lovey, and sit by the fire, though I don't know what I can tell you I'm sure. Joe, turn that telly off and put the kettle on. I can't get about yet as quick as I used to,' she told Abigail, 'though I never thought I'd be on my feet this soon after the op, I'm sure.'

Joe Totterbridge, with a look that could have killed at fifty metres, prised himself away from a riveting programme showing spiny anteaters tearing a termites' nest to pieces and devouring the inmates, switched off and shambled into the kitchen, where he could be heard dangerously clattering teacups in protest.

A lingering smell of cooking had issued from the kitchen when he opened the door. 'I hope I'm not interrupting your evening meal,' Abigail said, annoyed at the lack of forethought that had made her drop in, unannounced, at what might be an inconvenient time.

'No, we've had our tea, m'duck. Only one of them micro-waved lasagnes, I'm not up to doing much cooking yet, but it wasn't bad, considering, never mind what Joe thought of it.' Remembering Mayo's stringent comments on microwaved food, too, Abigail wondered if all men didn't share her superior officer's opinion. 'But I'd rather have something like that than have to depend on my daughters, they both have jobs, you see, though they've been golden over all this, bless their hearts.'

Joe came in with a tray on which were two mismatched cups and saucers, a teapot without a cosy. The milk, however, was in a jug. Abigail guessed he wouldn't have dared go so far as to leave it in the bottle. 'You won't want me for a bit,' he announced. 'I'm off down the Legion.'

'I might be in bed when you come in, Joe. It's been a long day.'

'Orright,' Joe said and left them.

'It embarrasses him when folks are poorly.' Mrs Totterbridge evidently felt some apology for her graceless spouse was called for. 'Doesn't rightly know how to cope, see. He's old-fashioned that way. Sooner I'm back to rights, the better, and that shouldn't be long, seeing I'm mending so nicely. Now, what can I do for you, lovey?'

Keeping her opinions of men like Joe Totterbridge to herself, and her own fresh embarrassment at having come here without previous warning, or giving enough thought as to how disruptive such a visit might be at such a time, Abigail said gently, 'I really think it might be better if I came back later –'

'Don't you think of it, m'duck! A bit of different company'll do me a power of good. My Kath's coming round at eight but until then I'm on my own.' She drew breath and gave Abigail a speculative look. 'It's about Mr Wetherby's murder you've come, isn't it? I knew, when I told that policeman in the hospital I worked for them, that somebody would want to see me – you always do, don't you?' she said, her opinions of how murder investigations were conducted evidently coloured by TV police dramas. 'How is he, then, the copper? Nice chap.'

'Oh, he's mending, too, thanks. Yes, it's about Charles Wetherby I'm here, or rather Mrs Wetherby.'

'Yes,' Mrs Totterbridge said thoughtfully, pouring tea and passing Abigail a cup. 'Though to tell you the truth, I wouldn't have fallen over backwards if I'd heard it was the other way round – that she'd been the one to be murdered, and you wouldn't have had far to look for who'd done it! But there, I shouldn't have said that, should I?'

'You mean because of the way he treated her?'

The old lady eyed her speculatively, but seemed relieved that she didn't have to explain what she'd meant. 'I couldn't understand it, to tell you the truth. My Joe's not much of a one for the lovey-dovey stuff, but he's never raised a finger to me, nor ever would. He knows he wouldn't see me for dust if he ever tried anything like that on! But as for Hannah – oh, I don't know . . . if she'd been one of my own daughters I'd have given her a good talking to, but somehow, I never could get near her, if you know what I mean. She was nice enough to work for, always pleasant to me, but not like my other lady, that's Miss Lockett, Dorrie Lockett down Kelsey Road, who I've known ever since she came back home to look after her old father. And was he grateful? Was he heck, miserable old sod! But best not say too much about that, eh, lovey, what's past is gone.'

For all the old lady's garrulity, Abigail's heart warmed to her. 'How long have you worked for Mrs Wetherby?'

'Hannah? Ever since he got the job at the school. I never saw him do anything to her, mind, only had the evidence of my own

182

eyes, when I saw her poor arms bruised, and sometimes marks on her neck. Mind you, I don't think she always let him get away with it – I've heard them having words, more than once, and she can be a bit sharp-tongued herself. But she had plenty of provocation – I wouldn't have blamed her if she *had* wanted to get her own back. Though it's daft to think she'd have *killed* him!' she added hastily, as though afraid she'd said too much. 'I mean, she'd have left him before it came to that, wouldn't she?'

'Why do you think she didn't? Leave him, I mean.'

There was a silence, a long one for Mrs Totterbridge. 'Well, you know, us women, we're funny that way, aren't we? Who knows what makes us put up with what we do? It might just have been because she still loved him.'

'Do you really think so?'

'Well, it was a funny set-up. She didn't have many friends to speak of. Moped around the house most of the time, she did. But she had her compensations, I suppose. He didn't beat her up *all* the time, and the way he treated her in public, butter wouldn't melt in his mouth. He never kept her short of money – and can she spend it! Beauty treatments and hair-dos are the least of it – and she must keep them mail order firms going, the stuff she orders! You should see the catalogues that come through the post, parcels arriving every day! I've teased her about it, but you have to be careful. As I said, she can be a bit sharp at times. Like last week, when this heavy box comes. "What've you been ordering this time, then, lovey? Feels like a hundredweight bomb!" I said. "You don't want to joke about things like that, Eileen," she says, "it'll only be those shoes I ordered." Hobnailed boots, they must be, then, I thought to myself, but it turns out later it was a new pair of kitchen scales with brass weights, just like my old mum used to have, though what was wrong with the others I don't know.'

'You say she hadn't many friends, but she was quite friendly with John Riach, the Assistant Bursar, I gather.'

'Yes, and friendly's all it is! She wouldn't look twice at him, not when –' She stopped abruptly and busied herself with the teapot. 'Another cup, lovey?'

'No thank you. What were you going to say?' Mrs Totterbridge shook her head, looked flustered, and Abigail supplied, 'Not when there's someone like Sam Leadbetter around?'

'Don't you go thinking there's anything going on there, either! I've let my tongue run away with me again. It's these pills they've given me, must be. I wouldn't say a word against Sam, not if you strung me up I wouldn't! I've known him since he was a baby, and a nicer chap never drew breath. All that was over before he left to go the South Pole, and I can't say I was sorry. Nothing could've come of it.'

18

When Mayo had a problem, he walked. Tonight, he had several, and one of the most pressing was Angela Hunnicliffe. She was becoming a source of intense frustration to him, mainly because of the feeling that he didn't know quite what they were dealing with here, he couldn't pin her down, or the circumstances of her murder. Apart from her name, her identity as an American citizen and wife of Brad Hunnicliffe, he still didn't have any idea what sort of woman she'd been. She appeared to have made no contacts, other than with people she'd met at the school through her husband's work there. They had found her pleasant, bland, and unmemorable. The only surprising thing about her was that she'd had an affair with Wetherby.

Three can keep a secret, if two of them are dead. A line he'd read somewhere, God knows where, a leitmotif that kept running through his head, so that every time he heard its notes, he thought of that third person who was still alive, in the form of – who? Who had killed the other two, Wetherby and Angela, what had happened between the three of them to cause it? Something trivial, a small twist of fate, a few angry words, one thing leading to another? As banal as that? Or had there been some deadlier intention, on the part of the one who still held the secret?

He couldn't, as his daughter Julie used to say, get his head round it. Odd, that, he felt more in charge of himself than he had been for weeks. He felt himself rested, complete, whole, returned to being a member of the human race. Reunited with Alex. Two weeks apart, then a peaceful weekend, a walk in the country, a dinner at their favourite restaurant, and his life was suddenly back in clearer perspective than it had been since the Fermanagh affair. A salutary little lesson to be learnt there, that his entire outlook on life depended so entirely on the naturalness and rightness of their being together. He didn't know why it worked out like that, but he wasn't going to knock it.

Walking homewards through the sodium-lit streets on Monday evening, leaving behind the busy main thoroughfares, he found a desire to see for himself the house where Angela had lived, though he'd been assured she had left no legacy of her tenancy other than a pair of pyjamas, a toothbrush – and her luggage, of course, which had been examined and found to contain no clue as to why she'd ended up, dead, in the River Kyne, rather than in Boston where she'd obviously intended to be.

Elton Street ran at a sloping angle off the main road, a short terrace of small houses that was the only one left of dozens of similar terraces built on a grid system around the turn of the century. Sooner or later it, too, would be pulled down, presumably for space to build more of the same sort of pretentious but, when it came down to it, tacky detached houses which spread out below it, unless the council got there first and built more of the high-rise flats which stood out like sore thumbs and ruined the skyline above Elton Street. Meanwhile, it stood alone, dwarfed but unbowed among its more brash neighbours, several of its houses sporting fresh paint, new front doors and window boxes.

Cleo had set up her small PC with her back to the window. Consequently, she didn't see his arrival. It was the knock on the door that made her lift her eyes from the screen and then reluctantly get up to answer it.

Oh, damn! she muttered, saving the file and blanking the screen. She hoped it wasn't Daphne, calling for a chat on the first totally free day she'd had since she'd seized the chance to quit working for Maid to Order. It had become evident that the chickenpox epidemic had run its course, children were going back to school and mothers returning to work at MO . . . Val Storey had been generous enough to thank her for helping out (though Cleo feared she was just being polite) and given her an extra tenner in her wages – to help out in case she did decide to move to London.

Which was still not certain.

It had taken some doing the other day, to convince herself it wasn't simply self-righteousness that was prompting her to make the first move. She reminded herself that Jenna had said sorry once, hadn't she? When she, Cleo, had been too hurt, too furious with her sister to listen. So now it was her turn. When she'd finally psyched herself up to dial Jenna's number, it had been continuously engaged. She gave it up at last and immediately, her own phone rang. Jenna. Her first words were, 'I hope it's not you who's paying for all those calls you've been having, or you'll have a bill like a Third World Debt! I've been trying to get you all evening.'

Neither of them was in any way surprised at this evidence of telepathy, this tuning in to their personal hotline. It happened all the time, it always had.

Jenna rarely allowed herself to show excitement, but her cool tones had sounded appreciably less so than usual. She began before Cleo could get a word in. 'I've found you a job.'

'Oh, Jen, not you as well! I've had this out with Mum more times than –'

'Not that kind of job, Cleo. Listen, I met this woman who runs Emu Publishers. Have you heard of it?'

'Yes, I have,' Cleo said cautiously, after a moment's thought. As far as she could recall, it was a small but reputable publishing house with an interest, though not wholly so, in women's fiction, not yet taken over by one of the big conglomerates.

'When I say the job is yours, naturally she wants to see you first. But she's looking for someone, and she was *very* interested. Especially when I told her about *Bough of Cherries*.'

There was a long, fraught silence. 'Did I hear you properly, Jenna Atkins?'

'Don't get uptight, she wants to read it. There's a chance she might *publish* it!'

'You'd no right even to mention it!' Apart from herself, Jenna was the only one who knew what she'd been doing during the months she should have been working for her exams. Not even Toby had realised the extent of what he called her scribbles.

'Of course I've a right, I'm your twin, aren't I?' It occurred to Cleo that this was Jenna apologising again, and her fury subsided. 'You should do something about it,' Jenna went on. 'It's never going to be published, sitting in a drawer or whatever!'

Not in a drawer, but its equivalent. Stuffed into an old briefcase for six months, her first, precious, unpublished novel. Twice she'd taken it out and read it through, and afterwards felt her heart beating with excitement and possibilities. Yes! It *was* good. It *did* have something fresh and new about it. It wasn't as naïve as she'd thought. Twice she'd put it back, telling herself she wasn't in a position to judge it objectively, there was too much of herself in it, how could she have the nerve to think anyone would want to read what had, admit it, been done before, and better . . .

'This woman's name is Laura Boyd. She's going to write to arrange an interview. It isn't in the bag yet, but you can't turn that sort of chance down, Cleo – it's something a lot would give their eye-teeth for. Decent salary, and you won't be too pressurised. Plenty of time to write in your spare time.'

'There's a little matter of where I would live, of course.'

'You could share with me, I'm moving to a place of my own.' She went on impulsively, as if afraid she might not say it at all if she didn't say it quickly, 'Toby's gone to India, he won't be back. Not into my life, anyway. What do you say?'

Silences between them were not usual, but here was another, in the space of a few minutes. 'Cleo?'

'I'll think about it. And Jen – thanks a mill. For the flat-share offer, too.'

Afterwards, she'd read through the manuscript once more. *Bough of Cherries* charted a young girl's progress into adulthood, her first love. Yes, it *was* autobiographical, to some extent, in the way they said all first novels were. She felt herself light years away from the girl who had written it. The serious, intense person who'd believed Toby was equally serious. India! She hoped he'd found enlightenment there. She laughed.

And because she'd been able to laugh, she didn't put the book away again. A little stab of hope pierced her and she'd left it lying on her desk. Right up until this morning, when she'd decided to give it a final editing and reprinting, just in case . . .

She knew he was a policeman as soon as she opened the door. He was stamped with it in some indefinable way, like her father, though anyone less like George she found it hard to imagine. Perhaps it was something in the eyes, that looked straight at you as if trying to read your mind. A big, sober-looking man with dark hair going grey at the temples, and those matching dark grey eyes with crinkles at the corners. Which showed he could probably smile if the occasion warranted it, and that the smile might be nice.

He told her pleasantly that he was Detective Superintendent Mayo, as if she hadn't already guessed it, an ex-colleague of her father's, and please could she spare a few minutes of her time? She'd been right about the smile. It quite transformed him.

She was wary, all the same. She'd heard about Mayo, that you were safe if you played fair and worked at least half as hard as he did, that he didn't make waves unnecessarily, but that you were wise to reach for your life-jacket when he did. What did he want with her?

Only to talk about that gun she'd seen, or so he said.

Oh, crikey, that gun! That bloomin' gun. She wished she'd never set eyes on it.

No, he said (his eyes *did* crinkle up), he didn't want her to repeat herself, just to read this through and tell him if that was exactly what she'd told Inspector Moon. He unzipped the leather document folder he was carrying, and handed a paper to her. 'I should pull your curtains,' he advised, 'you're on view to anyone outside.'

She thought for a moment he was being paranoid, acting like someone from MI5.

'That's just what my mum says,' she answered. Sassy. Saying she could take care of herself, thank you very much, and he saw that although she was nothing like her mother to look at, she had something of Daphne's spirit. He could imagine them clashing.

'Then your mum's right,' he told her, amused but slightly irritated. No one nowadays sat in a lighted room that faced directly on to the street, its contents on view to any passing villain, not if they'd any sense. Didn't she realise she was a sitting target, in front of that window, an open invitation, if only to any delinquent who might want nothing more than that PC she'd been working at? She still looked rebellious but she did draw together the thin, unlined, flowered curtains which he saw immediately weren't going to make things much better. There would still be that young, defenceless head silhouetted against the light.

He refused with thanks her offer of coffee, and watched her, assessing her while she read, aware also of the impact of the glowing room, the decorating of which had been young Gilchrist's unsustainable alibi for the time of Wetherby's murder. He looked particularly at the painted window in the alcove, acknowledging its cleverness, and saw why Tony Gilchrist's artistic ability had been reckoned outstanding at school, but thinking, with a wry smile, that the effect of the intended deception was lessened by its depiction of sunny skies when the night outside was black as your hat. A false window like that also ought to have curtains which could be drawn over it at night.

'Yes, that's what I told her,' Cleo agreed, handing Moon's report back when she'd read it. 'And I really *don't* remember anything more.' She looked at him candidly. She seemed, as George had said, to have her head screwed on. A pair of amazing blue-green eyes, a firm chin. Pretty girl. Pity about the hair.

'OK,' he said, 'I know you think we're being a pain over this but I'd like you to tell me again, if you can, exactly what happened when you spotted the gun in the drawer.'

'What happened? Oh, well, a lot of Mrs Osborne's furniture had been taken upstairs when it looked as though the ground floor might be flooded. After we'd finished cleaning up, Sue – she was sort of in charge – suggested we move some of it back downstairs. Tone went upstairs to have a look around and when we went up, he'd already moved this chest of drawers to the top of the stairs – but I could see it wasn't going to be easy getting it down. They're narrow and steep and there's a bend in the middle. I thought it would be easier if we took the drawers out, make it lighter, and I started to pull the top one out. I know I should have asked first, but I did it without thinking. Anyhow, Mrs Osborne was there in a flash, covering up what was in it. Her daughter arrived just then and she said never mind moving the furniture down, just to leave it.'

'Did you mention what you'd seen in the drawer to the other two?'

'No. I didn't think it was any of their business – mine either, come to that. I didn't tell anybody, except Dad, later.'

'You say Tony was upstairs alone, before you and the other girl went up?'

'Oh,' she said, 'I see. It's because of Tone you're asking me all this, aren't you?'

Her chin rose challengingly but he only said, mildly, 'Maybe he opened the drawer before you came upstairs, for the same reason as you did, and saw the gun.'

'If he did, he left it there, didn't he? Otherwise I shouldn't have seen it. But why are you suspecting him? All because of what he did two years ago? This isn't the same thing at all! He wouldn't go around killing anyone!'

'Maybe he wouldn't, Cleo, and if it's of any interest to you, we've now let both of them go.'

'Both?'

'Tony and his brother, Dave. We brought Dave in, too, because he's been going around quite recently shooting off his mouth about Wetherby. In fact, he's never stopped making threats against him ever since Tony got himself into trouble. Which, if you know anything about it, involved both brothers.'

'Yes, I do know, Dad told me. Dave was caught breaking into the safe in the Bursar's office, and Wetherby went around saying Tony had given him the lowdown on how to get in. So in retaliation Tony took Wetherby's car, just to cause him some hassle and – and unfortunately crashed it.'

'Very unfortunately,' Mayo said. 'Especially for Tony.'

'Well, so it was. I wouldn't like to think I had to live with those scars for the rest of my life.'

'Nor I,' he said. Nor I, Cleo. 'And Dave, at least, has never forgiven Wetherby. Sworn he'll get him, one day, for that – and for landing *him* in prison. Logic isn't what Dave Gilchrist and his ilk are renowned for.'

'Dave may be like that, but Tone isn't. And he would never have shot Wetherby, the one thing he wants to do is put that incident out of his life. You might as well suspect me.'

'But supposing he'd mentioned to Dave that he knew where there was a gun?'

'Always supposing he saw the gun at all.'

'As you say, always supposing he did. It does seem unlikely, I admit, and we didn't find any reason to keep him. Or his brother . . . for now, but Dave'll be back with us sooner or later, on some other charge, or I'm a monkey's uncle.' He kept his tone light, not wanting to ruffle her further. 'Right now, it's Angela Hunnicliffe who's interesting me, that's principally why I came here tonight. Er – if I can change my mind, I *will* have that coffee you offered me, after all.'

'Yes, fine, it won't take a sec.' She stood up. 'But I'm afraid you'll be wasting your time. I never even met Angela.'

'I know you didn't, but I had the thought,' he said, for some reason not feeling foolish in admitting it, 'that some fresh idea might come to me, that I might pick up something if I saw where she'd lived. Find some reason why she should have been out there at Kyneford, the night before she was due to return home. You haven't by any chance come across anything at all she might have left behind? Things you mightn't have thought important? Scribbled telephone numbers, things like that?'

'There wasn't a thing. The place was clean as a whistle, everything just as it had been left. Mum had been through the inventory with her, you know, a couple of days before, and everything was in order. Oh – hang on!'

'There was something?'

'Ye-es. Something I seem to have a mental block about. I keep remembering it and then forgetting it again, though I don't suppose it's important. Have you ever heard of Clarice Cliff?'

It hadn't surprised anyone when John Riach categorically denied that his car had ever been in the vicinity of Covert Farm. It was what suspects routinely did when confronted with evidence of their misdemeanours, after all.

'There must be some mistake,' he'd said dismissively.

'Mr Riach, the Police National Computer doesn't make mistakes,' Abigail told him. Not when it had been double-checked against input from the DVLC at Swansea.

'I'll have to take your word for it. But if that's so, this person – whoever it may be, the person who thinks they saw my numberplate – must have made one. Perhaps they got the combination of numbers they actually did see into the wrong order so that this computer came up with mine.'

A blue Fiat, the same letters and numbers, referring to the vehicle of someone who was a suspect in the investigation . . .? That level of coincidence was too great for either Abigail or Mayo to swallow, or even for Riach, they could see, but Riach nevertheless stubbornly stuck to his story, swearing that he had never in his life been anywhere near Covert Farm or Wych Cottage. He had never heard of either of the Bysouth brothers, nor of Mrs Osborne. He could, moreover, prove that he had been pursuing his lawful employment at the school at that particular time all that week, and could produce witnesses to support it.

'Let's move on to something else, then,' Mayo said. 'Your alibi for the day Wetherby was killed.'

'Alibi? I thought that was something only needed as a defence against an accusation.'

'I'm using the word loosely. No one's accused you yet,' said Mayo, in a way that Abigail could see him thinking: this joker's getting too clever for his own comfort, time we took the spring out of him. 'Perhaps you'd prefer excuse?'

She knew now who Riach reminded her of, when he did that offended, haughty, pinched-nostril routine: Kenneth Williams in a snit. To the life, really, but she didn't laugh: the image reduced him to someone playing a part, covering up the real truth.

She could never quite decide how far it was ethical to use her femininity, in any circumstances, in order to manipulate, but she had no qualms about using it now. She smiled at Riach and managed to get a faint smile back. 'Would you mind if we went over your statement again? It would help me to get it absolutely clear in my mind.' As if she were the token woman on the team, there for form's sake, not her ability. Riach wasn't going to be fooled by this sort of behaviour, as no one would with half an eye, nor by her dazzling smile, which she could always use to good effect when she wanted to, but it was disarming. In the face of it, few could keep up the sort of aggressive defensiveness Riach had been showing. He wasn't going to collapse and give anything away, but his tight face relaxed somewhat and he allowed her to take him through his original statement with a reasonable show of good grace.

Yes, he had gone to Wetherby's house for the papers Wetherby had forgotten. He had told his wife to expect Riach and she'd unlocked the private gate ready for his arrival. He explained impatiently what he'd told them in the original statement: there were only two entrances into the school grounds, the main entrance, and a gate in the chain-link boundary fence at the end of the playing fields which opened on to a narrow pathway between two houses at the top of Vanson Hill. These two houses had originally been purchased for masters at the school, for the convenience of whom the gate had presumably been let into the fence. The gate was kept locked, and the Wetherbys now had the only key, the neighbouring house having been sold when the master who lived in it moved to take an appointment at another school, and the school having decided that a policy of tied accommodation was retrograde and uneconomical.

He'd arrived just after twelve, had a sandwich and a glass of wine with Mrs Wetherby, and had left just before half-past. 'She was expecting one of the High School girls – Rosie Something-or-other – for a costume fitting for the school play, at twelve thirty, so I made myself scarce.'

Confident now that his next movements could be supported, he told them that it had taken but a few minutes to walk back to the school, where he had joined Geoffrey Conyngham, the school Secretary, for coffee, over which they'd discussed certain matters relating to school administration. It was about quarter to two when he returned to his own office, where the elderly, retired master who looked after the school stationery supplies was waiting to see him. They had still been talking when the news of Wetherby's death had been brought to them. 'So there you are,' he said, confident now in the knowledge that what he had just told them could be supported. 'Nothing I haven't told you before.'

'Statements always bear repeating, just in case something's been forgotten,' Abigail said easily. 'You get on well with women, Mr Riach, don't you?'

'Not particularly.' Realising how this might be interpreted, he added, flushing, 'What I mean is, I get on well enough with them, in a civilised, normal manner. Unlike the late Mr Wetherby.'

'No, of course not, but you seem very friendly with Mrs Wetherby.' Even to the extent of playing errand boy for his hated superior, she thought. 'Sandwiches, wine . . .'

'She's a nice woman. It's the sort of thing she does.'

'How did you get on with Angela Hunnicliffe?'

'I scarcely knew her. Met her at school functions, when I must say I found her singularly unattractive. How Wetherby could have preferred her to Hannah totally escapes me – but I don't think I ever exchanged more than two words with her.'

194

All the same, her name had made him twitchy again. He didn't like talking about Angela Hunnicliffe, not at all.

'You're thinking what I'm thinking,' Mayo said after he'd let him go.

'That it was certainly Riach's car, but that doesn't mean it was Riach who was driving it? He could have lent it to Angela.'

'Or she could have taken it without him knowing. Find out where he keeps it.'

It was true that two witnesses had thought the driver of the Fiat had been a woman, but anyone seeing Riach's slight figure through the window might have mistaken him for a short-haired woman.

'Supposing it *was* Angela? What was she doing there, at Kyneford? And why borrow Riach's car? As far as we know, she still had her own.'

'We don't know that she had.' There had been no record of it being taken back to Automart for resale. Nor of it having been disposed of elsewhere, at least legally. The Driver and Vehicle Licensing Centre at Swansea had reported no change in the registered owner.

'Maybe she didn't want it recognised.'

However it was viewed, Riach's entry into the equation didn't make much sense. But enquiries were still going on, reports piling up. They were still interviewing at the school, though they hadn't yet reached the point where they needed to interview every boy; there were plenty of others who had not yet, for one reason and another, been seen.

Thinking of that, Abigail said, 'An interesting point's emerged about Riach. The lads have been keeping their ears open at the school while they've been interviewing folk, and word's going round that he hasn't yet got Wetherby's job.'

'I guessed as much.'

'It's not cut and dried, anyway. It's going to be advertised nationally and Riach will have to apply with the rest. He's saying that's a fair way to deal with it, but everyone who knows him believes he's seething that he didn't automatically come in for it. Apparently, it's not the first time it's happened to him – Riach was assistant to the previous Bursar and when he retired,

195

the same thing occurred. And Wetherby pipped him at the post.'

'So if killing him was a way of stepping automatically into his shoes, he made a big mistake. But I still can't see him putting himself at risk, even for that. He's too careful for that.'

'Yes, his alibi's watertight enough, but he left Hannah Wetherby at half-past twelve. How long did this girl, Rosie, stay with her for this fitting? Could it have taken an hour and a half? Has anybody checked that?'

'Scotty.'

They exchanged wry looks.

'So I'd better send Jenny over to talk to her before we see Hannah again, hadn't I?'

'Do that – and have a word with Vernon about that candle-stick, will you?'

19

'*How* much did you say?'

'If it had been genuine, Vernon says around £3,000.'

Mayo and his inspector stared uncomprehendingly at the garish object sitting on top of the filing cabinet, the safest place in the office, just in case Vernon had been wrong and the candlestick wasn't a copy, after all. Marvelling that a mere piece of household pottery, even if it was the real McCoy, could be worth that much. But Vernon Walcott, a knowledgeable auctioneer and valuer with fifty years in the trade, who ran the local fortnightly auction mart, was unlikely to have made a mistake. When Abigail had showed it to him, and he'd finished laughing, he said there was no way anyone he knew could have been fooled into thinking this was authentic. He showed her a teapot that was, and invited her to make a comparison and form her own judgement, but she couldn't for the life of her see the difference.

'Three *thousand*? For *this*?'

Vernon laughed cynically. 'It doesn't have to be beautiful. Just collectable. And that's nothing. I sold a Clarice Cliff vase a few months ago for nearly ten thousand.'

'Do you know Iris Osborne?' she'd asked.

'Good heavens, yes, known her for years! Everybody in antiques around here knows her – and takes cover when she enters the lists! She terrifies me,' said Vernon, whose unruffled urbanity had never been disturbed by anyone or anything. '*She* certainly wouldn't have made a mistake over this, if that's what you're thinking.'

'But would she buy it – would she buy a genuine one, I mean? It doesn't seem like something she'd bother with – the sort of stuff she likes to specialise in.'

Vernon Walcott's eyebrows rose cynically. 'It's not a case of liking, m'dear. No antique dealer worth their salt, certainly none I've ever met, and that includes Iris, would pass up *anything* if they saw the chance to make a bob or two on it. She didn't have to keep it, it's just a matter of finding a customer for it.'

'Have you come across an American woman called Angela Hunnicliffe, who's been collecting antiques for the last year?'

'Let's see . . . no, I don't think . . . Just a moment – American? Tall blonde? Yes, I do know her, vaguely. She comes along to the Saturday auction every couple of weeks, and she usually buys something. Small things, easily portable, things she can take back to the US, she says.'

'That's her. Would she have known Iris?'

'I don't know that she *doesn't*. Iris is often around the sale-room. The American lady could have bought one or two things from her, I suppose.'

'She won't be buying any more.'

'Gone back home, has she?'

No, Abigail told him, she had been identified as the woman who'd been shot and then found in the Kyne.

'My God!' Even Vernon's famous coolth was shaken.

'She wouldn't have bought this candlestick here?'

'*Here?* Try the market,' said Vernon Walcott. 'We deal with antiques, not junk.'

Mayo thought about that. About the clocks and clock parts he'd picked up in junk shops and on market stalls all over the place. One man's rubbish was indeed another man's treasure. He wouldn't have given tuppence for a piece looking like that candlestick up there, and wondered who might, but fashions came and went in antiques as in anything else. And if it were, as Walcott had suggested, worth something, it might, it just might, provide the missing link between Angela Hunnicliffe and the place where her body was found – in other words, a place very near Iris Osborne's cottage.

'Mrs Osborne?' Abigail repeated. '*Mrs Osborne?* Shooting Angela, then a week later going out and shooting Wetherby?' For all the jokes about Iris being trigger-happy, for all her reputed hard-headedness, she couldn't see the old lady deliberately and cold-bloodedly committing murder. 'She must be knocking eighty!'

Mayo gave her an old-fashioned look. 'Never known such a thing happen?'

'With respect, you haven't met her.' But the objections were only token. It was being naïve in the extreme to believe that you couldn't tell a murderer by their age, their face, the way they spoke, or how they lived their lives. Like Mayo, she'd known frankness, innocence and charm to conceal the vilest of human deeds. And she hadn't yet forgotten the look Iris Osborne had given her when she'd asked about a replica gun. She also remembered two pairs of small-sized gumboots, and one larger, in Mrs Osborne's porch – and that the body hadn't been shod when found.

'Then perhaps it's time I did meet her,' Mayo said.

'But why? I mean, why would she do such a thing?'

'Emotions run high when money's involved. Supposing Angela stumbled across some extremely valuable antique that she tried to sell to Iris – no, not that candlestick! – something really valuable. Say Iris wouldn't offer her enough for it and they quarrelled about it, culminating in Angela being shot? And supposing Wetherby knew Angela had gone to offer this antique to Iris? When she disappeared, and a woman turned up dead in the vicinity, he would immediately have been suspicious. Perhaps Iris silenced him for that reason.'

'It's a theory.' Abigail did not look convinced.

'Actually, more of a guess. But guessing's a step up from nothing, and isn't that where we start from every time – what if this, what if that?'

There was truth in his half-serious remarks. Educated guesses, suppositions, hypothetical theories, a shot in the dark, call it what you will, they all came to the same thing when there was a lack of hard evidence. Surprising, really, how often they led to logical conclusions – but usually only after a long, hard slog of trying, trying again and again. Abigail felt suddenly tired. She looked out at a sky heavy and sombre with rain clouds, thinking of the sun that was promised later by the weathermen, the predicted rise in temperature, longing for it, daring to hope the investigation would allow an hour or two of spare time again next weekend. Time to finish the tidying up of her winter garden that she'd started this weekend, before the For Sale sign went up. With difficulty, she brought her mind back to the present.

She said, 'Iris has never been properly interviewed. That cosy little session Jenny and I had with her doesn't rank as that.' But she thought, how could I ever have thought Wych Cottage cosy?

The stifling, choking sensation of unease as she'd stood there in the lane under the rose-streaked evening sky, looking at the dark silhouette of the house, came back. She was suddenly certain that the key to the whole affair lay at Wych Cottage, with Iris Osborne.

'What's getting at you, Abigail?' Mayo was suddenly very serious indeed.

She looked down and realised she'd moved from doodling on her scratch pad to folding what she'd scribbled on into smaller and smaller folds and was now trying to tear the result, impossible as tearing a telephone book. What *was* the matter with her? Tough, in control, Abigail Moon, police inspector, filled with silly fancies and imaginings?

She tried to smile. 'If we do go and see Iris again, what are the chances of a search warrant? It's probably the only way to get anything out of her.'

'Remote. Non-existent on present grounds. But we're a long way from that yet.'

Though maybe not as far away as all that. Facts were piling up – not an avalanche yet, but Mayo knew from experience how a case could become a landslide once certain facts were established. Yet when it did, as if it were an undeserved stroke of luck, it usually felt like an anticlimax – perhaps because of that puritanical Yorkshire streak that told him nothing was worth it if you didn't have to sweat blood for it. Sometimes he suspected he was happier when he had to fight every inch of the way, dig for every little fact, put them together piece by piece, but he never dwelt on that. Especially not at the moment. Just now he was grateful for anything that would wrap this case up. 'Let's go for it,' he decided, suddenly, positively, with that authoritative certainty which energised everyone around. 'Wych Cottage and Iris Osborne.'

With a great effort, Abigail pushed aside the morbid reluctance to return there. 'OK, let's go.'

It hadn't been considered necessary to stop rehearsals for *The Beggar's Opera*, due to be performed in another six weeks, on Founder's Day, especially since most of the cast didn't yet know their lines, or their movements, including the handsome youth cast as Macheath, who'd no objection to playing a dashing highwayman, but had nearly withdrawn from the cast when he found he was actually expected to *sing*.

Were all school productions like this? wondered Jenny Platt, watching from the darkened auditorium. The cast fooling around, the girl playing Polly Peachum behaving like a bored diva, the teacher directing operations at the hair-tearing stage – an exceedingly tall, weedy-looking individual by the name of Roger Barmforth, who called everyone darling and uttered 'Oh God,' in a doom-filled voice at regular intervals. Remembering plays from her own schooldays, in which she'd always been cast as the maid, she decided they might be.

'*If with me you'd fondly stray, over the hills and far away,*' sang Macheath persuasively to his languishing Polly.

So this was Polly Peachum. Or Rosie Deventer, the girl she'd come to see. Evidently regarding all this as a bit of a drag. Nothing apparently in her mind except clothes, make-up, boys. Seventeen, going on twenty-five, and not doing anybody any favours by still being at school, not even herself. Wasting everybody's time. She looked intelligent enough – she had to be intelligent to have reached the Lower Sixth at Princess Mary's, where most of the girls were expected to go on to university or vocational career training – but Rosie didn't seem to be going anywhere, except heading for marriage and two kids before she was twenty – well, kids, anyway. Unless somebody got hold of her and shook some sense into her. Jenny guessed it was only parental pressure that was keeping her on at school.

'You like acting, Rosie?' Jenny asked to break the ice when the rehearsal had dragged to a close, and she had guided Rosie to a seat at the back of the hall, though she was thinking on the same lines, had she but known it, as Hannah Wetherby, some time before: that Rosie was not much overburdened with the necessity actually to *act* in this part she'd been selected for. And she did have a good soprano voice.

Rosie rolled her eyes. 'It's all right. Better than school. *Boring*, that is. Dead boring.' She had a painstakingly concealed middle-class voice and, out of her stage clothes, still looked like a tart. She had on a red, black-spotted skirt so tight Jenny wondered how it could contain her substantial bum, decorated with a baby frill round the curved hem which was split to her crotch at the front. With very little fabric to speak of between that and the end of her cleavage. Hair growing out from a blonde tint, a mane of permed curls. Big brown eyes.

Jenny explained why she was here. 'Just to check on the time you went for your costume fitting at Mrs Wetherby's. Your lunch hour, wasn't it? Which is what time?'

'Twelve to half-past one.'

'That's school dinner hour?'

'Right.'

'So you'd finished eating by . . .?'

'I don't eat that grot! I had a Mars bar.'

'And how long did it take you to get to Mrs Wetherby?'

'Ten minutes.' Jenny raised her eyebrows. 'I have a mountain bike.'

'Which way did you go?'

'Same as always. Across Danvers Street and up Vanson Hill.' The girl looked at her watch. 'If that's all, I have a date.' She glanced towards the door, where the handsome, sulky youth who was playing Macheath was hanging impatiently about.

Jenny, who'd gone to some trouble to talk to Rosie here rather than embarrass her by interviewing her during school hours, or at home, was annoyed. She thought of her own date, put off yet again. Rosie snapped her chewing gum, which annoyed her more. She said sharply, 'No, you didn't go that way, Rosie. Think again.'

'Oh yes, I did! I remember, 'cos I always stop and look in Benetton's window, in case they have some new things in. I saw a fantastic top and I went in and asked how much only they were out of my size.'

'Rosie, there was a diversion on Danvers Street that day, all day. A burst water main, and traffic was directed round by Victoria Road. You couldn't have called in at Benetton's.'

'Must be thinking of the wrong day, then.'

Jenny clenched her teeth. This was like chipping cement with a nail file. 'I don't think you went to see Mrs Wetherby at all, did you?'

Rosie snapped her gum again and Jenny resisted the impulse to shake her, hard. 'Rosie,' she said, 'I asked you a question. Where were you when you were supposed to be having that costume fitting?'

Rosie's glance strayed once more, very briefly, towards the door where Macheath still lounged.

'Right. Macheath!' Jenny called. 'Have you a minute?'

'He has a name of his own, you know! But there's no call to bother him.' She raised her own voice. 'Be with you in a minute, Andy!'

'Well?'

'OK, the sodding costume didn't need fitting, it's not too tight, never mind what old Barmpot says!' She glanced scornfully towards where the released Roger Barmforth, with a young female teacher, was collecting scripts and props. 'So I rang Mrs Wetherby and she said it would be all right, I needn't go. She told me she wouldn't say anything if I didn't.'

'So where were you?'

Her eyes strayed to the door and back again. She said hurriedly, 'If you must know, I was with my boyfriend.'

Jenny would have bet her next month's wages that it wasn't Macheath.

She wasn't a vindictive young woman, but she couldn't help feeling a malicious pleasure as she rang into the station and relayed the information she'd just obtained before going thankfully off duty. Oh, Scotty, she thought, Mayo'll have your guts for garters. He'll have you back on traffic duty before you can say Caramello.

Strangely enough, now that darkness had really come, the cottage looked ordinary, unthreatening, a small chocolate-box affair, not at all inimical. Or perhaps, Abigail thought with a vestigial memory of her earlier apprehensions, that was simply because its owner wasn't here. She hadn't answered the door, the cottage was in complete darkness. As they walked round to the back, and Mayo pointed to the hard standing, the concrete slab tucked discreetly out of sight and just large enough for a small car, she saw it was vacant.

A vehicle drew up as they walked round to the front of the cottage again. It proved to be driven by Jared Bysouth, returning to the farm, blocking the lane with his Land Rover. Being a good neighbour once more, nosing around and preventing anyone who'd no business at the cottage from escaping.

'Oh, it's you, Inspector,' he called, leaning out of the window. 'I wondered what was going on. If you're looking for Iris, you're out of luck. She was backing her car out when I passed about half an hour ago.'

He stuck his elbow out of the window, looking ready for a chat, but Abigail said, 'Thanks, Mr Bysouth, we'll come back in the morning.'

Deflated, she looked back at the house as she slid back into the driving seat of the car. She had screwed herself up to a pitch of expectancy, and now, prosaically, the interview would have to be put on hold. Finding out whether Iris was a killer or not would simply have to wait until morning.

As they drove back, Mayo sat next to her, picking up messages, one of which was to lighten his days for some time to come, the other to prove crucial to the immediate situation. Acting Sergeant Farrar came though, jubilation triumphing over the crackling static, with news of a patrol car, responding to a 999 over a fight outside the Lion and Lamb which had arisen during a drugs handover. One man had been stabbed and was in a critical condition, several others were in custody and one of them was offering information about the man suspected of shooting and killing Danny Fermanagh in exchange for leniency. 'We've got him, gaffer,' Farrar exclaimed, forgetting in his excitement to sound like the world-weary, seen-it-all sergeant he aspired to be.

'Hallelujah!' said Abigail when she heard the glad tidings, saw Mayo punching the air. And then fell silent and listened, as he did, when Farrar started speaking again.

'Jenny rang in a report on that interview she did. Want to hear it?'

20

Sam Leadbetter never knew what sudden urgency drove him to push aside his writing and immediately leg it out for Hannah's house. He only knew that the need was as imperative as a sneeze, something he couldn't have stopped and had no control over. And that he had to prevent her: Hannah, at the moment, was dangerous, volatile, and liable to go off at any moment, with who could say what disastrous consequences?

He could have saved himself fifteen minutes if he'd been able to cut across the playing fields and use the gate near the house. But even Sam didn't entertain the possibility of scaling the school's chainlink fencing, behind which grew a robust hawthorn hedge – and to drive via the ring road would *add* at least fifteen minutes. No alternative but to walk along Kelsey Road and turn right into Vanson Hill.

The night was soft and springlike after the day's rain, the sap was rising and even in his hurry he noticed the faint flower scents drifting from the gardens he passed. He had to pause at the hospital gates for an ambulance to turn out and gather speed as it raced urgently down the hill; the hospital itself stood berthed like a great, lighted ship in the lee of the hill, giving out its subliminal message that here the desperate business of life and death went on all the time, separate from the rest of the world, regardless of its material pressures. A sense of nameless panic caused him to lengthen his strides into a jog.

A full moon sailed high, sending a wash of cold light over the garden as he turned into Hannah's drive, the delicate scent of a single daffodil made nauseous when multiplied into that of a thousand, naturalised as they were under the trees here, increased year by year . . . a heaviness of lilies, funeral chapels, hints of mortality. As a sitting tenant, it was rumoured that Hannah would now have the legal option to buy at a reasonable price. How would she be able to bring herself to continue living here?

The front of the house was in darkness. He didn't bother to

ring the bell but tried the side door, tutted at finding it unlocked, but then, seeing a wedge of light driven out into the darkness from the conservatory, he moved quietly round towards the back.

Fifteen minutes earlier, Hannah had been sitting in Charles's study, from which led the conservatory extension. Drawers were open, piles of papers were stacked on the desk in front of her, but she felt incapable of doing anything except stare in front of her. There wasn't much she needed to do in actual fact; he had typically left his affairs, as was to be expected, in perfect order.

She sat facing the conservatory, where the expensively installed uplighting and downlighting mutated the spiky leaves of palms and other nameless plants into rapiers against the glass, and limned the twelve foot high cheese plant she hated, throwing demon shadows of its monstrous holed leaves on to the walls. That, at least, was weeping for him, dripping sticky honeydew from the points of its leaves on to the floor and on to a small polished table beneath it, something it had never done before. She hadn't either moved the table or wiped away the secretion.

She'd had the lighting, the whole extension in fact, copied from an illustrated feature in one of the magazines devoted to showing the interiors of other people's homes, but now she hated it. There was garden lighting, too, but rather than enhance the features there, the coloured lights had the effect of making the waving branches of the trees seem menacing and grotesque. Charles, who rarely commented on her choice of furnishings or decor, had, strangely enough, liked it.

What had it felt like to be Charles, sitting here, night after night, his Wagner CDs going at full volume, looking out across the conservatory? Had he, too, been trying to push back the jungle that was just outside? Had he had any intimations of his own death? Her Catholicism had always induced a certain fatalism in her, she had believed you died when your destiny was fulfilled, but now her beliefs were being strangely tested.

Why did he have to die? Why did he have to be what he was? They could have had such a wonderful life together. Instead, for

206

years she had been like a rabbit transfixed in the headlights of a car, held in thrall. Until she had, suddenly, found herself able to move again, felt life coursing through her veins. Alive. Vibrant. Active and powerful. But it had all drained away, leaving her empty again.

The house was so quiet you could have heard a fly crawling on the ceiling.

Then she saw, or imagined she saw, some movement in the shadows of the garden. She squeezed her eyes shut, like a child who thinks if she can't see the menace in front of her, it won't be there, as she'd done every time Charles lifted his hand to her. Put her hands over her ears to shut out words that wounded like arrows. But now, her eyes flew open, fancying she heard the faint creak of the conservatory door handle. Heart jumping, she remembered it wasn't locked. She hadn't yet become accustomed to going round the house and locking up, every evening before supper, as he had always done. Meticulous in that, as in everything else. After that first leap, her heart settled into a slow, hard, painful thumping, and she strained her ears for the next, slightest sound, sitting as if turned to marble.

A clock chimed. Unnaturally loud sounds penetrated the silent house. The traffic, whooshing by on Tilbourne Road. A wailing ambulance siren, a sound so common in this house that she normally never noticed it. Charles's long-case clock sounding a measured tock, tock. The house was very empty.

Gradually, she heard it, no imagination this time, a halting footfall exploring the dark, finding it hard to discover the step up from the conservatory into the study. Still she sat motionless as the door opened and the air from outside lifted the fronds of a huge fern, making it shiver like a live thing, and the figure moved slowly forwards, out of the shadows.

A small figure with white hair.

She was wearing grey, unlike the sweet-pea colours she and the Queen Mother normally favoured, an old-fashioned suit with a Gor-ray skirt she must have had hidden in her wardrobe for years. Indeed as she came nearer, a faint, sickeningly sweet smell of orris, patchouli, strawberry, of Body Shop clothes-protector sachets, came with her.

Hannah felt a shiver of something almost akin to anticipation. Keep her talking, wasn't that what they always said you must do in these sort of situations? Calmly, as though you felt no astonishment at this invasion of privacy from someone you hardly knew.

'Goodness, you gave me a fright!' Leaning back, fanning herself exaggeratedly, she let her other hand trail over the chair arm. 'What are you doing here?'

'Well, I'm beginning to think it's about time we got our act together, as my grandchildren say. I've been visited by the police, Hannah, and I've no intention of taking the blame for something that was no fault of mine.'

She was mad, barking mad, but Hannah had suspected this from the beginning. Mad, or dangerous. Had been certain of it ever since she had received that parcel she'd had to pretend was a new pair of scales.

Remembering what it had actually contained, again she felt that shiver of excitement, a remembered thrill of fear, almost sexual. Her trailing hand sought for her handbag, on the floor next to her chair, while she spoke: words, something, nothing, anything, it didn't matter. The soft leather bag had a magnetic catch, and opened easily. She pulled the flap open and her hand curled around cold metal. Pulling it gently out, she felt its solid weight in her palm. She raised her arm, her finger on the trigger, and brought her other hand up to it. She squeezed, once.

This is a nightmare; the day Angela died, all over again.

The unexpected pull that had made her stagger, the bang that had made her ears ring and ring, the smell of cordite, Angela, toppling forward, like one of those target dolls at a fair . . .

And now . . . the same thing, happening again. Iris Osborne this time, with blood blossoming from her chest.

The conservatory door was still open and Sam came charging through. He stopped at the sight of the gun in her hand.

'Oh, Sam! Oh, my God, Sam! She would have killed me if I hadn't got the gun from her – just like she killed Angela, and Charles.'

'Let me have the gun, Hannah.' His voice was stony.

She looked at her hand, holding the weapon. It was quite steady, when it should have been shaking. For a moment, she hesitated. It would be so easy. Then she allowed her hand to tremble as she passed the gun over to Sam. Let herself cry, big tears spilling from huge, frightened brown eyes as she raised her head to him. In the circle of lamplight, with the old woman's body on the floor six feet away, she stood waiting for his arms to encircle her.

Instead, he walked away from her, towards the telephone. 'What are you doing, Sam?'

'I'm ringing the police, what do you think?'

21

The tape recorder in Iris Osborne's hand was slippery with sweat. Hospitals were always overheated. She felt under the pillow for one of her lace-edged, freesia-scented hankies and wiped it fastidiously. Normally cool and calculating, she was unused to nerves, and the fact that she was shaking disorientated her. But she had to get this recording right, listen to it over and over again before committing herself to making that statement the police needed. She would think it over, carefully, do it in her own time, in her own way. They weren't pressing her too much, yet. She was off the danger list but far from well. The bullet that madwoman had fired at her had missed any vital organs – the shock had done far more harm.

She must do this before Eleanor came and began fussing and lecturing her again on how foolish she'd been. Then she could concentrate on getting well and being allowed to go back to her own home and her own affairs.

She pressed a calming hand to the bosom of her fluffy turquoise bedjacket, drew a deep breath and took her mind back to the day when she'd first met Angela Hunnicliffe, through one of Iris's own advertisements. That was where it had all begun, when Angela had rung and asked whether she was interested in buying a piece of Clarice Cliff pottery.

Iris herself didn't admire Art Deco in any shape or form, but she had customers who did. Clarice Cliff was avidly collected and fetched phenomenal prices. She couldn't afford *not* to be interested. She'd said she would very much like to see it and arranged for Angela to bring it to Wych Cottage.

'Where did you come across this?' she asked interestedly, when she'd examined the candlestick and calculated what she could get for it.

'Oh, a car boot sale,' Angela answered evasively, with the irritating giggle Iris was to become familiar with. She was a rather colourless blonde, and her little girl ways sat oddly with her height. Iris didn't believe her. Maybe she had picked up a similar candlestick, but not this one. She knew Angela was lying for some reason, and trying to cover up rather clumsily – people at car boot sales in the past had let fortunes slip through their fingers for fifty pence, but not nowadays. The lie made her wary. Anyone capable of lying about one thing could lie about others. But a simple thing like a lie never worried Iris too much and, thinking of the profit she was going to make, she didn't press the matter.

As they chatted over the tea and biscuits Iris always provided for her clients as part of the general softening-up process before the hard bargaining started, Iris learned that Angela had come over here from America with her husband and while he'd been very much taken up with his job, she'd been left with nothing to occupy her empty days. As a way of overcoming her boredom, she'd started going to auction rooms, markets and antique fairs to pass the time, and discovered an interest in porcelain and pottery. As her collection, and her knowledge, grew, she gradually become more discriminating, and dissatisfied with her earlier, naïve, 'finds'. She had begun a little modest trading to offload some of them. And that was how it had come about that she had telephoned in response to an advert of Iris's in the back of one of the glossy magazines devoted to antiques.

Iris found to her surprise that Angela could drive as hard a bargain as she could herself. This was something she understood, and she looked at the young woman with more respect than she had at first. Their meeting started an association that was to their mutual benefit. Angela looked out for anything Iris might be interested in buying from her, and Iris did likewise for her. She was quite sorry that Angela would be returning to the States within the year, when Brad Hunnicliffe's exchange here ended, they'd become quite good friends.

The last time Angela had knocked on the door of Wych Cottage she had been sheltering from the pelting rain under an umbrella, having paddled through the widening mud-scree the ceaseless downpours of the last week or two had made of the lane. 'My, you're going to be under water if this deluge doesn't stop soon!' she announced, prophetically had she but known it, as Iris ushered her in.

'Pray that it *does* stop, then.' Iris was beginning to be very worried indeed at the amount of water that was sweeping down the lane to the dip where Wych Cottage stood.

'This weather is something I shall *not* miss when I've gone,' said Angela, taking off her rubber boots and leaving them and her umbrella in the porch.

'Gone?'

Angela then told Iris that she was in fact returning to America the next day. Her husband had unexpectedly been called back to the States – had already left, in fact, to spend a couple of weeks with his ailing father before taking up his new position in San Francisco. Angela had arranged to stay behind for that period, in order to attend a country house sale she didn't want to miss, where there might be bargains to be had, and also to arrange for her china collection to be shipped over to America. 'My suitcases are packed, all I have to do is leave the keys with our landlord. But I can't say I'm sorry to be going.'

'No doubt you'll be glad to get home, quite apart from leaving all this rain behind.'

But Angela said not really, in fact she'd rather begun to enjoy being over here, now that she'd found – now that she'd found such an absorbing interest. She'd flushed a little and Iris thought, shrewdly, she hadn't been going to say that, there's a man. She'd suspected before now that Angela, if not her husband, Brad, was finding their marriage a strain. But lately, Angela went on, she hadn't been so comfortable around Lavenstock. She'd hesitated, as though not expecting to be believed, and then rushed on . . . We-ell, it sounded paranoic, but she'd had the definite feeling lately that someone had been following her, and not just once or twice, but several times. 'It's weird!' Her hands twisted nervously and she shivered, but then she shrugged it off with a forced laugh and unpacked the latest piece of china she'd acquired for Iris.

They'd struck an amicable bargain, and Angela had been ready to leave, standing in her stockinged feet waiting for Iris to fetch her mac, when the knock came at the door. A strange woman stood there, dripping, rain streaming from her unprotected hair and from the light, showerproof jacket she wore, useless in such a deluge, her eyes wild.

'You have Angela Hunnicliffe in there!' she announced, accusingly, and before Iris could stop her, had forced her way in.

212

Iris, protesting, hurried after her into the sitting-room where Angela and the woman Iris later learnt was Hannah Wetherby faced each other like a pair of tigresses. Iris was outraged, being forced to endure this vulgar cat-fight, here in her own pretty sitting-room, but could do nothing to prevent it: Angela, pale as death, and Hannah, hair plastered to her head, her inadequate shoes squelching mud all over Iris's precious Persian rugs with every movement she made. Spitting out, in a low, furious voice, that she knew all about her husband and Angela Hunnicliffe, and that it was something she would not tolerate any longer. This was obviously the person who had been following Angela – she hadn't imagined it, then.

If Angela had simply said, in answer to the accusation, that she was going away the following day, maybe the other woman would have calmed down. But Angela didn't. She retorted that if Hannah hadn't been such a frigid bitch in the first place maybe Charles Wetherby wouldn't have had to look elsewhere.

Hannah could barely contain herself. She hissed furiously, 'And maybe if he'd treated you like he's treated me, you'd be frigid towards him, too!'

Angela didn't draw away as Iris would have done, but took a step nearer. 'You're hysterical,' she said coldly, and slapped Hannah's face.

However Iris searched her memory, she could not be quite certain of how it had appeared to her then – whether Hannah deliberately shot Angela, had meant to do so all along (though if not, why had she come equipped with a gun?) or whether it was, as she said afterwards, an uncontrollable impulse that came over her, that she'd only meant to threaten Angela. Iris, in view of what had happened to *her*, now believed it was certainly the latter. But whatever the truth was, she had pulled a pistol from her bag and in a moment it was all over. Angela was dead.

Iris couldn't believe it. Ten minutes ago, in this lamplit room with the dark weather comfortably on the other side of the windows, she'd been sitting in front of a roaring fire, having a cosy chat and a cup of tea, eating shortbreads. And now, here she was, with an armed madwoman in front of her and the dead body of her friend at her feet. Her heart was pounding ominously. She shook with fear and reminded herself she was no longer a young woman. And then she looked at the intruder and

213

saw she was also trembling, even more uncontrollably, staring at Angela's body with horror and with the gun dangerously hanging from her fingers.

Iris breathed deeply and took two courageous steps forward. 'I think you'd better give me that,' she said, and took the gun from Hannah Wetherby's thankfully unresisting grasp. She pressed the safety catch, as her husband had always taught her to do with firearms, and then, not knowing what to do with the weapon, she pushed it into the nearest drawer, which happened to be the top one of the walnut bow-front chest which the Bysouths had later carried upstairs for her. And with so many other things to worry about, her brain had promptly blanked out the memory of ever having seen it; she'd totally forgotten it until her mind and body acted almost in unison to prevent that girl from the contract cleaners seeing what was in the opened drawer.

She had eventually, not knowing what to do with it, simply wrapped the gun in layers of cotton wool and bubble-wrap, put it in a shoe-box and posted it back to Hannah. Let her find the means of disposing of it!

Hannah was standing as if rooted to the spot. 'Oh God,' she whispered, almost soundlessly. 'Oh God, what have I done? I *never* lose my temper.'

'Come away,' Iris said, averting her eyes from the body, putting off the decision she knew would have to be made, later, when they were both calmer. Taking refuge in practicalities because the woman frightened her to death. She could go off at any moment like a time bomb. 'You need to dry off.'

Hannah allowed herself to be led into the kitchen, where Iris found some cooking brandy and poured generous measures into two glasses. 'Drink this,' she ordered, sliding one across to Hannah, before reaching for a couple of dry towels from the tumble-dryer. Hannah stood like a doll while Iris helped her off with her jacket and pushed it into the dryer. Her sweater, underneath, was damp and her skirt was sopping, too. 'Dry your hair while I fetch you a bathrobe, and we'll put everything else in the machine,' Iris commanded. She wanted this woman out of her house, as soon as possible, but there were things to be decided and she wouldn't be any help while her teeth were chattering and she was in that near catatonic state. Iris's feet, as she went upstairs, felt leaden; she had to pause for breath on the landing, and wait for her heart to resume its normal pace. She was very much aware that she was too old for all this.

Hot, sweet tea might have been a wiser recommendation for shock than spirits, but after the first sip or two of the brandy, Iris began to feel better; Hannah downed hers as if it were lemonade and the return of some colour into her cheeks showed it had done her no harm, either.

While her visitor was stripping off her skirt and sweater, Iris couldn't help noticing how underweight she was; neither did the long thin cicatrix of a healed scar right down her upper arm escape her notice. There were also the faint yellow marks of a fading bruise on her neck. Iris looked at her huge dark eyes and facial bones, and the hair that, now it was nearly dry, gave hints that it might be thick and glossy, and thought this woman might once have been very beautiful, but that it had been some time since.

'Well, don't you think you owe me some sort of explanation?' she demanded at last. 'Your name, for a start?'

'Yes,' Hannah said, an unnatural calm descending on her, and began to speak. When she'd finished, Iris said, 'If he's treated you like that, why do you want him back? Why didn't you just leave him?'

'You don't understand. If I left him now, I should have nothing. After all, I've put up with him for all these years, provided a front for him, pretended to be a model wife for a model husband – why should I have to leave everything, be reduced to skimping and saving, having nothing? He owes me for that. I've had a life of sorts. Now I can have a better one . . .'

Could she possibly have *forgotten* the corpse lying bleeding into the hearthrug in the other room?

Iris had asked herself a dozen times since why she hadn't called the police, then and there. But she knew the answer, really. The police were the last people she wanted around, poking their noses where they weren't wanted. In the event, it was Reuben Bysouth she rang, not sure how far she could trust him, but knowing no one else to turn to, after she and Hannah Wetherby had dragged Angela to the cold-room door and tipped her down

215

those wicked stairs to get her out of the way until they could think of what to do with the body.

'I'd like you to get rid of that car in the lane for me, Reuben,' she said when he'd sloshed down the lane in the Land Rover and come in, shaking off water like a dog. 'Anywhere, anyhow, as long as it can't be traced. You can have what you can get for it.'

Angela's car. His bribe for listening, without comment, to her carefully edited account of what had happened; for his complicity in what would later have to be done. Unshockable, he understood perfectly well, without her saying so, why she hadn't contacted the police. He did ask her who the woman was who'd done the shooting, but when she refused to give either her name or the dead woman's, he didn't press her. What he didn't know, he couldn't be forced to tell. No one understood the need for keeping schtum at times better than Reuben Bysouth.

'And you can drop these keys in at the Atkins Inquiry Agency.'

Iris had typed a short letter, as if from Angela, signing it with a reasonable facsimile of her signature, copied from a receipt for china, explaining her departure the following day, and put it in an envelope, together with the bunch of keys that were labelled, with foolish disregard for safety, in Iris's opinion, '9 Elton Street'.

'All right,' Reuben said, 'I'll do that, and I'll see to the car, but what you going to do with *her* then?' He jerked his head towards the low door that led into the cold-room. 'Can't keep her where she is.' He stared reflectively out of the streaming window, where the rain still lashed down. 'I could get rid of her for you.'

Iris followed his gaze, across the sodden fields to the pig units. 'No!' She wasn't squeamish, but even she couldn't contemplate that. 'Leave her where she is, until I have a think what to do.'

'Don't leave her too long,' Reuben said. 'She'll smell worse than a slaughterhouse by tomorrow.'

But that night, the waters rose and rushed down the lane and swirled and sucked around the cottage and in through the cold-room's air space. The pressure forced in and broke away the rusty iron grating covering the vent. And as the water level rose even further and eventually seeped in under the doors to cover the ground floor of the cottage, the body in the cold-room rose with it, floating on the surface, until it was level with the vent and was sucked outside with the current, to be borne away on the flood.

22

Hannah had never in her life been in a police station but its severe impersonality, she thought with that new, not-part-of-all-this feeling, made it an appropriate place to tell her bleak story, unemotionally and without passion. That story which had been leading up to this point for years, if she had but realised it, but she had only known it with certainty after she'd fired that first shot.

She had, since being arrested, discovered qualities in herself, a courage she hadn't dreamed she could possess, that made her ready to accept the consequences of what she'd done. She *was* afraid of breaking down, however, of letting her defences crumble in front of these accusing strangers. No – she quelled the trembling within – she would *not* do that: she'd learned the hard way how to keep a rein on her emotions, not to show outwardly what she was feeling, even when she was being ripped apart, mentally and physically, and she could summon up the endurance this last time.

She'd already told, as calmly as if she were talking about another person, her version of what had happened on that wild, unforgettable day at Wych Cottage. The worst day of a life that had long since ceased to have any joy in it. They told her that Iris Osborne – not dead, she'd made a botch shot there, and that had been her undoing – had also made a statement, and it must have tallied with hers, because they seemed basically satisfied, up to that point.

But there were still questions, questions. Finding herself capable of unexpected determination, she had demanded that the questions should not be put to her by a man and they had, amazingly, agreed. Her interrogators were the russet-haired inspector, Moon, and a younger version, deceptively gentle, soft-eyed and pretty, a detective constable called Jenny Platt. Hannah had asked if Tracey Matthews could be there as well, she who'd been so bumblingly kind to her before, and to her surprise, they'd eventually agreed to that as well.

The first thing they wanted to know was why she'd been following Angela, and she knew immediately this was going to be the hardest question of all, because it was something she'd asked herself again and again, and she still didn't know the answer. What had she expected to gain from following that woman – and why had she picked on that gawky, unattractive creature, out of all the others? Perhaps it had been just because of that – that even such a Plain Jane as Angela Hunnicliffe was more alluring to Charles than his own once-adored, once-beautiful wife. Stalking, they were calling it. Why were you stalking her?

It wasn't only men who stalked, through revenge at being sexually spurned. That she knew. Then why? To put some sort of hex on to the woman? She deliberately hadn't been too careful, she had *wanted* Angela to suspect someone was behind her, a shadow, knowing what she did, where she went, who she met, to be frightened, even though she'd had no means of knowing if it had worked. Confrontation, then? It must really have been that, though she had never intended to go so far as to kill her. But when she told them this, she could see they didn't believe her, and who could blame them, when she'd had the gun, so ready to hand, so snugly convenient, sitting in her bag?

'Where did you get that gun?' asked Inspector Moon, watching her every expression, while DC Platt took careful notes of everything that was said, shared the questions, and the tape recorder whirred at the side. She had refused a solicitor, despite their advice. She didn't want to be prevented from doing this her own way, however deeply it would incriminate her.

'Please answer the question. Where did you get the gun?' the inspector repeated.

'The gun? Oh, I've had it for years. It belonged to my father and I found it after he died, when I was clearing out his things. He used to be a member of a gun club, I didn't know he still had it. He taught me how to use it, he said you never knew when such knowledge might come in useful.'

Target practice in the garden. A dartboard nailed to a tree. Shooting at magpies and squirrels. Bang, bang. Watching them fall, dead. Vermin, her father had said.

'Why did you keep it?'

'For the same reason. I thought it might come in useful some day.'

'You mean you intended to use it on your husband?'

'My husband? Don't you understand, yet? I *loved* Charles!'

'But you've admitted you shot him dead.'

'I'm not denying that. I would never have killed him – but you see, I found out that he knew . . . He knew that I'd killed Angela.' But that was only the half of it.

You fool, Charles had said, she would have been gone the next day. Why did you have such a fixation on her? It was all over anyway, bar a farewell drink after she'd been to see that woman at Kyneford about a plate she had to sell. But she had never turned up. Philosophically, he'd accepted he'd been stood up, that Angela had gone off to America without bothering to say a proper goodbye, but then a body had turned up near Kyneford, and he'd known. That it had to be Angela, that Hannah had killed her. How had he known that? Well, how did Charles always know everything about her? A process of osmosis? Black magic? More simple than that this time. He discovered she'd been using John Riach's car – some busybody had seen her in it and told him – and he would not stop until he found out the rest of it, employing his usual subtle methods.

'Why did Mr Riach agree to lend you his car?' the young DC asked.

'To spite Charles.' The truth, out before she thought of the consequences, to both of them. 'He thought the reason I didn't drive was simply because Charles didn't approve. He saw encouraging me to do something Charles didn't like as a way of getting at Charles behind his back – he's always detested him. But you mustn't blame John, he didn't know –' She shouldn't have said that, it hadn't been necessary, but what did it matter now?

The inspector was looking at her with that look all the police seemed to have developed, that intent, steady look that made you say stupid things, muddle up the truth, unless you were a better liar than she was. 'Didn't know what, Mrs Wetherby?'

'He didn't know that – I'd lost my licence.' For the first time she felt herself falter. 'I lost it after I once nearly killed a child, driving while I was drunk. She ran out from behind an ice-cream van, I didn't have much chance, but I might have avoided her altogether if I'd been sober.'

I drank because my husband had stopped loving me. Or did he stop loving me because I drank? Who knows which came first? Can either of these three women begin to imagine what it felt like to live in the same house as someone you love and never to be kissed tenderly, not even when you were having sex, or hugged, or even touched, except to hurt? Year after year after year? No, they would never understand that particular kind of hell. How desolate you felt, so that drink became a comfort, then a necessity?

'I didn't care about having my licence taken away, in fact I was glad. I felt I didn't ever *want* to drive, not ever again. The accident stopped me drinking, though – next time, I might have really killed someone. Not someone who deserved it, but someone innocent, like that little girl.' A nightmare for the rest of my life. 'But I needed a car to follow Angela . . . and John Riach asked no questions.'

She'd learned, some time since, that John would have done practically anything she asked. Implicit in this was the expectation that some day he would be repaid . . .

'Angela Hunnicliffe's body was found on 4th March,' said Moon. 'You say your husband was immediately suspicious and confronted you, and the truth emerged. You knew that he knew what you had done, and was prepared to keep silent, yet twelve days later you killed him. Had he threatened to tell the truth?'

'No, no – it suited him to have a hold over me!'

'Then something happened between you and John Riach when you lunched together that day, to make you act as you did?'

It had quite suddenly become clear to Hannah what she had to do. She had almost laughed, wondering why, when it was so simple, she'd never thought of it before. 'I saw him staring at a bruise on my neck. I saw the expression on his face and I knew he was going to say something, to sympathise with me. If I'd told him what was going on, there would have been no going back from then. I could see the words almost beginning to choke him, but I managed to stop him from saying anything. I . . .'

'Why, Mrs Wetherby? Why were you afraid of him knowing that your husband had been hurting you? He was a friend.'

'I *was* afraid – of what he might do. There's a violence in his nature. I'm an expert at recognising that. Not the same sort of violence as Charles used, but cold, and in the end even more deadly, I should imagine. You see, I knew he – I knew what he felt about me, though he'd never said anything. I didn't feel that way about him, but even so, I couldn't let him do something he might regret, just for me. He has been kind to me, in his own way. So I stopped him from speaking and packed him off.'

'He might have been able to help,' Tracey Matthews said, unexpectedly. 'Or somebody might have. If you'd told some-body what was happening.' She blushed and subsided, with a quick apologetic glance for her intrusion, but the inspector smiled at her.

'I couldn't,' Hannah said. 'I could never tell anyone. It was a matter of pride, for one thing. Don't you see how *humiliating* it is to admit you've allowed your husband to beat you for years?'

'Yes,' said DC Platt, 'I can see that's hard, especially if you try and bear it alone.'

'I couldn't leave him. Nor tell anyone. My faith meant that my marriage vows were sacred. As for help . . . I did try, once. I went to a nun, when I was on a weekend retreat. I was told I must try and forgive.'

For a long moment, nobody said anything. The tape whirred, the workaday sounds from outside continued. Hannah heard her own voice repeating in her head what she'd just said. It sounded hollow. She'd tried so hard to believe in it: the sanctity of marriage, turning the other cheek. And what had it led to?

She said, 'For a while, it worked. I did everything he wanted, turned a blind eye to his philanderings, became a good wife again, so that even he could find no reason for hitting me. I listened to him. Oh, how I listened to him! Sermonising, lecturing, pontificating. All for my own good, of course! It wasn't easy, but I'd had years to learn submission, and I had my compensations, as I've always had, freedom of a sort, plenty of money. He was never mean. I tried to see him as the man I fell in love with. The peace didn't last. And when he found out about Angela, it was worse than ever.' Suddenly, Hannah wanted this done with. She said, almost impatiently, 'Something had to break, sooner or later, and it was me. I have never been able to stand pity, and when I saw it in John Riach's eyes, something snapped. So when Rosie Deventer rang a few minutes later, to complain about having to come over for a fitting, I told her it didn't matter. I had already decided I was going to kill Charles.'

A different quality of silence fell. Hannah felt it hanging now, like a heavy curtain of condemnation. These were women, she told herself, just as she was, sisters under the skin, and she had, up to now, felt their sympathy. But now she had trespassed even the boundaries of their understanding. They were, after all, also officers of the law, committed to upholding it. Then the inspector, the one she had thought was the toughest of the three, put out a hand and touched hers. Brief as the touch was, swiftly withdrawn, so that Hannah thought she might almost have imagined it, it gave her the impetus she needed to go on.

'I went upstairs for the gun, put it in my handbag, and walked across the playing fields to the school. I didn't care if anybody saw me, but nobody did. The dinner hour was over, school was beginning again, though the admin people hadn't returned from their lunch. I walked into Charles's office, gave him some reason for being there, a book I knew he had in the office. I walked to the bookshelves behind him and I said, "This is for all the things you've ever done to me, dear Charles," and I shot him.'

Bang, bang. Dead. Vermin.

'The paper – in his mouth?' asked the inspector, gently, after a while.

Hannah laughed. 'Oh yes, the paper! I tore off the top page of that report he'd been yammering on about for weeks, and it gave me the greatest pleasure to make him, just for once, eat his own words. And then I went home.'

But that wasn't how it had felt. She had never knowingly broken the law before . . . except to drive the Fiat without a licence, and when she shot Charles, she was amazed at the violence in herself, all the violence that had been used on her turned itself inside out and spewed out of her. Until she was empty inside. Empty.

The tape machine clicked off. As DC Platt leaned forward to replace the spool, gently, as if she were afraid of breaking something, Hannah said, 'Shall I tell you something? I can't be sorry for anything I did, except for hurting Angela. That was done in a split second, never to be undone. But it wasn't like that with

223

Charles. The world seemed new when I walked out of that office. There was a smell of spring and there was a music lesson going on in the chapel when I crossed the quad, some of the younger boys singing. There's nothing in the world so beautiful as young boys' voices, is there?'